Praise for
River Spirit

"Dazzling . . . One of the great pleasures ⟨...⟩ novel tells us how to read it. The pace is swift, galloping over momentous events, stating profound changes with unsettling directness . . . Aboulela has written a novel of war, love, faith, womanhood, and—crucially— the tussle over truthful public narratives."  —New York Times

"A blazing historical epic of war, love, and revolution . . . A magnificent novel about the price of unwavering devotion and the inexhaustible pursuit for freedom."  —Los Angeles Review of Books

"Evocative and delicately composed."  —Literary Hub

"[Aboulela] has written a novel about one of the most important events in Sudanese history, the Mahdist War, and has centered women while doing it."  —Ms. Magazine

"Action-packed . . . Aboulela casts a scrutinous and perceptive eye on the motives of religious leaders and colonial forces, and she layers the narrative with a rich blend of languages and cultures. This brims with drama and nuance."  —Publishers Weekly

"Rich and moving . . . captivating."  —Kirkus

"Historical novels are often most successful when they focus on ordinary people experiencing extraordinary times, and that is the case with Aboulela's latest. Zamzam and Yaseen's love story is moving and gripping, sweeping the reader along hoping that they will end up together against the odds . . . Highly recommended."  —Library Journal, starred review

"[Aboulela] explores themes of faith and conquest without compromising on rich characterization or compelling plot development. She also centralizes women and their experiences in a larger sociopolitical context that is most often viewed in terms of men's lives . . . Aboulela reveals the thin lines that can demarcate religious zeal and patriotic fervor, social crusade and personal recklessness, as she creates a finely wrought and compellingly in-depth drama about a land and its people."  —Booklist, starred review

"River Spirit is—like the rest of Aboulela's oeuvre – flush with stunning, complex portraits of people."  —The Skinny

"Captivating . . . Aboulela unspools the fraught story of Sudan, as freedom and faith do battle."　　　　　　　　　　　　　　　　　—*Daily Mail*

"Although the story she tells is harsh and often horrific, her narratives, sometimes offered in the voices of those close to Akuany as well as in the third person, also glow with a rare beauty, a shining sensual awareness of the joy of life . . . In the shimmering quality of her prose, we glimpse the peace and joy that underlies her world view, perhaps a vital one for our time; clear-eyed, realistic, and sophisticated in recognising the world's horrors—but never without hope, or the underlying sense that our conscious existence, here on earth, is a miracle to be celebrated, every day that we live and love."　　　　　　　　　　　　　　　　　—*Scotsman*

"A novel of extraordinary sympathy and insight . . . a wonderful achievement."　　　　　**—Abdulrazak Gurnah, Winner of the Nobel Prize in Literature**

"*River Spirit* had me gripped from the first page. This is real history, imagined in splendid detail, a story of ordinary people caught in extraordinary times. The characters' interwoven narratives create a book shaped into twists and turns all the way to its thrilling end. A triumph of storytelling."
　　　　　**—Aminatta Forna, author of *Happiness* and *The Window Seat***

"In rich, evocative detail, Aboulela captures one of the most important moments in Sudanese history. But ultimately, this is a story about people. Everyone—from Akuany to Yaseen to Musa to Fatima to Robert— reminded me of the hearts and minds affected by the winds of imperialism. You must read this."
　　　　　**—Dolen Perkins-Valdez, author of *Wench* and *Take My Hand***

"Leila Aboulela weaves together strands of Sudan's history in this fascinating and unforgettable tale. By far my favourite of all her works, Aboulela employs elegant, poetic prose to create yet another masterpiece. This is a story that demands to be read. It is an excellent novel."
　　　　　　　　　**—Goretti Kyomuhendo, author of *Waiting***

"Painted with the words of an artist who loves and understands their subject, this novel is a historical portrait of freedom. Aboulela skillfully draws the uncertain colours of what freedom means to different individuals in a Mahdist Sudan to the last full stop."
　　　　　　　　　　**—Zukiswa Wanner, author of *The Madams***

# River Spirit

Also by Leila Aboulela

# River Spirit

A NOVEL

## Leila Aboulela

Grove Press
*New York*

*Published simultaneously in Canada*
*Printed in Canada*

First Grove Atlantic hardcover edition: March 2023
First Grove Atlantic paperback edition: March 2024

Library of Congress Cataloging-in-Publication data is available for this title.

ISBN 978-0-8021-6275-5
eISBN 978-0-8021-6067-6

Grove Press
an imprint of Grove Atlantic
154 West 14th Street
New York, NY 10011

Distributed by Publishers Group West

groveatlantic.com

24 25 26    10 9 8 7 6 5 4 3 2 1

*For Nadir, who also remembers*

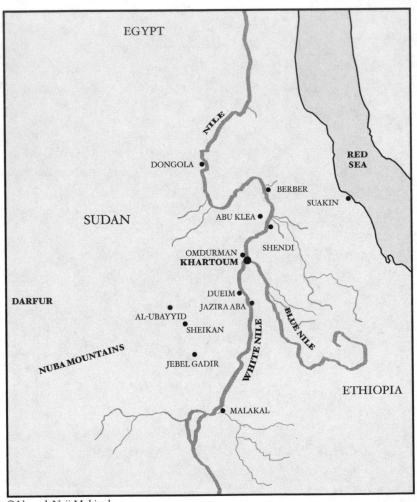

EGYPT

NILE

DONGOLA

BERBER

RED
SEA

SUAKIN

SUDAN

ABU KLEA

SHENDI

OMDURMAN
KHARTOUM

DARFUR

DUEIM

JAZIRA ABA

AL-UBAYYID

SHEIKAN

WHITE NILE

BLUE NILE

NUBA MOUNTAINS

JEBEL GADIR

ETHIOPIA

MALAKAL

©Ahmed–Naji Mahjoub

The Prophet Muhammad ﷺ said, "I give you good tidings of the Mahdi. He will be sent at a time of conflict and earthquakes. Then he will fill the earth with equity and justice as it had been filled with tyranny and oppression. The dwellers of the heavens will be pleased with him as will be the dwellers of the earth. He will distribute wealth evenly among the people. And Allah will fill the hearts of Muhammad's nation with contentment."

—Musnad Ahl al-Hadith

The Prophet Muhammad ﷺ said, "If there was only one day left in this world, Allah would extend that day so that He sends a man from me or from my family, whose name matches my name and whose father's name matches my father's name. He will fill the earth with equity and justice as it had been filled with tyranny and oppression."

—Sunan Abu Dawud

# Prologue

## The Nuba Mountains, December 1881

Rabiha steps out of her hut, sets out to warn the Mahdi. The night is lit by a full yellow moon. She must not be seen by the soldiers surrounding the village. The governor of Fashoda is on the move, intent on annihilating the Mahdi once and for all. She must get to him first. Sounds of a shuffle, a pant: she turns to see the old hunting dog following her. She bends down, rummages on the ground, finds a mango stone, and throws it at the dog. She picks up a chewed bit of sugarcane. It is still in her hand when she reaches the outskirts of the village. The vegetation thickens and rising out of the shadows is a Shilluk warrior, posted to ensure that no one leaves the area, certainly not before the planned surprise attack against the rebels. Spear in hand, muscular torso above his loincloth, the physique of a wrestler. She stiffens, drops the bit of sugarcane. Fight or run, fight or run? She reaches for her knife. She turns so that he can see her in full. Curves, breasts, glow of shoulder, long braids. She forces her body into limpness, hangs her long neck in submission, hides her hand behind her back, palm tight over the knife. He approaches, first with caution, then the start of a swagger. Makes low soothing sounds as if she were a skittish calf, lone antelope, stray prey. He must be near enough now to scent the sandalwood she uses in her hair to drench the smell of grease; she can see the decorative row of bead-like scarring across his forehead. He drops his spear; she waits a beat and aims down at his stomach. There is hardly any sound apart from the thud of his body on the ground. She looks around, grabs his spear, and runs.

She knows this land, every path, where it is smooth and where it is rocky. She had discarded her usual layered shoes, slipped her feet in flat tanned leather, tied the strings all the way up her calves. She can move faster like this, and she needs to be fast. Needs to warn them. Herding her goats as she did every morning, she had passed the hut of the village chief and overheard the conversation. The Turkish binbashi sent by Rashid Bey, the governor, to say that the assembled force intends the village no harm, they come in peace, passing through Kinana land, and heading up the mountains where the rebels have fled. The binbashi requested volunteers from the village but sensed a reluctance. Hence the imposed curfew, the prohibition against anyone leaving, in case they alerted the rebels.

Last week the Mahdi with his community had been received warmly by Rabiha's tribe. She had been one of the many who gathered to listen to him preach, entranced by his manners and compassionate smile, pierced by his words. She had pledged allegiance to his cause, to renounce material things and not shirk from jihad. These promises felt like a weighty responsibility she would carry forever. She was an orphan, brought up in the care of her older sister. Her father had died worn out by the tyranny of the Ottoman invaders, their cruel incessant taxes, their disregard for people's circumstances. Rabiha remembered his anxiety the year his sugar crop failed; how could he pay what he didn't have? Crushed by debt and made small, always.

Rabiha keeps striding, bloody knife stuffed into the wide cloth she had wrapped around her hips and thighs. The new spear in her right hand. There are poisonous snakes, and she must be careful. There are thorny bushes, scattered rocks jutting out; there could be, if she were unlucky, a lion or a hyena. She can hear their cries. All these dangers but the most pressing one is that she might not get there in time. Jebel Gadir is far away, normally a two-day journey. And she must cover that distance in one night. She runs.

When she runs, she feels the amulets she is wearing bounce against her chest and biceps, sacred words in tiny leather pouches, the red tassels that tie them fluttering against her skin. The newest amulet was given to her by the Mahdi himself. Not enough that the Expected One smiled at her but to give her this special protection too! First, she had asked for amulets for her two daughters. Then she asked for one for herself. It had been a special day when he arrived, the sky soft, the world bright. Every day of his visit had been charged with a particular aura, his sermons changing the daily life of the people, stirring hopes in them. He was the one they had been expecting, he was the Guided One mentioned by the prophecies. But Rabiha's husband had been skeptical. He was cautious by nature, and she respected him for that. But his concerns—fear of disruption, fear of change—were what they

3

were, just fears. So, she did not tell him that she was going out tonight. He would have stopped her. Forbade her or at least dampened her resolve. And to cover all this distance, she must not be distracted, not by a marital disagreement and certainly not by lack of confidence. So, she had slipped out of their warm bed as soon as he started snoring. He would not notice her absence until dawn.

The cold breeze scalds her face and bare arm, the right one that isn't covered by the brown muslin shawl. The breeze finds its way through to her thighs. Running is making her warm, though, and she must keep it up. To cover distance and keep warm. Searching for the flatter paths up the mountain, but perhaps there will be a delay in doing so, better take the shortcuts. Shortcuts she had taken as a child. Not for her the sitting still, clinging to her mother's clothes. She did not remember her mother clearly. Always ill, spread out on a mat, calling out for water. Enough to break the heart or make you want to run away, up the green mountain, under the sun. *Rabiha, Rabiha*, it is as if she can hear her mother calling her. Feeble voice, a hint of reproach.

She feels thirsty. The sky is clear, the moon near. She can see the pockmarks on its surface, brown frizzles, unruly. No time for gazing, she must run faster. Her shawl is caught by brambles. Irritated, she yanks it away and hears it rip. Never mind. She can mend it later. When dawn breaks, her absence will be noted. But they will guess where she has gone. All day, as the news spread around the village, they had been whispering about Rashid's impending attack. When volunteers didn't step forward, or at least not enough of them, it had been clear that the village was sympathetic

4

to the rebels. Rashid's next strategy was to encircle it with warriors from the Shilluk tribe, loyal to the government, and enforce a blockade. No one allowed to leave. For the attack on the rebels to succeed, the element of surprise was essential.

Surely by now, if the man she killed had been discovered, they would have been after her. She is safe from Rashid's men but not from the animals of the forest. Run and stay alert for the gleam of an eye, listen for a low growl. Loud are the frogs, on and on they croak, insects chirp. Pass through the forest or circle round it? The quickest route is the priority, no matter what. She has done this trip before but never so quickly, never with this much urgency, never alone or at night. The moonlight is less yellow now, more silver. On such a night, the moon overshadows the stars. She could have used them to navigate her way too. No matter, memory serves her well. She will not get lost. She must not get lost. There is no time for errors.

This is why she does not stop when she feels the sting. What sting? No, nothing. Her right heel. Must have scratched a tree trunk, picked up a thorn. She is desperate to stop, sit down, cradle her foot, squint to see if there are, God forbid, two puncture wounds made by fangs. Or grope with her fingers to take the thorn out. But she cannot sit. She is halfway there. Pulling herself up on hands and balls of her feet. It could be that she had upset a nest, aroused the one animal she dare not name.

Fatigue. It is to be expected. How many hours ago did she leave her hut, leave her village, encounter the Shilluk fighter? She is definitely more than halfway there. Too late to go back. Too late to go back means she will go forward, she will keep going, she will arrive in time. She stumbles and falls. The spear rattles down next to her, pain in knees. Facedown, she smells the rich, dark soil. How heavy she breathes and wants to stay there just like this, crouched in this ludicrous position, as if prostrating in prayer—a variation of that, distorted, not quite right. Not comfortable either, but she is catching her breath, and it is pleasant not to move, to feel drowsy, to be still, leg muscles burning. How is her foot? She is not sure, the sensations in her body a blur. A distinctive pinch in her right foot. Not good. She should look at it, treat it. Speed is essential for such a bite. But who says it is a bite? Speed is essential, too, for tonight's mission. She leaps up and smiles because she can leap up. She is not beaten. She runs.

If she had packed some dates, she would have stuffed one in her mouth now. Imaginary sweetness and she runs. Spits out the stone that doesn't exist, emerges into a clearing. Yes, she remembers this place, a favorite, gives the impression of a small village abandoned, though it might not be so, just her fancy, just because it is flat and clear. Not long to go now, another few hours. She picks up speed.

Her foot hurts. She can't deny it now. There is a throb in her right foot. There is a strange feeling as if the skin is stretched. She slows down to a walk. Chides herself and starts to jog until she cannot bear the hard impact on her swollen foot. It reminds her of when she was pregnant. The first time, her ankles swelled a week before the birth. She stared at them in fascination, peering over her rounded stomach, wondering why they were suddenly so fat. In the second pregnancy, the swelling started a month earlier than the birth. She would dig her finger in the top of her foot and leave the imprint of

6

a pit. Her feet pliant as mud. Perhaps this is how it is now, but she has no time to sit. Walk fast if she cannot run. Walk faster and faster and faster.

Nothing in her hand. Where is the spear? She must have dropped it but can't remember. No matter, she can see her destination. She can see her destination now. She sprints, her foot protests, she hobbles, she runs, lopsided, drags her foot. Dawn breaking and she is there, there, at her destination, passing those sleeping in the open air, makeshift tents, live-stock, thatched huts built in haste—all that she expects of a new community. Fragile, fledgling, fresh with hope, alive with promise. And where is he? She will speak to no one else. She will report to no other.

People are waking up, the clank of water pitchers for ablu-tions, time for the prayer. She is sweating, wants to quench her thirst, but she must speak out first. She makes her way through, keeps going, asks for directions, arrives, requests to see him. Her progress is blocked. They ask, *Why do you want him? Who are you? Who sent you?* She is panting. Best to pause until she gets her breath back. If she wants to be taken seriously. The sky lights up, night recedes. She dares not look down at her foot. Instead, she looks at the ivory bracelet on her left arm. It has high ridges, and she can make out the engraving of the lion in the middle. She can distinguish people's faces, a nose knocked out, a wild white beard. *Woman, what do you want from him?* She can make out people's expressions. One lanky fighter after the other looks her up and down, assesses her, approves her body, doubts her story. Rage flares through her. She hits out against this wall of belittlement and disregard. Because she's a woman. Is that why she is doubted? No, she will not be silenced; she will not be brushed aside, not after what she has gone through. She stands her ground, stands her ground tall, though the pain in her foot is intense now, sending up waves of nausea. She must not be sick, not now. Not now.

She will speak to no one else but him. She will not be patronized, brushed aside, doubted. She raises her voice and demands. Insists. What she has to say is crucial. No, it cannot wait. Yes, she is sure. Where is he? She pushes her way. She pushes her way into a space where there is not a single woman. There is nothing to be afraid of. She has transcended shyness, politeness, anxiety. Even femininity. There is only her urgency and there is no time.

He will see her. He has just finished praying and he will see her. She must not look at those surrounding him, those who judge her a waste of time, label her a distraction, brand her an entertainment, even before she has opened her mouth. It is to him she had been running all night and to him she will talk.

She starts, "I am Rabiha from the Kinana tribe. I came to warn you."

"I remember you," he says, and around him those who had been skeptical start to listen. Those who were distracted and talking among themselves pay attention.

He remembers her. He remembers her. Confident now, she says what she knows. The planned timing of the impending attack, the size of Rashid Bey's army, the route that they are taking. He believes her. She knows he does because of the way he listens, the questions he asks. The way he says, "You ran through the night."

When she is done, when her words result in men leaping to their feet, in action being taken, in plans being set in motion, preparations being made, when she is done, she can look down at her swollen foot.

She can see what she didn't want to see, the two puncture wounds from the snake's fangs. The poison is spreading as she staggers around, not knowing where to go. She has fulfilled her mission, said her piece, and now this pain. She gives in to it, after holding out for so long, there are no defenses, no need to fight, no need to run. She does not faint, she chooses to stretch out on the ground. How tired she is!

She wakes up in a tent. There is movement outside. "You are our guest," a woman says. The Mahdi's guest. She is his wife and looks down at Rabiha with concern. Offers her a drink of water. Rabiha swallows and wants to know what happened. Did Rashid attack? The woman replies, and Rabiha visualizes what she tells her, sees images of the forest where the Mahdi's men hid, the brilliant trap he set. Divided his men into three groups. Arranged them in a crescent. Springing out just as half of Rashid's army were emerging from the forest and the other half still inside it. Chaos and victory. Rashid Bey killed. Hundreds taken as captives. Spears and sticks overpowering guns. And the booty—a lot of it— the booty! Firearms, horses, uniforms. The news spreading across the country, another spectacular victory for the Mahdi and, consequently, more tribes joining his cause. *Rabiha, you saved us.* Strengthened and saved us all. We will drive these foreigners out of our lands. It will be Al-Ubayyid next. Sennar, Darfur, Khartoum.

She swims in and out of consciousness, her whole right leg now swollen rigid. She hears the whispers, grim. The poison has spread; we've called for her family.

It is her sister who is hugging her, tears in her eyes. She has brought with her the girls. Rabiha basks in her daughters' sweetness, breathes in the scent of their youth, draws them close to her, close, close. *Where is your father?* He is on the way.

Rabiha understands his reluctance. It is disapproval that makes his feet slow. Disapproval that she had done what she had done without telling him. Let alone asking for his permission. But he will come. She knows he will. When she sees him, he is a shadow, sitting at a distance. It is the girls who are with her, their lips near her ear, "Yumma, Yumma," their arms heavy on her neck.

"Ask your husband for forgiveness," her sister says, but Rabiha twists away from tradition. With each last breath, she is a rebel, striving to become more than an obedient wife. She is Rabiha, the woman from Kinana who changed the course of a revolution.

Later, with the sun high in the sky, the Mahdi leads her funeral prayer.

# 1

# Akuany

**Malakal, September 1877**

The river was her language. Eleven-year-old Akuany stood in the shallow, humming Nile, listening to what the water was saying, believing. Reeds moved in the breeze. The river smelled of fish; its surface was silk. Akuany pressed her feet in the sticky mud, looked down at the shifting cloth that covered her hips. The raised tribal decorations on her stomach were now in the water. She bent her knees, and her breasts became wet. They were uncomfortable these days, the areolas soft and stretched. Older boys pinched them and laughed even though it pained her. Women looked at her with sympathy. Motherless child, her toddler brother, Bol, perched on her hip. They thought her mature for her age, but here in the water she was carefree, teasing the fish because they were too slippery to catch. The river was a place to draw water and wash, to fish and set sail, and for her it was more, the spirit of who she was. The place that kept her safe when they raided the village.

On the bank she could see Yaseen, the young merchant from Khartoum, her father's guest, sitting reading. Bol was squatting near him, reaching to clasp his ebony prayer beads. A wisp of smoke rose over the village, more than a wisp. She saw it, but it did not alarm her at first. Hitting her palms against the water, she could hear Bol babbling, the merchant saying something to him in return. The woman who was washing her clothes admonished her daughter. None of them heard the horses neighing, the huts catching fire, the screams of those who were speared and those who were shackled to be driven away to the slave markets farther north.

When the woman washing the clothes turned and saw the smoke, she cried out. She ran up the bank, anxious about her younger children, hurling herself toward danger. Yaseen, the merchant, called out to her, but she didn't listen, and her daughter went with her too. Akuany and her brother stayed with Yaseen. He understood the meaning of the smoke. The three of them waited for hours. Akuany's skin dried, and she held Bol on her lap. At first, she was soothed by the songs of the river. Then she felt hungry and Yaseen had no food. Her brother whined and Yaseen told him to be quiet. "Go to sleep, both of you," he said. And they did. They curled up next to him and fell asleep with their stomachs rumbling.

Akuany had always liked Yaseen. He came from Khartoum to buy gum from her father, carrying back the balls in large baskets hitched to his camels. He came once a year after the rains stopped and the roads dried. When he was younger, he used to come with his father, but Akuany had only shad-owy memories of the older man. Yaseen brought sweets for Akuany, and because he smiled and had a nice way of talking, their home would change in his presence. It would feel like feast days even though it wasn't. Yaseen usually stayed with them a week but to Akuany it always felt longer. There was the excitement of preparing for his arrival. For days her father would pick or tap gum from the acacia trees that grew wild. How beautiful the gum looked, glistening in the sun! She had tasted it once and it got stuck to her teeth. There would be a special welcoming meal for the Khartoum merchant, which, now that her mother was gone, was cooked by the neighbors with the millet flour and vegetables brought by her father. After Yaseen finished eating, he would look up, his fingers still sticky with food and say, "Akuany will take me to the river." He said it as if he could not go there on his own, as if he had forgotten the way. She would lead him, charged with pride. When she was younger, she chatted all the way. This time, though, she had been uncharacteristically shy. He did not go into the water with her. He never did. He would sit with a toothpick in his mouth or his prayer beads or book, the folio pages held between hard covers, which he was careful not to smudge with water or mud. He would gaze at the water or if it was late afternoon up at the sky, and often Akuany, playing in the water, would forget his presence.

Fearful, they spent the whole night at the river. The merchant kept saying, "Some of the raiders might still be there. They'll take us too." Then he would sigh and say, "Oh the loss." Then he would pray. On the morning of the following day, he went back on his own. He was not gone long, but Bol would not stop crying. When Yaseen came back, he looked like he had been crying, too, but he had food with him. Sesame seeds, a bruised mango, and dried bread that the children gobbled while he sat away from them with his face in his hands. He told her not to go back with him to the village, and when she insisted, he said she must close her eyes. "Don't look, don't look, Akuany." But she did look and saw things broken, upside down, distorted and in their distortions lopsided and looming up at her. Homes burnt to ashes, beddings and utensils smashed, livestock vanished. Healing powder knocked out of a horn, cracked mortar, grains of millet scattered on the ground. The elderly roamed like ghosts in the remaining smoke. The disabled and ill tossed aside. Not a single beautiful white cow to be found. All the vitality gone or going, for it was not safe to remain in such a vulnerable spot. The raiders might come back for the remaining able-bodied. She choked on the smoke, gulped fire; tears ran down her face. Yaseen kept saying, "Close your eyes, don't look!" She closed them and still saw horrors, could not keep them closed. Opened them to see the worst thing of all. In the epicenter of the devastation was her father, splayed flat in front of their hut, speared to death.

Yaseen buried their father and took charge. Akuany and Bol were his responsibility now. He would take them back with him to Khartoum. A month ago—a week ago—such a prospect would have filled her with adventurous delight. To be with him on a journey, to be taken to his home, which must be grander than hers. His city, which was bigger. To be with his family eating the same food. A day ago, she might have been beaming, but now she could hardly understand what he was saying. His voice, his orders, reached her from a faraway place, his face close to hers repeating her name. "You must stop crying and look after your brother. We must pack what we can and get out of here!" Where is this, where is that? In one surreal moment he found her mother's jewelry and pushed bracelets up her arms and around her ankles, strung beads around her neck. She would sink and he would yank her back. She would drift, and he would pull. She would drown if he lost his grip.

A storm in her body, still wailing, and they were on the road. He had lost his camels of course, lost his merchandise. There was one donkey left and they set out on it. The three of them. No lingering aunt or distraught villager disputed the merchant's claim over the children. An adult rescuing two orphans? Or human flesh as compensation for his material loss? He seemed to know what he was doing, and the alternative was to remain in the carcass of the village with neither means nor protection. He was the children's savior and now they were his.

The road was not without its dangers either. Or raiders. The donkey might collapse before they reached the next village. Her little brother was not well; he fidgeted and fretted for water. Sometimes, he felt listless in her arms. In the villages they passed, people knew the merchant and he knew them. The travelers were given food and hospitality, Yaseen holding court, repeating the tragic events, enumerating his losses. This was not tribal warfare in which prisoners were enslaved until they were ransomed. These were unscrupulous raiders looking to sell human flesh up north! His listeners shook their heads in sympathy or muttered prayers for the coming of the Expected Redeemer, the promised Mahdi, who would pull them all out of their misery, who would bring justice and peace to the world after it had been filled with tyranny.

Akuany could not grieve for her father. She could not remember how he looked or sounded before the spear struck him. That was the most vivid memory she had of him now, horrific and evil. Everything before that faded. When her mind drifted toward him—and it did so often—his murder obliterated everything else and she was gripped with pain, the kind that didn't bring tears to her eyes. Instead, it made her shiver in a strange way so that the merchant would ask, "What's wrong with you?" He would put his warm hand on her forehead and throat, which she found comforting, and then say, "But you don't have a fever."

She was afraid of the men who had killed her father, who had destroyed the village and taken the other children away. She had heard about how the boys were shackled and thrust into the army and how the girls were sold as concubines. She had heard that they were never ever reunited with their families again. Was this what was happening now to her best friend, Alek? To her neighbors, Kenyi and Deng? To Taban, the bully?

After days on the road, her head began to clear. Her father's death withdrew from the rest of her body and settled as a concentrated pain in her chest. She could look around and see the land they were traveling through, the different browns and lesser greens. She could feel the burning sun on her head and the weight of Bol leaning against her. She could bathe in the small streams and waterways they stopped at. She could watch the merchant giving water to the donkey. He had been tense; now slowly he was becoming more like his usual self. She felt a new ache for him that she didn't understand. It came from the loss of her father, the wildness of the past days. He held her when she screamed, until her eyes turned red and her voice rasped in her throat. He brought her water and said, "Drink." He lifted his finger and said, "One thing. Only one thing I want from you. Do you know? I want you to eat." Repeated it until she was, at the end, able to chew and swallow.

After a couple of weeks, soothed by the rhythms of the journey, she began to note her new life. At sunset, the merchant would start to find a suitable place for the night. A shelter from wild animals and potential enemies. He would pray, and then they would settle under the starlight. He would lie down, toothpick in his mouth, and she would sit next to him asking questions. "What is Khartoum like? Does it have a river?"

"A mightier one."

"Does it hum like our river?"

"It roars."

"Are there boats on it?"

"Lots. Steamers too. Government steamers."

"I saw a steamer once in Fashoda. My father took me there." The whole family had gone to visit the homestead mound of the Chollo king. But she could not talk about her father without breaking down.

They traveled northwest. Away from the White Nile, circling the Nuba Mountains, heading toward the desert. On the outskirts of a village, they stopped at the hut of a woman who seemed to live on her own. She was effusive in her welcome, warm, and plump; her lower lip and gums were tattooed with indigo, breasts big and soft under her wrapper. She greeted the merchant with familiarity, then lamentations at his story.

"And these two were all you gained!" She put her hands on her hips. Her food was better than they had eaten for days. Asida freshly pounded, spinach stew with goat's meat. The woman held Bol in her arms, cleaned the mucous from his nose, poured warm oil in his ears, fed him mouthful after mouthful. She bathed him and he slept after that, the kind of peaceful sleep he had not enjoyed for a long time.

The children lay down in the clearing in front of the hut, while the woman and merchant chatted by the fire. Listening to the sounds of the night, searching for the tunes of the river and not finding them, Akuany started to doze. She woke to the laugh of the woman. "How old are you, anyway? Eighteen?"

"Twenty."

"Because you're penniless, that's what's keeping you from going in the hut with me?" The merchant's reply was inaudible.

"I can take the boy."

Akuany now heard his sharp reply. "Of course not."

She fell asleep after this until the pale light. When the merchant was busy feeding his donkey, the woman spoke to Akuany. "You are a fresh pretty girl and valuable too. Do you understand? You can't go around like this covered only in a skirt! I will give you something."

It was an old and tattered piece of cloth, but its color was still bright. She showed Akuany how to wrap it crossways over her chest. "Anytime now you will bloom, and your virginity is precious. He is your master now, and you must save it for him. He is still young, without a wife and children; he will get them in time, but you are separate from all that.

You understand what I'm saying, don't you? Your body isn't for anyone else."

Akuany turned to see him walking toward them. He looked grumpy, impatient to get going.

"Aren't you going to tell Akuany she's pretty, all dressed up?"

The merchant grunted. He was not interested in Akuany's clothes. "I suppose I now owe you for that."

She laughed, such an attractive laugh, which captivated Akuany. "I don't trust you. Men are fickle. The cloth is between me and the girl." She touched one of the blue bead bracelets on Akuany's arm. Akuany took it off and gave it to her. The woman looked at it and smiled, then shook her head and handed it back to Akuany. "And wrap up your mother's jewelry too. You can't go about laden like that."

They continued to travel. Days squashed against him in the saddle, nights gazing up at the sky. She watched how he lit a fire, the way he hoisted her brother up in the air, the way he opened his palm, and it was full of peanuts. It was his custom to have a nap at midday. He would find shade and barely disembark before passing out on the sand. She liked watching his face when he woke up, how his eyebrows twitched up high before he opened his eyes. He would then raise a hand to swat away a fly or wipe his face. There would be a confused look in his eyes, one that she cherished, as if he did not know who she was and when he realized he would smile and say her name. She did not know that she was living some of the sweetest days of her life. How would she guess, crushed between the horror left behind and the unknown future, the discomforts of travel, the disorientation? They were often thirsty, now that the river was behind them, now that they were treading sand and dry scrub. The merchant bought water from other travelers who carried large waterskins on their camels. Once a camel knelt and rolled over a waterskin. It punctured and they watched as the sand soaked up every drop, while the camel's owner tried in vain to hold on to what remained in the damaged waterskin. The merchant knew the way and they never got lost. They passed villages whose languages Akuany couldn't understand, whose ways were different, and the only two people she knew were her brother and the merchant.

The town of Al-Ubayyid had a color; it was reddish brown. Rows of mud and straw houses stretching out, a brick tower in the center surrounded by a low government building with an arched entrance, the bustle of western Sudan's most prosperous markets, soldiers on horses. There was a special excitement the day they arrived, and they found themselves caught up in the crowd that was gathered to greet the new governor-general of Sudan, Gordon Pasha. He had been seconded from the British army to the Ottomans, appointed by the khedive in Egypt. There he was on top of a lithe, feisty camel that he had purchased from one of the local merchants. A camel that was capering now and dancing to the delight of the crowd. Akuany had seen Europeans before, the overdressed, puzzling missionaries who built a large house in Fashoda, who planted roses and liked the sounds of bells. General Gordon was just like them. When he lifted his helmet, the rays of the sun caught the brightness of his hair. "That camel should run with him now to his palace in Khartoum," people in the crowd said. They chuckled at the delight he took in his new camel. They said that he had been listening to claims, that his remit was to end corruption and end the slave trade too. Akuany, listening, wanted to know if they would be set free then, her friends, her neighbors who were taken from her village? Alek, Deng, Taban, Kenyi? Would they go back home? The merchant didn't reply. How fine General Gordon's saddle was! Embroidered and with colorful tassels. How pleased he looked with his hopes and his camel.

The merchant's sister, Halima, lived in Al-Ubayyid. Her husband, Hassan, was an officer serving Gordon Pasha's host, the local Turkish governor. They had five children, all girls, the eldest ready for marriage, the youngest Bol's age, the middle ones close to Akuany in height. It was bewildering to enter this home. In an instant she lost her merchant. He became the honored guest, the bachelor uncle arriving empty-handed without his laden camels and usual gifts. But what did you bring us this time, Uncle? A scrawny, sickly toddler and an unkempt little girl.

She became an object of ridicule. "Don't you know anything?" they said. Although the family's house was simple—a hoash, a women's room, a men's room, the latrine—Akuany was confused. She could not feel the river, not a single note nor a whiff of its water. People lived like that! And water came to them from wells. When the cannon was fired to mark the departure of General Gordon, Akuany was petrified. She made a better impression helping with the household tasks, milking the goats and sweeping the hoash.

"I want to keep the boy," the merchant's sister said.

Akuany held her breath. It was getting dark in the hoash, and she was sitting with the other children. They had just finished eating.

"He needs his sister," the merchant replied. "I don't want them separated."

"Fine," Halima replied, and Akuany breathed. They would be back on the road, the three of them like before. He would take them to Khartoum.

But Halima then said, "Leave them both. The boy's health has just started to improve. He would be better off here. You can take them when you come again. You won't wait a full year, you said. So, it won't be too long."

Six months. She would have to wait months, live among strangers. In addition to the children, the household also included Halima's mother-in-law, who was bedridden. The elderly woman addressed Akuany as khadim, fetch me this and fetch me that. Halima corrected her, saying that Akuany and her brother were orphans and not enslaved. She corrected her mother-in-law once, twice, and then let the matter drop.

As for Bol, he was adored in this household full of girls. "Our boy," Halima would say, and soon she was feeling possessive about him, making plans for his circumcision ceremony. When he was a little older, she would do it. An opportunity to invite her friends, a celebration, a meal. "But we will be in Khartoum by then," Akuany said.

"*You* might be in Khartoum," Halima laughed. "But not our boy." She was not being unkind to Akuany. She gave her new clothes for Eid and medicine for her eyes when they once got red and scratchy; she showed her how to hide her mother's jewelry by digging a safe spot in the corner of the hoash. She was attentive and motherly when Akuany started her monthly bleeding. But Bol came first; he mattered. Halima wanted to give him a new Arabic name; she would send him with the other boys to the khalwa to learn to read the Qur'an. Perhaps in the far future she would arrange a marriage between him and her youngest daughter. Then he would truly become the son of the house. A legitimate son-in-law. At first no one took her seriously, not even Hassan, but with time her fantasies started to sink into the fabric of the house.

Akuany waited months for her Khartoum merchant. She learned from his nieces how to wear slippers, how to speak Arabic, how she must never shave her head. Buthaina, the eldest niece, was beautiful, with a full round face and clear skin. Akuany tried to copy her as much as she could, covering her hair and not laughing out loud. Sometimes Buthaina sneered at her, often she was kind, but she and her sisters were always superior because Akuany was an orphan, because they were dark brown and she was dark black, because they were circumcised and she was not. She learned how to fast in Ramadan; she tasted tea for the first time. The azan started to sound normal, so did the cannon fired at Eid, so did the fearsome sight of the Turkish governor's bodyguards, known as the Baltagiya, walking in town in their white tunics, brandishing their whips.

She loved running errands in the souq, the green courgettes and red onions, black aubergines and yellow peppers, sugarcane stacked high, sacks of sesame, senna, and tamarind, dusty ostrich feathers. The livestock souq was even better. There invariably would be a beautiful white cow, one she would gravitate toward, cooing even before she reached it. She could not help but rub her cheeks against its hide, speak her language, gaze into its eye and recognize a kind of sadness. Then the din of the souq would recede, the clamor of voices bartering and calling out, the smells of sweat and wares—and she would be back in her village, the cow prized and coveted, a measure of wealth and pride.

She avoided the slave market. The misery of it, pain pressed tight in human chests, the humiliation of the viewing. It filled her with dread. Instead of searching for familiar faces from her village, her instinct was to look away, to duck her head and move unnoticed. She was not capable of helping anyone. Violence was not far away. The governor's Baltagiya did not brandish their whips for show. Grown men (and sometimes women) yelping and slithering in the dust, their skin split open, their clothes stained with blood, watched by crowds made merry with relief that they were not the ones being punished.

News came from Khartoum of Halima and the merchant's father's death. She wept and the neighborhood women gathered round, came and stayed with her for a few days. Akuany served them water and tea. Some of them called her khadim and others would correct them and say, "Halima is bringing up her brother as her own child."

Did this mean that she would be going to Khartoum without Bol? Should she stay? But she could not stay; if she were staying, she would not be waiting, waiting like she was now, conscious of the months passing, heat, dust storms, rains. She belonged to him, but at the same time the tie with Bol was tighter; they were kin. But if he stayed in Al-Ubayyid, she could not stay here with strangers who didn't know about the river like her merchant did, who didn't speak to her like he did, who hadn't seen her as she truly was, mouthing the water words, naked and listening to the river. Oh, how she missed it and could never feel settled in a town where people could not feast their eyes on the moving blue or set sail or eat fish. Her merchant, her river—she yearned for them both.

He did come before the year was out, glorious on a camel as she used to see him arrive in her village. The rush of joy, but she was oppressed with shyness, struck dumb in his presence, silent as his nieces and Bol captured his attention. And why not let them? They could have him here in Al-Ubayyid as much as they wanted. She was the one who was going to travel with him. She was going to ride his camel, up high. She was going to listen to his voice and wake him up each day from his siesta. It was enough for now to meet his eyes as he spoke to others, to hold her breath when she overheard him saying her name to guests and family. "I used to barter with her father down south . . ." "Her father supplied me with the best gum, may Allah have mercy on his soul." She would smile and not be able to stop smiling because he was speaking about her; he was telling them who she really was. "Yes, from the Shilluk," he would say. "Chollo," she would correct him, wanting him to notice her, reveling in the description of her village. Verdant, green, lush, the White Nile pouring—yes, true, it had been like that and more.

He was busy in Al-Ubayyid. Every morning at the souq, every evening visiting other merchants or at the mosque with Hassan, or sometimes they would visit him, too, and chat by lantern light. Complaints about the extortionate taxes levied by the Turks, a story of how General Gordon granted mass liberation to the enslaved in Al-Fasher, all because Egypt had signed an anti-slavery convention with Britain. And what does that have to do with us? Bad enough the Turks and Egyptians are ruling us; now they went and got us a Christian to meddle in our affairs!

One night, after seeing his guests off, he found her in the shadows waiting, as she had been instructed by Halima to clear up after the guests. Alone with him for the first time. He said, "How are you getting on, Akuany? Are you happy here?"

She replied as his nieces would have replied, decidedly demure, "Alhamdulilah I am well and happy."

He said, "Halima is clinging to Bol. She will not let him go."

"Yes."

"And what do you say about that? Shouldn't you be with your brother too?"

"No."

She sensed him smile in the dark. "Why not?"

"Because I am going with you to Khartoum."

"You would be better off here, Akuany."

The tears rose to her eyes, but she would not make a sound. He continued, "You see, my circumstances have changed with my father's death. He left us, his children, a shop, and I decided to sell my share to my brothers and go to Egypt to study. The life of a merchant is not for me. It's too full of temptations and insecurity. This trading trip is my last. I'm doing it to settle my debts. You see, I want the peace in books. I want to study at Al-Azhar, and when I come back, there will be employment for me."

"I will come with you," she said. "I can serve you wherever." She reached for his hand. It was warm, just like she
remembered.

"You're far too young. It is better that you stay here with
Halima. Better for you and remember, you will be with Bol.
It is the right decision." He let go of her hand. She needed it
after all, to cover her face.

He was gone four years and in those four years many things
happened. Buthaina rejected a suitor with so little prospects
that his offer was deemed an insult; instead she married the
son of a local dignitary. Bol became Ishaq and started Qur'an
school. Dust storms came and the wells filled up in the rainy
season. People were taxed and they were taxed and they
were taxed. They comforted themselves with talk of the
Expected Redeemer, the Guided One who would appear and
save them from destitution. During these four years, Akuany
emerged from childhood to find that she could not be safe.
And though Halima had made promises to her brother—to
care for Akuany as if she were one of the family, to honor
her as an orphan should be honored—when the time came,
Halima could not protect her.

# 2

# Yaseen

**Cairo, May 1881**

At night, the streets are lit by gaslight and even after living here for years, I am still in awe. I walk among the throng of people heading to the Azbakeya garden pulled by the tunes of the military band. The air crackles with smoke from the vendors grilling. How can there be so much beauty in darkness, so much wakeful movement! Now that the khedive has given us this nighttime glory, no one wants to go to bed. His Majesty has built gardens and planted trees, extended neighborhoods. There are mansions here that I only imagined existing in Paradise. My heart fills with gratitude that I can be a witness to such progress, that I can return home to Sudan and tell others about this.

I am completing my studies at that most prestigious of universities, Al-Azhar. There are a handful of us from Sudan, like my good friend Isma'il, and many who are dark-skinned such as myself, brothers from Mauritania, Senegal, and the lands of the warrior Usman Dan Fodio. There are students from India and China, yes, China. And from islands that are even farther away. It took them months to get here. I revel in their company and respect the effort they put into studying the Arabic language, which is not their mother tongue. I attempt to ease their burden by reminding them that my mother tongue is a colloquial form of Arabic and that is the situation, too, with our teachers. We do not converse socially in the language of the Qur'an. We, too, need to be taught to understand it.

I excel at my lessons because of a natural aptitude, all praise to the Almighty; more than one teacher has remarked on my precision. I will return to a junior post in the central government or a position with a wider reach in the provinces, administering the religious affairs of the people. Justice, justice, justice. It is instilled in us every day. Without it the strong squash the weak, men tyrannize women, the rich steal from the poor, and corruption ravages the land. Daily I study Allah's words so that I can expand, so that I can be alive and not only living, so that I can tell the real from the fake. I pore over books and imbibe the words of the learned so that I can weigh options and choose the path of least harm. So that I can distinguish science from superstition, vanity from initiative, so that I can understand that even scholars make mistakes, act on ego; so that I can be suspicious of anger, mindful of self-interest, cautious of my instincts, and all that put together to uphold Allah's religion, so that His word can be supreme, so that His light can benefit my people. For years I dreamt of this student life, wanted it but was not certain I could acquire it. In Sudan, I traveled to the south and the west buying gum, cayenne pepper, sorghum, spices, and ostrich feathers to sell in Khartoum. Commerce never interested me, but travel did.

Travel is a component of our religion. If it were not so, then the Hajj would not be compulsory for every able man or woman who can afford it. We are commanded to travel the world and to contemplate Allah's glory in the vast differences of His creation, to see with our eyes the remnants of past civilizations. I myself have made a point of visiting the pyramids and of reminding myself of the tyranny Pharaoh practiced over the children of Israel. I stood on the shores of the sea in Alexandria. I visited the shrines of saints and companions of the Prophet Muhammad, peace be upon him. The world is an open book, but few know how to read it.

I have been here almost four years. To offset loneliness and protect myself, I early on took a wife. I believed that we were compatible, but it turns out that I am mistaken. Or at least the contentment was all on my side. Today she announced that she would never leave her parents or her city. When I finish my studies, she would not travel back with me to Sudan. "The day you leave," she said, "is the day you divorce me." I am not sure what provoked her to say this but then my wife is a mystery to me, and I have no idea what she hears from neighbors or friends about marrying a Sudanese. I had assumed she was content; she seemed to be, especially at first. I can't remember when she changed. Today her poisonous words coincided with the study of divorce in my fiqh class where I sat miserably learning that it was incumbent on me to release her favorably and to be generous with her maintenance. I am filled with bitterness. I would have been better off with a concubine (and they are still to be found despite the signed anti-slavery convention), but it's too late for that. Besides, thinking "if I had done this or that" is not only fruitless, but it is also the work of the devil. So, I leave her at home and roam these bright streets. They do lift my spirit.

The khedive had ordered roses to be planted, jasmine and white lotus. To walk at night in a perfumed garden—I would never have imagined this. I pass the opera house and see a young girl dressed in the European manner, laden with jewels. She leans out of a carriage window and calls out to her driver. "Bakhit," she says and then raises a fan to her lips. He dismounts and hurries to her side, tall and ample in expensive livery, and I recognize him as a eunuch. When he turns, having received his instructions, our eyes meet but we do not acknowledge that by virtue of our dark skin we share a homeland. If I greet him, I will only embarrass him, and so I stride in the opposite direction.

As expected, not everyone in Egypt is comfortable with these displays of Western culture. I hear the complaints within Al-Azhar itself. Earlier this year, our sheiks supported Urabi Pasha's nationalist mutiny against encroaching foreign influence. Egypt is for the Egyptians not the Ottomans and not the British, who are pulling the strings from behind them. As a foreigner, I am deemed trustworthy or at least impartial. Consequently, I am privy to sensitive conversations. I prick up my ears at the mention of money though. My years in trade have attuned me to this. Whether I like it or not, commerce flows in my blood.

The question is, where did Khedive Isma'il get the money for all the modernization required to claim that Egypt is no longer part of Africa but instead part of Europe? It's true that he borrowed from foreign banks; he was in such severe debt that shares of the Suez Canal had to be sold to Britain. But he had another source of revenue—the Sudan, which his grandfather invaded in 1820 and annexed to the Ottoman Empire. Ivory, gum arabic, ostrich feathers, tamarind, and senna—all these my country has an abundance of, but it is the taxes that are devastating the people. Taxes imposed indiscriminately without considering people's circumstances, a constant demand for livestock, slaves, money, alaf, boats, and then custom duties. When villages cannot pay, the khedive's army raids their durra stores and zaribas and I have heard that a punishment for a man who cannot pay his taxes can be a hungry cat stuffed down his underpants.

Justice, justice. It pains me to admit that it is lacking. My pain comes from divided loyalty. Progress cannot be stopped; it is the way of the world. And the progress of my country cannot be separated from Egypt and Turkey. We are enmeshed together. But injustice unleashes storms; injustice causes the kind of damage that perpetuates itself.

An eye for an eye, whether it is a prince's eye or that of the enslaved. Is this not what the law says? I am here for this. To learn better, to learn more. My dear mother said to me, "I understand your nature. Every mother knows her child. You were always the thoughtful, contrary one. So, what is wrong with that! Stay in your shop during the day, travel as you've always traveled, and at night spend time with like-minded friends. Why must you study? Why must you go away? Such unnecessary expense." My brothers were scathing: "You fancy yourself a preacher! Enjoying the sound of your own voice. Your father's job is not good enough for you!"

"Honest trade is a noble profession," I defended myself. The Prophet Muhammad, peace be upon him, rode the trade caravans in summer to the Levant and in winter to Yemen. I am not disparaging of how food had been put in my belly, but my heart leans toward more. I don't think they ever understood me. Or believed me, until I started to pack. My mother in tears, my brothers asking me to reconsider. I also felt the pangs of departure. Leaving everything that was dear and familiar, heading out into the unknown. But the thoughts of Al-Azhar were an impetus. The eagerness to walk its corridors, sitting cross-legged in a circle with my colleagues in this huge space with the columns and the arches, listening to the lessons, open books in my hand. And it was all like that when I arrived. The comfort of conversing with those who knew as much as I knew and the excitement of listening to those who knew more. My venerable teachers and the unfurling of my soul in their company, bending to receive the wisdom they had acquired, the science passed from one generation to the next. It is the law that keeps our religion from disintegrating; it is authority that makes it watertight. Justice paves way for the light.

Arriving home, I find that my wife has cooked. She is perfumed and dressed for a reconciliation. I soften and my appetite awakens, a few choice words from her or none would have sufficed. Instead, she juts out her chin and says, "I was teasing you when I said I don't want to return to Sudan with you. I was testing you, and you just turned glum!"

"I don't like being teased," I say, approaching the tray she had placed on the carpet.

"You were supposed to beg me to come with you or shout, 'Nonsense, you are traveling with me, woman, no matter what.'"

"I took you at your word," I say, reaching for a loaf of bread.

There is a mock surprise expression on her face, her arms folded on her chest. She sighs when she says, "Really, you are so easily hoodwinked. What have I married? A simpleton. But I should have known you were one when you gave all your money to your friend."

She is referring to my friend Isma'il who graduated before me and needed to pay off his debts before he could go back to Sudan.

I say, "Isma'il is like a brother to me. I could not see him in need and do nothing."

"Even at my expense."

"Yes, even at your expense. These are our traditions."

"And you expect me to go off with you, far from my own family! I will be at your mercy, and everyone there will be 'like a brother to me, like a brother to me.'" She mocks my accent.

I catch my breath in anger, the morsel dropping from my fingers.

"No, I won't. You will have to divorce me first," she says. "You might be a fool, but I am not."

When I stand up, the distance between us is greater than this home I can afford to rent. I cannot tolerate this provocation. "I will not be toyed with," I say. "You keep asking for a divorce and you shall get one. Now. Why prolong it until I leave? You're divorced."

After a few bitter weeks, during which I complete my studies, I return to Sudan without her and start my new life in

Khartoum. My mother is overjoyed to see me, and my brothers curious to know how I've turned out. I am eager to visit my sister, Halima, in Al-Ubayyid but prefer to wait until I am earning, so as not to go to her empty-handed. So scarce are graduates from Al-Azhar that I am quickly employed by the office of the distinguished chief of Sudan's ulema, Sheikh Amin Al-Darir. He is blind, as his name implies, but he has memorized a multitude of books in such a way that he need never refer to them again. Everyone knows him; his rank had been endorsed twenty years ago by the sultan himself in Constantinople. It is an honor to serve him and to my delight, he takes a special interest in me. "Oh, the scent of the honorable Azhar is on you, sublime and invigorating," he says the first time I present myself to him. He then proceeds to interrogate me on news of the faculty and the contents of my courses. I reply as accurately as I can; he is not a man to tolerate fudged answers. Eagerly, I take up my new duties as a jurist, finding satisfaction in the overlap between sacred law and human life.

I steadily catch up on the news. After three years, Gordon Pasha was relieved of his post as governor-general of the Sudan. Apart from establishing military outposts along the Nile, he had achieved little. The slave trade he set out to abolish is only dampened; corruption is still slithering. The gossip is that he had suffered a nervous breakdown of some sort; the more scandalous gossip is that he has become an alcoholic. We, the Sudanese, shrug our shoulders and move on. As far as I can see, things have not changed much in the years I have been away.

But I might be wrong. The current governor-general is the Egyptian Ra'uf Pasha. He had been in discussion with Sheikh Amin regarding a man in Jazira Aba named Muhammad Ahmed Abdallah who has declared himself the Expected Mahdi. Today matters came to a head when a telegram reached Ra'uf Pasha from the man himself. In it, Muhammad Ahmed claims that his position has been mandated directly by the Prophet Muhammad in a dream and that anyone who doesn't believe in him will be purified by the sword. In response, the governor-general wants a fatwa against him.

Sheikh Amin tells me this on his return from the palace. His jellabiya is stained with mud from the first rainfall of the season. It crosses my mind that he can't see his soiled clothes, but then again knowing him he would gather the evidence, the rainfall, the condition of the roads, the probability that his clothes have been smeared with mud. He sits, as usual, with his head tilted upward, his walking cane still in his hand. "I told the governor-general that the appearance of the Mahdi is one of the signs of the end of Time. There is no dispute about this. He didn't know the particular hadiths I referred to but concurred that I knew best. So, I will not be rushed into issuing a fatwa," he says. "We need to question this Muhammad Ahmed first."

"Will he agree to come to Khartoum?"

"He can't refuse."

"So, you'll have him arrested and dragged here in chains?"

The Sheikh smiles. "Perhaps we can send you instead. Meet him, hear what he has to say, debate him, and come back with a report. A charlatan? A deluded mystic? It's time to tackle him head-on."

To travel southwest. It will be an opportunity to visit my sister, Halima, to find out how Akuany and Bol have been getting on in my absence. I say, "Is there a probability that he is really the Expected One?"

The Sheikh tightens his hands over his walking stick. "According to the Sufis we must be always anticipating the arrival of the Mahdi. We must live each day as if we are living in the end of Time. It is their opinion and not a wrong one."

I say, "But after the death of the Prophet Muhammad, peace be upon him, people declared it was the end of Time. They were wrong."

He nods. "Perhaps it is healthy for us to assume that the world does not have much longer in existence. To remember that it is temporary as we are temporary."

I say, "The Rightly Guided Mahdi has certain characteristics. He comes with signs. Surely the issue is whether Muhammad Ahmed is truthful in his claim or not, regardless of the government's position."

The Sheikh smiles. "That is why you are the right person to question him. He's been sending me personal letters urging me to join his cause. I know him. I met him some years back."

I am surprised. "Was he here in Khartoum?"

"Yes. He is originally from Dongola, but he was here. His father was a boatbuilder, and he was one too. Trade didn't appeal to him, though, and he studied with Sheikh Mahmoud al-Mubarak in Burri village. Because the students' food was subsidized by the government, he refused to eat it. He almost starved waiting for his family to send him what they could!"

I picture him. Hard on himself and ultimately on others.

Sheikh Amin goes on, "He used to roam the banks of the Nile and even then, he was known for his effective amulets. Austere, rigid, and simple, one of those people who think in absolutes. That was my assessment of him. He hated Khartoum."

"How can anyone do that!" I immediately regret sounding like an adolescent.

The Sheikh smiles. "He hated the church bells and the European missionaries. He hated the Greek merchants, the bars, women walking unveiled. He hated the Turks ruling us, the villas they built, the palace overlooking the Nile. When Muhammad Ahmed says these things, he speaks as if he's the first to discover them, as if he's the only one taking offense, as if we don't have reservations ourselves! We have successfully curbed the influence of the Christian missionaries."

"It is common knowledge that their activities are restricted."

He is emphatic. "We are continuously disabling their efforts. He, though, would have us banish them altogether, as if that is practical!"

There is a silence and what is unspoken is our understanding of idealism and pragmatic reality. For Sudan to be part of the sprawling unity of Islam, to receive the blessing of the Ottoman Khilafa, we must bend to the diplomatic pressures imposed on the sultan from European powers. We must consider what benefits Islam as a whole and curb our discontents with Turkish Egyptian rule.

He goes on, "Muhammad Ahmed swore allegiance to Sheikh Nur al-Daim but then they fell out. Sheikh Nur al-Daim now calls him the Dongolian devil covered in human skin."

He chuckles, but I experience a sting of fear. Do I really want to meet the devil covered in human skin? Out of curiosity I do and out of duty too. "What happened between them?"

"Sheikh Nur al-Daim was having a celebration for his son's wedding. There was singing, music, and dancing. The usual way of our people. Muhammad Ahmed publicly objected to the music and the mixing. He brought the party to a halt and offended his teacher's guests."

"Disrespectful," I say.

"But others see this as gumption. Standing up for what is right. Forbidding evil. Sheikh Nur al-Daim kicked him out. They say Muhammad Ahmed did beg him for forgiveness, prostrating and shackling himself to the forked yoke used to punish runaway slaves but Sheikh Nur al-Daim wouldn't relent."

This does not surprise me. It is not undue harshness. The oath sworn by a novice on these Sufi paths is strict.

Sheikh Amin continues, "Still, Muhammad Ahmed won himself admirers. He proved himself pious and stern. He joined another sheikh in the same order, and when the sheikh died, he took over. He is popular, no doubt, charismatic. Then there are the miracles. They weary me insofar as they show how gullible the population is. Poor, simple folk, unlearned and therefore vulnerable. Yes, go to him and come back. A young, educated man like yourself, he might soften toward you and agree to cooperate instead of sending threatening telegrams to the governor-general."

"What if he doesn't?"

He pretends not to hear me and calls out to the young boy who leads him home every day.

My plan to visit Halima on my way to Jazira Aba succeeds because the roads are still dry. I see Bol at the entrance of the house, and I embrace him. How tall he's grown! Old enough now to play in the alleys with boys his age, no longer the clinging toddler. Halima had written to me about his progress. How she now calls him Ishaq and how he had recently started Qur'an school. She rarely mentioned Akuany. Once, perhaps just a vague comment to say that she is faring well. I look out for her as the others gather to greet me—Halima, her husband, Hassan (with whom I had never felt completely comfortable), and my delightful nieces, all except Buthaina, of course now in her husband's house. Where is Akuany? Gone to run an errand perhaps.

It is Ramadan and soon after I arrive, we hear the cannon fired to mark the end of the fast. The neighbors arrive to welcome me, and they stay for maghrib prayers and the iftar meal. The conversation veers toward Muhammad Ahmed, who had recently visited the city and garnered support for his cause. He is well respected and trusted. The women swear by the amulets he has given them; men are in awe of his piety. I listen, saying nothing of my coming mission to meet him; I wonder yet again where Akuany is.

As soon as the guests depart, I ask about her, and instead of a reasonable explanation for her absence, there is silence. We are sitting in the hoash, and it is becoming a hot evening, no sign of clouds or breeze. Hassan gets up and goes inside. Halima stares at the ground. "What's wrong with you all," I say. "What happened?"

"She's with the governor's wife."

"Whatever for?" I try to recall what I know of the governor's wife. Turkish? Circassian? Isn't she the one known for her tantrums?

"She took a liking to Akuany." Halima says, her voice flat. "Saw her one day in the souq and demanded that she stay with her. You know what these people are like."

Hassan is back now, and he chimes in. "You can't say no to these people. They take what they want."

"What do you mean 'take'?"

They are silent and I fight the realization that is building up in my mind.

Hassan repeats, "You can't say no to these people. Then they toss you a pouch full of coins to seal the bargain."

"You *sold* her. How dare you!" I am shouting at them both. Standing now. "How could you! I left her with you in trust. I knew her father. She's an orphan! Did I go to the south and raid a village? Am I a slave trader? Have you turned me into one? Was she yours to do with as you like? I trusted you." I am bellowing and the household is paralyzed before me. A neighbor peers over the wall.

I think I will hit Hassan. I will shake Halima so that she cries instead of hanging her head down in shame. I dart out of the house. I walk all the way to the governor's house. It is guarded of course. The Baltagiya are there with their whips. "I need to see the governor," I say. "It's urgent."

"Come back in the morning," they say.

"I said it's urgent. A mistake has been made. It needs to be put right."

"Go, and come in the morning," they say.

I push past them, and they hold me back. They say, "If you're a scoundrel, why are you dressed like a learned man?"

Hassan's hand is now on my shoulder. He must have followed me. "Brother, don't make a fool of yourself. Remember your position. We can sort it all out in the morning." I hesitate and shrug him off. I walk straight into the night. She is inside this house now and God knows what they've done to her, what they've made of her. I should have taken her to my mother in Khartoum, I should have taken her with me to Egypt, I should not have let her out of my sight. It is clear to me that I have been a negligent fool. Her wholehearted trust . . .

Hassan is hurrying after me. "You need to calm down. You need to see this in perspective. Is this such a misfortune? She's living now in more luxury than we could ever provide her."

"I will get her back. Whatever it takes."

He catches up with me. "I can't believe you," he hisses. "Are you going to be one of those men who initiates a dispute over a slave girl? With the governor! And even if he relents, do you have fifty pounds to spare? Because that's what he paid for her, and I won't lie to you, we've spent it all."

I turn around and, with all my strength, punch him in the gut.

# 3

# Musa

It started with a new zikr we could hear at night. A different kind of chanting, raw and catchy. Prayers wafting in the dusty breeze, sung by nomads and traders. Sung around campfires and flickering lanterns. Chanted near the big creek by men sitting on cool, clean sand, in starlight and moonglow. Carried through dunes and waterways, the words circulating under trees. And it would continue through the night. There was nothing foreign about this zikr; it was our own language, familiar and fresh like a newborn from among us. It spoke to me after midnight. It spoke to us all. It said, *Wake up, you've been asleep.* It said, *Wake up, you've been exploited.* It said, *This is but a dream and reality a step away.* It started with a new zikr that lasted until dawn, that came with promises, that came with hope and pride. It said, You've been pushed aside, pushed around, squeezed, butted, cowed, held down. You've been robbed in broad daylight, sucked dry. You've been fooled. You've been strangled, and the end is there, there across a burning stretch, across spikes rising from the ground, past

43

traps, across pits, over water in which you could drown. But you will not drown. You will fight and win. You will fight and own your enemy's weapon, take his women, ride his horses. You will win because you will not be alone; there will be angels fighting by your sides, jinn on horseback. They wait for you to spring forth and then they will rise.

But no, it started well before the zikr. It started with games that we youngsters played. Two banners. Two groups of boys fighting under different flags. The banner of the Turks and the banner of the Mahdi. Only the Expected One could challenge the beastly Turks. We children of Al-Ubayyid would make the banners out of branches and old, discarded cloths. Whatever we could find. And there was no consistency. One time the black banner would represent the Mahdi, one time it would represent the Turks. A red banner, a green banner. The day I took part in the game it was the green banner, and I was on the side of the Mahdi. We fashioned wooden swords and we beat our opponents, the sons of brigadiers and constables, who fought on the side of the Turks. The game turned violent; blood was spilled until a sergeant's slave ran to report us to his master. We were winning before the elders came to break up the fight. Gave us a telling off too. Then we knew that what we were doing was more subversive than a children's game.

People were always talking about the Expected One, the Rightly Guided Mahdi. Wishfully at first, then with urgent need, with anticipation. He was our last resort, the sure way of success. Only someone divine could beat the Turks; only someone backed by angels could face their savage whips and Remington guns. Only someone sent by the Almighty could drive them out of our lands. And so, the hopes circulated, and we bided our time. Except, of course, those of us who were in the pockets of the government, and they were many, for a colonial administration needed its workers, from officials to the lowliest water carrier. Those directly and indirectly employed by the government and those who supplied it with hay for horses, firewood, and the laden caravans that made their way north to Egypt. Whole tribes who were benefiting from the Turks—the Khatmiya, the Shaigiya—completely loyal. But for the rest of us, there were taxes we couldn't pay, land we farmed only to yield enough to keep us alive and the rest went to them, boys stolen to prop up their armies, girls taken for their harems. No, there were no benefits for us; there was the hate stewing in our bodies, waiting to explode.

I would be the first to admit that I was not a conscientious youth. I had no sense of direction. I was neither adept in my lessons nor especially fit. I enjoyed playing, that's true, but I did not have ambition for gaining money either. Neither did religion fascinate me, nor did I possess an urge to travel. There was nothing remarkable about me. My father was an ironmonger; he fashioned knives and spears. He was an honest man, skilled in his work, the best in Al-Ubayyid. He taught me, or at least he tried. I used to run away from his workshop to play with the boys around the creek. I would often return home to find a beating waiting for me. To be honest, I did not appreciate the need for a skill; I did not understand the reasons for reading and writing. School meant a whipping every single day, slates with jumbled words that neither stayed in my head nor on my tongue. Standing up and making a fool of myself every time the teacher asked a question, then getting caned afterward. I could not tell the letters apart, which one had one dot or two or three, whether the dots should be above the letter or below. Ya, ta, tha, ba—they merged, and I didn't care either way, so much toil for one single sound. I sat in class, hearing the drone of the teacher's voice, and there was nothing that I was curious to know. At other times, at home, outside school, I would experience similar confusion. Distinguishing between my left and right sandals puzzled me and infuriated my parents. So, I walked barefoot instead.

Everywhere I turned I found oppression, the strong wanting to hound me, step all over me. And I was not the only one. We were like mules pushing our weight forward to be watered and fed. Eating to serve. Serving to die for one master or another. Dust and sweat, my ears jammed with their own ringing so that I could not hear their scolding, their talking sense, so that I would not fear their threats. No one respects you, I was told. Did I respect myself?

Yes, I did the day I was whipped and bore it without a whimper, not like my father. When we were young, he was whipped by the governor's Baltagiya. He twisted on the ground and cried out for them to stop—just like a woman. His shame covered us all, seeped into our lives so that we could not look straight into each other's eyes. And I understood why afterward my father felt the need to beat up my mother at the slightest provocation, to kick me, to punch my eldest brother when he disagreed with him. I understood why he did that, but I despised him for it—though I could not rationalize my feelings. Later I came to understand that my father was fighting the wrong enemy.

The day I was whipped and took it like a man—became a man—was special for me, my own private victory. I was whipped for insolence. The governor was prancing on his horse, his Baltagiya thugs surrounding him, and I did not get my cart out of the way. I was heading to the market, pushing a cart loaded with onions and potatoes, one more attempt to carn a living. The cart was heavy and one of the wheels was broken. And suddenly there they were, the Baltagiya, hefty and brandishing their whips, their uniforms damp with sweat, clearing the way for their master. Left and right they swatted us aside like vermin. Make way for the governor, make way for the governor. Dust rose in the air. I knew what was expected of me—to hurry off like everyone else was doing, duck, get out of the way, stay safe. But I didn't. Rebellion rose in me. Why should I budge for that Turk? Why should a foreigner order me around? If he's the one on the horse, then let him scamper past my broken cart.

I held my ground. They tipped my cart over and pushed me on top of the scattered vegetables. They rained blows on me, and I lifted my arms to protect my face. But not once did I cry out, not a whimper, not a sound. They had to move off. They could not leave the governor, and he would not interrupt his tour over such a trivial incident. I stood up and shook down my clothes, streaked with dust and blood. Someone helped me set my cart upright. Most of the onions and potatoes were crushed. I didn't care, so proud of myself I was, firm with righteousness, rich with dignity. Not a single tear.

Later, the Mahdi would teach us that strength came from not needing, from the ability to do without. It was need that bred weakness. Our need for food, for wealth, for sleep, for this and the other. If gold means nothing to you, then you are strong; if pain means nothing to you, then you are mighty; if death means nothing to you, then you are invincible. But he was yet to enter my life. In those early years I was confused, searching for him without knowing that I was searching. In those early years I was like any other young man.

A girl caught my fancy once. I saw her in the souq. Buthaina she was; everything about her seemed to pour over me, toward me, her plump cheeks, her voice like liquid, her skin like treacle. My passion for her grew, but she wouldn't have me. Her father dismissed me. "What kind of life would you give her? I think, son, you're not ready for marriage." Even my father did not have an encouraging word to say to me. It was like a joke to them, but I held a grudge. I wanted that girl with the plump, round face; she could have been the incentive for me to change, to mend my ways. But no, Buthaina was not for me with a father employed by the governor and an uncle studying at Al-Azhar. She had expectations of her menfolk. After that I took to drinking merissa, earned enough here and there to sit by moonlight and sip the brew, waiting for the pleasure to reach my head.

And then he saved me. The man visiting from Jazira Aba. The man with the gap between his teeth, the one who knew me inside out, the one who moved with grace and smiles. But I told this story often over the years, through wars and illness. I told of how in those early days he spoke to the weak and the strong, urging them to join him. He had a word for everyone, including worthless me. I gave up my life to him. He deserved everything I possessed, and what did I possess but this sinful body, this unruly mind, this life that pulsed within my heart?

When was the first time I met Muhammad Ahmed, the Mahdi? I don't have a straightforward answer. There was the day I saw him far away, just a glimpse, as he entered a mosque. The first day I heard his voice, when I prayed behind him, way back in the last row. The first day I saw him close, he was sitting down, head to one side, listening to someone next to him. The first day he looked at me and how it made me feel small and significant at the same time. The first time he spoke to me. The joy on the day I found out that he had remembered my name. At first, I could not be in his presence for long. It tired me, it drugged me. Then slowly I built up a tolerance. I would sustain longer prayers, I could stay up later in the night for the zikr, I would linger when others left. I poured water for his wudu, ran errands that however small, tedious, or tiring were satisfying because I was doing them for him. Best of all was when I accompanied him, not by his side, for I was too lowly for that, but trailing behind, hanging on as much as I could. When he spoke, each clear word entered my soul. For him, only for him, I could sit still without fidgeting. I could learn.

I was with him when he visited the influential men of Al-Ubayyid. The richest merchants, the highest officials, he would go to them, he would ask to be admitted, he would beg to be heard. There was no arrogance in him, no hurt pride if he was turned away, no bitterness, no vengeance. On and on, indefatigable, he would circulate. After a time, everyone got to know him. I adjusted myself to the structure of his day—the hot morning hours in seclusion and study, the cooler afternoon and early evening visiting and speaking. Then after midnight, the new zikr. Day by day, the circle got wider, the attendance increased. People came from smaller neighboring towns, nomads on their way to the watering wells stopped to listen. *Who is he?* they asked. And they got their answers. There was no mystery about him, his lineage well-known and comforting; so-and-so knew him; Sheikh so-and-so vouched for him. This is his brother, this is his brother-in-law, this is the man from whom he bought a goat and some leather.

The people of Al-Ubayyid described him as the man from the White Nile. Jazira Aba was his home now though he originally came from Dongola. They said people from the White Nile were good people, generous and forgiving. They would tell him that to his face and he would reply, "May I always visit you insha'Allah, and through me you can experience the sweetness of faith, until it settles in your hearts and you find your way to safety with the Almighty." Women flocked to see him for amulets that would make them fertile, for prayers to cure the sick, for blessings. He always obliged in those early days when all this activity took place at night while most people were asleep. We his students (was I a student now? I, the lazy dropout, the loafer?) and those who were keen, who loved him and listened when he shared the secret words. "I am the viceroy of the Prophet, peace be upon him. He had come to me in dreams and told me that I am the Expected One. Renounce the world and follow me. Follow me and stop paying taxes to the infidel Turks."

I traveled with him outside the city. We moved around Kordofan as he spoke to the settled Fur who had suffered from abusive tax collection and the rugged Baggara, the free-spirited cattle nomads whose livelihood was threatened by Gordon's insistence to end the slave trade. I traveled with him farther as he won over the sheikhs of one order after another—the Sammania, the Isma'ilia, the Tijania. He won over the Arab tribes of the White Nile, Dighaim and Kinana. I was there in Rufa'a when he recited the Qur'an and fell into a trance, when he wept, moved by the sura of the Calamity, when his name started to fly and people sought him out, eager for his miracles and his blessing. Even the steamers passing on the Nile would slow down, blow their whistle four times, and captain, crew, and passengers would turn toward the shore and offer their respect to that well-known holy man.

I was one of forty men who drank from a small cup of milk he had blessed. We drank our fill and there was still some left over. Women pushed their sons toward him. Farmers found his name written on leaves, inside aubergines, traders found it etched on ostrich eggs, schoolboys found it scratched on watermelon seeds, and he was present in the dreams of the elders and in the hallucinations of the mad. Even in the dens of debauchery, within the vapors of opiates and merissa, his name was mentioned with tenderness. He was humble and fervent. He did not want prestige; he was neither pompous nor overbearing. He preached that the end was near. He said, "Nothing is left of Islam but its name; nothing of the Qur'an but its Arabic script." He wanted a revival. He wanted an awakening. He gathered us around him, riverine tribes and nomads, those from the Blue Nile and those from the White. We swore allegiance to him singularly and in clans. When chiefs swore allegiance to him, they did so in the name of the whole tribe. They brought their people with them.

I was one of the first to prepare to leave Al-Ubayyid and make my pilgrimage to Jazira Aba where the Mahdi was based. "One day you will return swathed in victory," he told me. "This is the hour of need for which you have been created." I made a point of saying my goodbyes to my family and friends. I made a point of telling them why I was leaving. Surprise on their faces, neither many questions nor comments. My father had washed his hands of me years ago. My brothers were weary of me asking them for money and meals, my mother no longer alive to plead my case as mothers usually do.

I urged my friends to join me. Those of us who, years ago, played by the creek our game of Turks against the Mahdi, well before he appeared, well before he declared himself. "The Guided One is manifest," I said to them. "I am going to him in Jazira Aba. Come with me."

# 4

# Akuany/Zamzam

**Al-Ubayyid, 1879–1881**

She was in the souq when the governor's wife saw her. She was talking to the cows like she always did whenever she was sent to run an errand. The ones in this market were ragged and thin. Some of them would be used for heavy work; they would be blindfolded and made to walk all day in circles drawing up water from the creeks and waterways. Without the blindfold they would get sick and dizzy, but hours of darkness must not be pleasant either. Akuany felt sorry for them. Suddenly a woman carrying a sack of tomatoes touched her shoulder and pointed toward a carriage. The driver had just disembarked and was walking toward them. The man tending the cows said, "Look girl, they want you over there. The governor's wife. Go, don't keep them waiting."

Akuany did as she was told. She walked toward the carriage and met the driver halfway. With him leading the way, her steps to the carriage were less tentative. The market crowd parted so that they could pass. Soon she could see a plump white arm reaching out from the carriage's window. And there was the governor's wife, kohl rimming her eager eyes, a tiny hat on her head, under which dark, heavy hair and a white gauze veil cascaded to her shoulder. She was saying things that Akuany couldn't understand. She was wanting something, and she was used to getting what she wanted.

Akuany became Nazli Hanim's girl. The governor's wife was bored and homesick. She was miserable because she had figured out that if her husband had truly been a great catch worthy of her, he would not have been posted to this dump. Her parents had been deceived. They had not done their research properly; they had sold her short. "Be patient, my darling Nazli," the governor had said to her. "We won't be here for long. It's a mistake. I'm doing everything I can to get us out of here."

He would do anything to pacify her, to keep her occupied and entertained. Anything to stop the sulks, the tantrums, the haranguing. A little black girl. Why not? With Gordon now out of the way, the unpopular anti-slavery laws could be ignored. He tracked down the family and tossed them the money, wrote out a bill of sale and had it witnessed. This was how Akuany started her new life. Officially enslaved.

The governor's house was huge, and Nazli Hanim's quarters were crammed full of things. Tapestries on the walls, huge bulky furniture, carpets to sink in. The windows were covered with curtains, and it was cool and dark. Akuany had never seen anything like this. On the first day, Nazli Hanim shoved her forward and said, "Walk straight ahead and see what you find."

Akuany found a girl from her village. The girl also had a nose ring and shoulder-length braids. Akuany smiled and the girl smiled too. Akuany reached out to touch her and the girl did that too. Suddenly with a shock Nazli Hanim was behind the girl, cackling and screeching and she was behind Akuany, too, at the same time. Both girls squealed.

"It's you, fool," screeched Nazli Hanim. "In the mirror." She hooted with laughter.

Akuany put her fist in her mouth.

"Do you like what you see?"

She nodded. Very much. The girl in the mirror was pretty. Especially when she took her fist out of her mouth and smiled.

"Fool," said Nazli. "Wait till I'm done with you. Wait till I fumigate you and dress you properly. And you need a new name too."

There followed a great deal of bathing and delousing. Nazli scrubbed Akuany so hard that she scratched her skin. She made her try one outfit after outfit and then marched her to see herself in the mirror. Akuany preferred how she had looked the first time, like a girl who could be her friend. But Nazli Hanim did not care about her opinion. She gave her a new name, a Muslim one. Akuany became Zamzam.

Compared to the others enslaved in the governor's household, Zamzam had an easy life. At least at first, before the novelty wore off and Nazli got bored of her. In those early days, she could not have enough of her. She continued to dress her in costumes that became more and more outrageous. She took great pleasure in designing and ordering these costumes from the tailor. At times she even dressed her up as a boy. She taught her how to sing and to walk up the stairs without being afraid. Seeing stairs for the first time in her life, Zamzam had at first sat down and pushed herself up one step at a time.

Nazli wanted her to perform even more acrobatics. Once she commanded her to climb up a tall cupboard and dance on top of it. Zamzam lost her balance, fell, and broke her arm.

This was the first time Nazli hit her. How dare you fall off! What a nuisance you are! With a broken arm (and the slap), Zamzam was not much fun to play with. She was tossed aside and so ended up with the others who had their quarters outside, across from the kitchen. Hadija, the older cook, befriended her. She took her to a traditional bonesetter who wrapped her fractured arm in fresh goatskin soaked in water. Hadija made sure that Zamzam had plenty of rest. Hadija could speak Chollo, and it was such a relief to listen, to understand, to talk. Hadija explained things to Zamzam, explained how the governors came and went. Some were Albanian; some were Egyptian; some had been stationed elsewhere in Sudan; some in other parts of the Ottoman Empire. They all served the big sultan in Constantinople. Everyone had someone higher than him. Hadija was special because she had been freed long ago. She was now earning her living at three Maria Theresa dollars a month, which Zamzam guessed must be a huge amount because of the way Hadija dropped her voice when she said it. She was a Muslim and had gone at her own expense to the Hajj, further enhancing her superiority. The others in the kitchen belonged to the government and to this specific compound in Al-Ubayyid. Zamzam's position was different, Hadija explained. She belonged specifically to the governor and his Nazli Hanim. Zamzam was treated better, but to some extent, the others could come and go as they pleased; there was something impersonal and collective about their predicament. One day they might all be freed en masse. It had happened before when General Gordon went to Al-Fasher. It could happen here.

Hadija was bald and she had a yellow string of beads around her head. She took them off when she made her ablutions and hitched up her dress over her head when she prayed, standing straight in her pantaloons. Zamzam would be allowed to hold her beads during that time, and she enjoyed their smoothness in her palm, their dull, honeyed color. In the late afternoon, Hadija would sit in the shade of the guava tree that grew in the backyard and smoke a red clay pipe. Zamzam liked to sit near her, smelling the pipe and eating unripe guava. Hadija was the one who braided her hair in the Fulani style with blue and orange beads. She took an interest in her story. "When your merchant comes back," she said, "he will ask about you for sure. But would he be able to get you back? Maybe, I've seen it happen. But then the governor is the governor, and Nazli Hanim has her whims."

This nevertheless comforted Zamzam. Seductive hope lightening the dreary outdoor kitchen where they worked. From dawn to sunset they cleaned, cooked, washed, ironed, and fed the considerable number of Baltagiya and staff living in the governor's compound. One of the young women, Hibra, tall and lively with hair extensions made of goat's hair and secured with gum, oversaw the governor's guest quarters. Whenever a guest arrived (all military men and there was a continuous flow of them) she would make sure that his room was ready. She would serve his meals and take charge of his laundry and mending. She would polish his boots. She would massage his back and press his feet. She would also make him feel truly welcome and to achieve that she had to be available and accessible. Expectations differed from one man to the next and could not always be predicted. Some men ignored her, some pinched and flirted, some pulled her to bed, some were brutal. A few would remember afterward to toss her a coin or two. Hibra must continue to smile, to lower her head, though not all men wanted subservience, she explained to Zamzam. Some liked her sassy and uncouth, some preferred the thrust of vulgarity, the thrill of coarseness, some needed a bit of help. She must tell these men apart, use her wits, find out what they wanted before they knew they wanted it. Intuition, sharpness, flexibility—these were the skills she honed. The others and even kindly Hadija admired Hibra and held her in esteem.

While Hadija mothered Zamzam, Hibra took on the role of the young aunty. "I will teach you all I know," she would say.

"Don't corrupt the child, Hibra."

"I'm telling you, Hadija, she has potential." She turned and winked at Zamzam. "Go on, tell them what the binbashi gave you this morning."

Zamzam had gone with her to the guest quarters to help serve the early morning tea. The major was a large, genial man, thinning hair offset by a bushy moustache and thick sideburns. Still in his underwear, he had fondled Zamzam's cheeks and squeezed her backside. "What a sweetie you are," he'd said. "Why do they hide all the new treats from me and fob me off with the same thing every visit." He laughed at his own jokes while Hibra tutted and fussed over him. He gave Zamzam a coin, which she handed over to Hibra because it seemed the right thing to do.

The anecdote was met with smiles among the kitchen staff and Zamzam was pleased to be in their company, their toughness, and the warm sadness they held inside. Their sorrow that seeped out in sunsets and in songs, that burst out in nightmares. Many of them shouted in their sleep, thrashed out at enemies. The pain in them was so deep it was almost forgotten, distant memories of loved ones and homes, those who died on the way, those who were God knows where. They only spoke about the here and now, the silly mistress, the governor who would rather be elsewhere, his Baltagiya with their whips that they could aim at the household staff if they were ordered to do so. Work and more work, dragging themselves at the crack of dawn to sweep the dust off the veranda, to polish the floor as the young mistress instructed them to do, to wash the curtains again, to chop, boil, fry, and break their backs over the fire.

When Zamzam's arm mended, she was whisked upstairs again, back to the card games, to the ridiculous outfits and acting the clown. There were outings to the foreign families deemed prestigious enough to entertain the governor's young wife. Zamzam enjoyed the carriage rides, the change of scenery. On one occasion, she suddenly missed Bol and gathered up the courage to ask to see him. Nazli's no was accompanied by a jab with her fan, and so Zamzam did not ask again. In these other houses, there were children for her to play with, if they wanted to play with her. She was not a guest and not a servant, something in between. If the games required a scapegoat, if the games required a loser, a punch bag, or something to kick, she was the best one for the role. When her outfit got stained or torn, she was punished by Nazli.

A year passed and Bol was allowed to visit her as an Eid treat. Halima brought him. "Alhamdulilah you are well, Zamzam," she said. She spoke in a formal way and looked out of place sitting on the governor's porch. She did not want to listen to complaints and was suspicious of questions about her brother. The matter was out of her hands. Ishaq, the Arabic name she had given Bol, was now the son she could not give birth to. She would make sure he got an education and bettered himself. In this grand plan, Zamzam was little more than an inconvenience.

A year passed. Another. Zamzam shot up. She became gangly; she became taller than Nazli, which irked her. Zamzam was no longer cute. She was no longer the pinch-her-cheek, pull-along toy. It was time for less fun and more work. When Nazli's mother visited, Zamzam was assigned to look after her. She carried water for her bath, she massaged her feet, and she learned how to prepare the hookah pipe, which the elderly lady indulged in almost every afternoon. At the end of the elderly lady's visit, both the governor and Nazli traveled with her to Khartoum and on to Suakin where she boarded her ship. Zamzam stayed behind. She was not their first choice; they took with them other servants who were more efficient and versatile.

Their absence felt like freedom. She was now with the other household staff and there was hardly any work to do. She slept more and ate better. She visited Bol whenever she wanted to. There were also some adventures for her to experience in this month. The time she went up to the roof of the district office and stood near the mighty cannon, whose blast had frightened her so much when she first arrived in

Al-Ubayyid. She could see the roof of the storeroom made of dom palm wood and the sentry at the door. The time she went with Hadija and Hibra to a wedding and danced for the first time as a young adult, and she did not need to learn how to dance, because the rhythm was in her and the movements felt so natural that it was as if all she had been waiting for was the drum. How well Hadija danced even though she said she was sixty-five and past her prime! How graceful, how supple was Hibra's body as if it were pure muscle and flesh without a single bone! The beat of the drum went inside Zamzam's soul, thrilled her with feelings she did not understand, raked memories of her mother's body and her mother's mother and her mother's mother's mother. All of them had known these breasts jiggling, their knees bouncing, sisters on either side. It was the zaghrouta though, which Zamzam could not master, no matter how hard she tried. Twisting her tongue, cupping her hand over her mouth, making an *eyeo eyeo eyeo* sound, but the joy cry would not come out. Hibra and Hadija laughed at her. "It can't be taught," Hibra said. "It just happens, you have a feeling, an excited feeling, everyone is around you, all together, and then it just bursts out of you. You go on and on until you are out of breath, and then you feel relieved afterward." Hadija spoke of the enslaved when they were freed en masse by General Gordon at Al-Fasher, the women heading out with bundles balanced on their heads and babies strapped to their backs. On that day you could hear their ululations from far, far away.

One of the young soldiers who guarded the province prison started to court Zamzam, sending her gifts of food. He interested her a little because he played in the military band, which seemed to her a fine thing, but whenever he spoke to her it was a disappointment. He didn't know her, nor had he ever seen a river. He occupied a small place in the universe; he was someone with little substance. Not like her merchant.

Her merchant would come for her one day. Save her. Whisk her away to his home in Khartoum. She believed in his ability to do so, in his sense of responsibility. She believed that their fates were entwined. That he was for her and she was for him.

And he must save her soon before she became like Hibra, serving in the guest quarters with no one to protect her, at the mercy of whoever was visiting, obliged to do what they wanted. Zamzam was Hibra's height now, still a little gangly but soon she would be graceful; she would fill out. The only reason that she had not yet caught a visiting general's eye was because Hibra, lately, had started to fear the competition. Instead of asking for Zamzam's help, she turned vicious if Zamzam ever ventured near her territory.

Hibra fell pregnant. There was much whispering between her and Hadija—Zamzam the wide-eyed listener. This was not the first of Hibra's pregnancies but certainly one worth keeping. If Hibra delivered safely and her lover, the binbashi, acknowledged the child as his, it meant freedom. Manumission for Hibra and a status for the baby equal to that of the major's other children. She would become Umm al-Walad, mother of the master's child. It had happened before to so-and-so and so-and-so. Hadija named lucky women, heads held high in Al-Ubayyid society whether anyone liked it or not. And when the son grew up, even better, who would dare insult a gentleman and call his mother an ex-slave! They might whisper it among themselves, but the law was the law; and if you dig deep, you will find that in every Sudanese family there is a branch that trailed back to a manumitted woman who went through agony to deliver a free child.

Perhaps Hibra should have waited until she gave birth, but she did not; she could not. She sprung the news on the binbashi, who turned purple with rage. Accused her of playing a trick. Did she not bed every guest who passed through the governor's compound? How on earth could she be sure that the child was his? He whipped her with his belt, knocked out her front teeth, and because this was not enough to quench his fury, picked her up and flung her against the wall. A hefty muscular man in his prime. She was left bleeding and it was not an accident that she lost her child. It was the intended outcome of the attack, a strategic blow executed by a military man.

For days, Hibra was ill. Raving and feverish, then broken, knowing she was broken, staring into space. Zamzam nursed her. Normal chitchat had no effect on Hibra. She barely returned a greeting. Zamzam thought her latest news must surely pique Hibra's interest. She herself could barely sit still or focus on any task after finding out that Yaseen had returned to claim her. "My merchant is back," she told Hibra. "He came yesterday and spoke to the governor about me. They are negotiating." Zamzam kept babbling, and Hibra kept staring into space. She did not ask any questions.

The whole of Al-Ubayyid heard about the merchant, now Al-Azhar graduate and one of Khartoum's jurists, coming to take back the orphan girl. Or at least having the audacity to claim her back! How gracious the governor was to receive him, to listen to his side of the argument! And then to say,

"Oh well, you could have her back if you return the money I handed over to your brother-in-law. A new bill of sale could be written, no problem at all."

There was, though, a problem. In that Yaseen did not have fifty pounds. He must return to Khartoum, spend time earning or raising the money and then come back to Al-Ubayyid. "No problem," said the generous, reasonable general who had no personal stake in his wife's discarded toy. "Take as long as you need. The girl can continue to live with us."

Zamzam did not accept this decision. She had waited before, and she would not wait again. She planned her escape on the night Yaseen was due to leave town. Without letting him know (they had not even seen each other during his days in Al-Ubayyid), she resolved to catch up with him at the outskirts of the city. His date and time of departure was easy to find out. It was not a secret.

It was dark when she left the compound, while the Baltagiya were busy eating their evening meal. Covered with one of Hadija's shawls, she slipped past the guards and kept walking in the starlight. The recent rain had left behind a breeze, small tufts of grass beginning to grow in the dark reddish earth. She knew where she was going. She hurried past the lepers who lived in the graveyard, past the last of the wells, stood still under a tree when a group of men walked past carrying lanterns. She waited for him after the huts started to thin. Soon, she saw him on his camel and gestured for him to stop. He seemed to expect her to speak up to him, ask him a question and get a reply. He could not tell who she was, and this came as a surprise; she was so used to him knowing more than her. She had to raise her voice, gesture for him to disembark. With reluctance, he instructed his camel to kneel. The camel lowered itself to the ground and he disembarked. She pushed her way into his arms.

"It's you," he said, and he said her name over and over again. She had not heard it for a long time, her real name. She laughed and he laughed and gasped at how much she had grown. "Is it possible?" he kept saying. "Masha'Allah. Akuany. Akuany." His smile, the same smile she had recalled every single day, his kind attention, the rightness of being with him—but all for too short a time. The sweetest interlude before he blurted out, "Oh no, no, no, you are not coming with me!"

"I am. I am. And you can't force me to go back there. I won't go. You don't know what it is like."

Her heart was pounding from the escape, being with him, the night. Her tongue was loose with what had been jammed inside her for years. "I must go with you. I want to. You can't stop me. Aren't I pretty enough for you? Don't you desire me? I know I am, and I know you do." She scrambled onto the kneeling camel, clung to the saddle, and said, "Here I am. Already. I will not get off, whatever you do. I am not going back. I will go with you to Khartoum."

He watched her with wonder. He had never looked at her that way before. He scratched his head and at one time looked around as if searching for help. He began to explain, but she interrupted.

"Oh, he has money, that governor. He doesn't need yours," she said. "They have gold hidden in locked trunks; I have seen Nazli Hanim's jewelry with my own eyes. He has seven thousand pounds hidden in a box in a secret part of the inside wall. Hibra told me about it; she knows where it is. And then

he insists on getting fifty pounds from you! I will go with
you, and you can pay him later. That's what you have to do.
Because I want you. I want you very much. I want you and
no one else. Ever."

"Are you sure?" he asked.

"Yes, I am sure."

He sat on the ground. "But now that you've escaped, why
tie yourself to me? Why go from one master to another?"

This was a trick question and she paused. There was the
wide-open space of the desert in the starlight. There was a
north to Khartoum and a south to her village. There were
routes to the White Nile, the Sobat River, streamers, boats,
riverways, and small villages all dotted along the river. She
paused to take all that in, to breathe the possibilities. Of
making it on her own, free and away.

Time passed with her sitting on the kneeling camel and
he on the ground. She was used to him being quiet with his
prayer beads. Memories of their journey—this was why she
was here, taking a risk, to live again those days and nights.
The time when they escaped from her burned village, moving
to safety, dodging danger, never settling in one place, never
having enough to eat and drink, the river too far away for
her liking and home far away for him.

Stalemate. She on the camel, he on the sand. Neither of
them shifting. Oddly enough, they started chatting about other
things. It was perhaps she who commented first on the camel.
An ugly creature, hideous compared to a cow. Ridiculous
hump, frightening face. He laughed and said, "We Arabs love
our camels. They are our ships of the desert. They are miraculous creatures, one of the signs of the Almighty." He then

told her a story about her father helping deliver a neighbor's calf. A long, difficult delivery, but then the most luminous of newborns. She had not known that story and listened intently. "Was that before Bol was born? Was that when I was a baby?"

"Maybe. I didn't know your father then," he said. "I only came to your village five seasons."

She thought that he had always been coming, all through her life. This made him laugh. "You think me an old man then. I am only eight years older than you, maybe ten. I certainly wasn't trading on my own as a child, though I did accompany my father on trips."

They spoke about Bol; they spoke about things that did not make her sad. Then the stalemate silence again, neither of them budging.

When he finally spoke of their disagreement, he said, "I am not going to Khartoum. I am going to Jazira Aba on government business. I can't take with me a runaway slave. I have been putting things right. The governor and I came to an agreement. I will raise the money and come back for you. I give you my word."

He was being reasonable, but she fought back. "You will need to drag me off this camel," she said. "I will not go back to them." He left her to say all she wanted to say, did not budge an inch. Gave her all the time she needed. Cool, he was. She had not thought he would reject her, resist her, turn down a chance for them to be together. And when she realized that he would—that he had—she cried, and when she cried he won the argument because if she genuinely believed she were traveling with him, why would she give in to disappointment?

She got off the camel on her own but not silently. She cursed him with rotten luck, wished out loud that his camel would become lame, that robbers would cross his path, and that his mission, whatever it was in Jazira Aba, would fail. "You're not brave," she said. And he agreed with her and said, enigmatically, "I hope I have not wronged you. Allah answers the prayers of those who have been wronged." She left him and after walking a distance turned and saw that he was still sitting on the ground. She waited—because hope is always hard to kill—until he settled on the camel. It lurched up and forward; he went on with his journey.

Her absence was noted, as was the red chemise she had stolen from Nazli Hanim. The red chemise never did achieve its purpose, which, in Zamzam's mind had involved nights of passion and stars. "Acting like a slut," Hadija admonished her, pinching her thighs.

"I am not a slut."

"Chasing a man! Stealing. You're the governor's khadim. Treat this position with respect."

"I'm not a khadim! I'm not meant to be here. I belong to Yaseen and no one else."

Hadija pinched her hard enough to make her scream. "Oh girl, you deserve a severe punishment." She was punished with imprisonment in the dark storeroom with only bread and water. "Until she weeps in repentance and kisses my feet," Nazli Hanim said. Zamzam refused to do this. No days in the dark, no bread-and-water diet would make her repent. No, she would never kiss the Hanim's feet. And she was full of rage, with everything and everyone, including him.

# 5

# Yaseen

**Jazira Aba, August 1881**

I am told the man I am seeking is in a cave. He had been in seclusion they say, but he might receive me now. They give me directions. As I approach the cave, I am surprised by the numbers gathered. Whole families who seem to have traveled from elsewhere, camping alongside their meager belongings. They are Muhammad Ahmed's new followers. Disparate groups gathering and there is something touching about their earnest hope, a mixture of dogged determination and the resignation of those whose demands are often thwarted. I make my way through the throng until I reach the rocky riverbank and the guards at the entrance of the cave. They take my name and ask for the purpose of my visit. Then they ask me to wait.

There are others waiting for an audience and with delight I recognize my friend Isma'il, whom I had not seen since our days in Cairo. Because he had graduated ahead of me, he is already an established judge in West Kordofan. We acknowledge in whispers that we are here for the same purpose.

What is this Muhammad Ahmed all about—could he really be the Expected One? Is he a threat to law and order? The second seems unlikely, given the state of the motley crowd surrounding us, unarmed beggars, young men with nothing but the axes they use for chopping wood and the knives for slaughtering chickens. We wonder if the holy man will receive us together or separately and agree to discuss our assessment afterward. Isma'il will travel to Khartoum with me as he has business there. I start to look forward to our journey together and to hosting him in Khartoum.

Muhammad Ahmed receives us separately. Isma'il is summoned in first, and I wait my turn. When he comes out, he shields his eyes with his hands and squints. "It's dark in there," he says.

I discard my sandals and stoop to enter the cave. I give my eyes time to adjust to the darkness. It is cooler here, the ground pleasant and soft under my feet. I reach out to touch the wall and it feels damp under my palm; I shuffle toward the murmur of voices. I recognize him straight away. There is a group of men seated on birch rugs, dressed alike, but it is obvious who their leader is. There can be no mistake. That smile so often mentioned in descriptions of him is directed at me. Handsome face, mole on the right cheek, gap between his front teeth, square figure, light skin. What I find new is the energy emitting from his eyes, an endearing approachability. I cannot help but warm to him, want to hear more from him, want to see more. He wears a patched coat, straw cap under his turban. He tells me to sit, and his voice is as attractive as his bearing.

"Our guest from Khartoum," he tells the gathering. "A graduate from Al-Azhar. One of the younger generations of ulema. Welcome. You are indeed welcome."

His tone is warm and sincere. I imagine if it were not Ramadan, I would have been offered refreshments. I sit with my back pressed against the wall. I had prepared a speech. I have more than a dozen questions, but suddenly my tongue is heavy in my mouth.

He speaks in low, soothing tones. He is not speaking about himself; he is, to my surprise, speaking about me. "That young man turned his back on the life of a merchant in order to get an education. In order to serve the Almighty. Admirable."

I wonder how he knows so much about me. Could it have been Sheikh Isma'il? Doubtful he would waste his precious audience detailing the background of a friend. Still, it feels odd, flattering but odd.

"And you distinguished yourself in Cairo. A diligent student, a quick learner. But all that you learned there you could have learned here. I never went in search of qualifications from any institution. Such validation means nothing to me. Do you think you know more than me?"

I do think that, but it would be impolite to say so.

"But you did right in giving up your past life," he continues, as if I had asked for his approval. "The life of a merchant is a loose life, traveling here and there. All the way to the south and up again. Plenty of temptation, plenty to cause a young man to stray down the paths of sin and debauchery. Is that not the case?"

There is a silence as if I am under interrogation. As if I stumbled and my clothes accidently hitched up to reveal my privacy. A fault on display. Her arms around my neck and her flesh radiating, a woman who was neither lawful wife nor concubine. But how can such a vivid picture come to my mind of something that did not take place? A temptation I resisted? In this company, a sin I wanted to commit but did not commit, internalized, seeps out of me like sweat.

"Because you settled for second best," he says, "supping at the sultan's table. The Turks pay you a high salary. Three hundred piasters a month and two ardeb of sorghum?"

"Oh no," I protest. If it were so, the fifty demanded by the governor would have been within reach and I would not have sent Akuany back! "My salary is far lower than that." I dislike the tone of my voice. How I sound disgruntled, eager for what my superiors earn, what I might qualify for in the future. What he quoted is what a high court judge in Khartoum earns.

He goes on, "The government that is employing you is not Muslim. Would Muslims open the door to the Christian missionaries? I saw the schools they established in Khartoum. For slaves and Christians they claim, teaching them Italian and music. But this is a cover, a front for proselytizing and for slavery. The Turks abolished the penalties for adultery and the drinking of alcohol. And you now administer their laws? Are you not ashamed?"

I look ashamed enough for him to continue. "Do you know what I am offering you?" he says, "the magnitude of it? I am offering you freedom from oppression and everlasting life."

There is a misunderstanding between us. I am not here for an offer. I am here to investigate him. I am here to advise him to relinquish his claim of being the Mahdi and instead fulfill his religious duty by setting out on the Hajj. Travel would broaden his horizons, enable him to see the world in perspective. I open my mouth to speak and close it again. The reverence of his followers is thick in the cave. They hang on every word he says. It crosses my mind that they would kill for him, they would die, and they would do anything in between.

He goes on, "Whoever opposes me will be humiliated by thunderstorms and drowning. In my audience with the Prophet Muhammad, peace be upon him, the second audience, he told me that."

A ripple of devotion passes through the seated men. They raise their voices in praise. They laud him as the Expected One. He continues to describe his "audience." How he lost consciousness of this world, how he entered a state swathed in light, and what he heard he heard with his heart, so that there was no doubt after that. No doubt that he was the Expected One the corrupt world was waiting for, the necessary salvation, the Guided One who would fill it with justice and equity. He is convinced by what he is saying. Totally. The certainty is fiery and contagious. One of his followers, a thin youth, swoons into a trace. Water is splashed on his face, but he remains immobile.

Ah . . . this is now a laughing matter. In theory at least, for I have not the slightest inclination to laugh. It is dread instead that emboldens me to speak.

"The Expected Mahdi has signs and characteristics," I say. "Certain conditions, his place of birth for instance . . ."

"I fulfill them all." His tone is cooler now but still patient. The smile unchanged. He proceeds to enumerate his signs. His name, the mole on his right cheek, his lineage traced back to the Prophet, peace be upon him. There is no documented evidence of the latter, but I do not refute his claim.

"Your vision, the one that prompted your public manifestation," I start to say. "Tell me—"

He interrupts me. "It is not only the Prophet Muhammad who was present but the souls of all the other prophets and messengers, the saints of the times. And in front of them all he said that I was his viceroy on earth, that I was the Expected Mahdi. He told them that whoever doubts me has disbelieved Allah and His Prophet, whoever does not support me is an infidel."

The weight of this pronouncement hangs in the air. The abomination of the word "infidel" levied at a Muslim. Whoever does not support him is an infidel! He delivers it lightly, still smiling, but I know and he knows the consequences of charging a Muslim with kufr, casting them out. There would be endless repercussions on their property and family relations, on even their right to life. The consequences are extreme. Reeling, I take my leave and stumble out of the cave. It takes self-control not to quicken my steps, not to appear as if I am fleeing.

It is comforting to find Sheikh Isma'il waiting for me. He looks grim, surveying the gathered crowds, travelers waiting for hours to glimpse the Expected One, waiting for him to lead them in prayer, to make more pronouncements that would change their lives. We had been given special treatment, granted interviews because of our Azhari titles, but ordinary people must wait. Muhammad Ahmed seeks the gravitas that an endorsement from us would grant him. He did not get it and if we are allowed to leave unscathed, it is because he still has hope that in due course we will come around to his cause.

We take the ferry to the mainland and depart on our camels straight away. After a few hours we stop for the noon prayers and exchange impressions. Isma'il says, "I was reminded of al-Nabulsi. Have you heard of him? From Damascus. In the seventeenth century he was the most famous of the scholar poets. He said his sacred knowledge came to him in dreams. Visions in which he met the companions of the Prophet, peace be upon him. An eccentric man who at times shunned the communal prayer and kept himself to himself."

I say, "This is different. Muhammad Ahmed is basing law on a dream. Imagine if on the month of the pilgrimage, someone, no matter who, the most pious, the most learned and well respected wakes up one morning and says that the Prophet came to him in a dream and told him that today is the start of Ramadan. What then? The whole umma abandons the Hajj and starts to fast? The calendar is readjusted? Would Islam have lasted through the centuries if such madness has ever been allowed? I am not questioning his visions. They are his, but they are his alone. He has no right to extrapolate laws from them. They have no basis on the fiqh or the shariah. Dreams are not evidence."

Sheikh Isma'il agrees. "I came with an open mind. In the sense that I was ready to believe that an intense spiritual experience had addled his mind. A case of jadhb, an effortless pull so strong and sudden toward the mystic that it is detrimental to a man's sanity. In that case it would be unfair to judge him by the outward law and it is best to leave him, to give him the time and space to come to his senses. But this is not what I find today."

"Not at all," I say. "He is in complete control of his faculties. Articulate, thoughtful, he has a purpose based on his visions."

"And what is worse, what I take against him is the takfeer. He is sentencing as infidels all who don't and won't accept his claim," Isma'il says, "insisting that anyone opposing him is an unbeliever!"

I tut. Belief in the Mahdi is not a vital component of faith. It is not one of the six pillars of iman: belief in Allah, His Angels, His Books, His Messengers, Judgement Day, and Divine Decree.

Isma'il says, "The true Expected Mahdi would never make such a pronouncement. There is no doubt in my mind. Muhammad Ahmed is not who he claims to be."

We mull the consequences of takfeer. Declaring that a Muslim is an unbeliever carries huge consequences. On individuals, on tribes, on the whole of the Turkish Egyptian administration, on the sultan sitting in Constantinople. It does not bear thinking about.

Isma'il knows the signs of the Expected One more than I. He enumerates them in detail, his features, place of birth, place of manifestation. I grow drowsy and move away from him to have a nap. I curl up in the shade that my camel throws and instead of the prominent matter we are pursuing, instead of the cave and the remarkable man I had just met, I dream of Akuany. In the dream I am enticed by the young woman she has become, and I do not turn her away.

In Khartoum, I enjoy Isma'il's stay and the resumption of our friendship. Sharing meals, going to and from the mosque. We have so much in common. How I relish talking about our studies in Cairo, comparing experiences, discussing books! The fact that he is my senior makes me look up to him. When he maps a career path for me in the judiciary, I pay attention. Day by day, his visit passes quickly, and though we often mention our encounter with Muhammad Ahmed in Aba, we are lulled by the ever-cosmopolitan character of Khartoum. My superior, Sheikh Amin, has moved on to other matters and my report about Muhammad Ahmed is well received. The government is taking matters into its hands, Sheikh Amin tells me, and a high-ranking official, Su'ud Bey, is himself going to Jazira Aba by steamer to convince Muhammad Ahmed to come to Khartoum and face the ulema.

A week later, Su'ud Bey returns to Khartoum empty-handed and furious. The meeting had gone badly. Muhammad Ahmed had sneered at the suggestion of coming to Khartoum. "Who should come to whom," he'd said. "I am the representative of the Prophet on earth and whoever disbelieves in my mandate will perish."

So now a whole squadron is going to sail against him. A Turkish general, Su'ud Bey, and six hundred Egyptian soldiers to arrest him. His followers are pitiful and unarmed. Let this be the end of the nonsense, to nip this threat in the bud before it gets out of hand.

After Isma'il's departure, my mother springs a surprise on me. "I have selected a wife for you," she says. "It is high time you got married. This girl is irresistible, a relation of Sheikh Amin Al-Darir, also from Tutti Island. Would you not agree that this would be an honorable union?"

I do not disagree. My mother is a strong-willed woman, even stronger since my father passed away. If he was tempering her, then now no one can. I am frank with her and explain the situation with Akuany.

She is undeterred. "You will not be the first bridegroom with a concubine nor the last. This is not a valid obstacle."

"The money is," I say. "Am I to pay the governor in Al-Ubayyid or prepare for a bride? I already gave my word."

In other households, this would have been sufficient for a woman to back off. But my mother is undeterred. She persists and says, "I gave my word too." She drags her gold bangles off from her arms and tosses them in my lap. "Don't use money as an excuse."

I am annoyed by this gesture. I hand her back the bangles. Delays lie ahead of me; promises I will have to break.

# 6

# Musa

## Jazira Aba/Jebel Gadir, August–December 1881

We waited for the steamer. Our master, the Mahdi, told us
that the government would come. We had scouts all along
the river and since Su'ud Bey's visit we had not been idle.
We rallied the Fellata, the Husunat, and the Dighaim, all
the tribes on both sides of the White Nile. We spread the
word, the message; we talked and urged. We explained and
answered questions, soothed misgivings. It was not difficult
to convince them. Life should not be a foot on your neck
pushing you to the ground. My master, the Mahdi, spoke to
their hearts, spoke their language. They knew that he did not
want riches; he did not want power. A holy man who fasted
and prayed—why would he lie to them?

Before the steamer arrived, the Mahdi ordered banners to
be prepared. Five of them. I knelt on the ground and spread
the material out on the grass. Above us the clouds were
milky with rain. He dipped his quill in ink and wrote on
every banner: "There is no god but Allah and Muhammad is
Allah's messenger." Then on each banner he wrote the names

of righteous saints, the intimate friends of the Almighty, all related to the Sufi paths of the tribes—al-Jilani wali Allah, al-Rifai, al-Dusuqi, al-Badawi. Four names that were familiar to the people, tariqa leaders whose orders were established and followed in Sudan. On the fifth banner he wrote his own name because he was one of them, like them, but his mission was higher and more concrete, his miracles powerful and tangible; the reins he was beginning to grasp were vast and still beyond our imagination. He wrote Muhammad Ahmed al-Mahdi, khalifat rasoul Allah—the successor of Allah's messenger. The wet script gleamed in the sun. I could distinguish every letter and every word. He had cured me, banished the jumble, eased the difficulty, and made me see. I ducked to kiss his hand and swore that I would follow him to the ends of the earth. He laughed and squeezed my shoulder. "Al-Ubayyid first," he said. "Then Khartoum, Berber, Cairo, al-Kufa, Jerusalem—my beloved, you will pray by my side in Mecca's sacred mosque."

My whole body vibrated with his prophesy. I would fight and not be harmed. We would win, we would win, we would win. He knew what he was saying. Let not these Al-Azhar scholars try to undermine him. They came puffed with pride and he sent them back with their tongues tied. Not one of them able to raise their voice to debate him. That was a sign of his power too. To transfix his enemies, to vanquish them and keep his opponents at bay.

He divided us into ten groups. He led us far from the women and children because of compassion for their safety. The steamer arrived at sunset. It settled on the swampy bank. Their plan was to break their Ramadan fast and then attack by twilight. But darkness fell swiftly, and in unfamiliar terrain they fumbled. We were waiting for them, crouching in the grass, having broken our fast and prayed taraweeh. We had prayed for success; we had prayed for help. There were only two hundred of us, while they were triple our number, well-armed and trained. What did we have going for us? We had the Expected One.

In the yellow moonlight we could see, but they were almost blind. Eventually the flutter of one of our banners caught their leader's eyes. I heard him call his soldiers to a halt. He was about to give the order to fire. And then another one, who I assumed to be the second in command, called out, "These are graves, sir. The locals pitch banners in their graveyards. I've seen it time and again." So instead of firing, they kept advancing toward us. We were invisible in the night, we were spirits with knives, we were thin and agile while they were bulky and heavy on the muddy ground. We stood up.

It was as if the first soldier walked into my dagger. Just gave himself up to me. I pushed it deeper in the cloth of his uniform, I pulled it out and in again. Cries now and their leader realizing our presence, called out, "There are men under those flags. Surrender, you disobedient villagers! Surrender, you imposter." Our master was among us, blessed sword in hand. He had refused to stay back, to command from afar. He was here in these bushes in this night. To deflect attention away from him, I called out. I taunted their general. "It is you who is disobedient, not us. We are not your subjects." My voice rang out. "This is not your land; you are a long way from Khartoum." From my throat, a war cry rang out and others copied.

They had formed themselves in a square, but we broke through it and hit left and right. Disoriented and frightened, their shots were out of control, did little damage. Our banners held high; touched by starlight, they ignited our hearts. We were bolstered by his prophecies—that we would win, we would win. He was sure of what he was saying, shining eyes and not a single speck of doubt.

The government soldiers bore the weight of their rifles, uniforms, boots, their heavy conscience. We were in tattered rags, barefoot, farming utensils in our hands, a hoe here, a fork there, knives if we were lucky. The steamer itself was loaded with gunfire, more than one cannon, reinforcements. But this did not frighten us. Our master's plan had succeeded. We had lured them to a dense place that worked against them. It had been raining for days and the ground was soft, puddles of water soaking up the grass, stinking the air. Where did the river end and where was the solid bank? We knew, but for them water and mud fused into one.

Through the night the fighting went on. There were pauses and gaps. I picked up my first gun from a wounded soldier. I hurried back away from the fighting, made myself familiar with it, practiced shots, and then I was back on the battlefield, aiming their own weapon against them. We pushed them back to their steamer. They retreated and we followed. Even when they were on the steamer firing at us from above, they were the losers.

We sent that general back to Khartoum defeated. At dawn, I picked up the first of my booty. A revolver and a signet ring from a finger that I hacked off. The rest was rich pickings for the whole village. Uniforms, boots, bayonets. The dead government soldiers were not true Muslims, never mind that they were fasting Ramadan and praying. As long as they did not accept the Mahdi, all their worship was a sham. The only true Muslims were on our side. Our triumph was a miracle. Twelve of us martyred while one hundred and twenty of them felled. We did not even owe them a decent burial.

I did not get to keep the ring or the revolver. We had to give everything up to a collective wealth. A new lesson to learn. Not to care about possessions but to care instead about the needy and the weak. Not to think of myself but to consider the circumstances of others. It was not easy for me to give up the ring. I felt as if I had earned it. Also, we learned that it did not behoove us to use firepower. Rifles were foreign tools, not fashioned by our hands. Brave warriors did not kill from a distance but thrust themselves in the face of the enemy. So, I surrendered the ring and the revolver to the treasury. There was no time to dwell on the loss; we were moving. The Mahdi ordered a migration. All of us to Jebel Gadir. We must escape the Turks, he said. They will come back with an even mightier force; they will want revenge. We must all travel, women and children, the new tribes that joined the cause. They were many because news of the victory spread, carried by the river, carried by the special breeze of this most auspicious rainy season. It was a miracle. What else could it be? Our triumph at Jazira Aba was a turning point. Those who had wavered before came running. Those who doubted shook off their misgivings.

At the western inlet on the White Nile, we found a fleet of boats waiting for us. The Mahdi's brothers, all boatbuilders, had prepared them specially for this journey. Our whole community boarded the boats and went on to safety. All of us traveling south, by boat and by land, our backs to Khartoum, our destination the Nuba Mountains. I looked up at the sky. There, right up there in the clouds was our tangible support. The rains that would turn the grounds swampy and hinder the government's army from catching up with us.

After seventy-nine days, we arrived at our destination. Jebel Gadir, high in the Nuba Mountains. It had been a grueling journey. We had passed through hostile lands and through tribes who welcomed us and pledged their support. Now at Gadir we could settle. I had never seen such greenery. A place where we could build a new community, turn our backs to the evils of our oppressors and build an ideal, equitable way of life. We were ready to start afresh, all of us together. The Mahdi wanted us united as brothers, our bonds warmer than those of tribe or kin.

But even high on the mountains we were not safe. Jazira Aba was part of Rashid Bey's administrative jurisdiction and so as the governor of Fashoda, he took it upon himself to crush us. He would have succeeded, but Rabiha, a woman from the Kinana tribe, foiled his plan. That day I was sure that the Mahdi had not taken part in the fighting and yet his clothes and sword were covered in blood. Our days were swathed in mists of miracles. We lived a frugal life and rarely allowed our stomachs to be full. Those who farmed lived on the fruits of their labors; those of us fighting gave our booty to the treasury and only took what we needed. The Mahdi loved those who were steadfast and hardworking. Those like me who itched for battle. Knowing I was restless, he would send me with his proclamations to kingdoms all over the Nuba Mountains, to riverine tribes, to spread his word and gain followers.

I got married at Jebel Gadir, encouraged that the dowries were now officially reduced. I married a widow because a virgin's dowry was double at ten rials. With my people all in Al-Ubayyid, I had been lonely, but her family—brothers and parents—took me in and we all lived together. My wife's first husband had been martyred. "I hope I bring you the same fortune," she said coyly the first time I bedded her. I was taken aback at her zeal. Her words chilled me, but she was right to wish me the best of endings. It was her duty. I did not see her do any wrong. She could not, though, drive the picture of Buthaina's plump face out of my mind. That girl in Al-Ubayyid who had rejected me. I still nursed a grudge against her and her family. Vague thoughts of revenge that I was too busy to formulate into plans.

The Mahdi was strict, and he did not take kindly to impropriety. Calling a fellow Muslim a dog or a pig or a Jew warranted eighty lashes and seven days of confinement. Twenty-seven lashes were the punishment for a woman with uncovered hair or one who spoke with a loud voice. New judges were appointed. The laws of the Turks no longer applied to us. We had our own generals and lieutenants. A khalifa at the very top, followed by tribal chiefs and commanders who were now to be known as emirs. We trained and we prepared for the time when we would descend from the mountains to drive the Turks out of all the lands of Sudan.

# 7

# Fatimah

I said to him, "You won't be the first or last bridegroom to show up with a concubine." He did not know that I was referring to his father. His father also had a concubine who was dear to him. Subhan Allah, like father like son. And even though Yaseen, being the youngest, might not remember Bakhita clearly, here he was repeating the same pattern. For sure not deliberately, but somehow it was also his fate. Of course, I resented my husband's position. She, my rival, though everyone told me not to see her as such, was also from the south, dark blue. He traded there, too, but she had grown up with him, was the first woman in his life; he had known her long before we got married. I entered his house, both his parents were alive then, his unmarried sisters and married brothers, sisters-in-law, a grandmother, poor cousins, and servants with the enslaved Bakhita among them. Now my son's story was different. I said, "Leave her to her fate, son. Let her make her own way in the world. She's not for you." He glowered and then I knew that he was more desirous of her than he would admit. All this talk of responsibility and justice was just what he did best—talk.

Today I boarded the ferry and headed out to Tutti Island to see his prospective bride. Who knows, a wife might distract him from that girl in Al-Ubayyid! I saw that when I mentioned that the Tutti girl was a relation of his superior at work, Sheikh Amin Al-Darir, he became interested. He would want this, a marriage officiated by the blind old man himself. It would be a seal of approval for him. To be part of a group he always aspired to, those who were educated and established. Not like us, the merchants of the souq, bowing low to market forces, haggling and pleasing our customers above all else. Never mind, his brothers and sister were easy-going. If he, the youngest, was the most difficult, I must not complain. All his life he was difficult. A tiresome pregnancy, a birth in which I almost died. I didn't die, but I never birthed another child either.

That day . . . for hours squatting over the birthing hole, clinging to the rope with all my strength. At first the women around me were joking. "What's wrong with you, Fatimah? Why are you acting like a young woman giving birth for the first time? Yalla, push him out and let's get this over with." There was no gush of water to help me like with Halima. For a week, the water had been dribbling out of me and I thought it was urine. I was not more tired than expected. I had done this before, over and over. What now? The midwife who should have been in front of me, waiting to catch the newborn, moved instead to crouch behind me. That's when the others shut up and realized that I was not acting, something for sure was wrong. I moaned and pleaded to be allowed to lie down. There was nothing more that I wanted than to stretch out on my side. I wanted it even more than for the pain to go away. To give up. But no, I had to cling to the rope, with them now propping me up and the contractions stinging like fire but without strength. It should be an irresistible urge; that's what I remembered from the other times. An irresistible urge to push, a violent stretching, all for the baby supreme, and a trampling over me, until the birth takes place. But with Yaseen, I did not want to push him out. Hours passed with a pain that was leading nowhere, as if I were suffering for the sake of suffering, on and on, with my strength ebbing away and I heard them say, *She will die, she will die.* I believed them because how else could this blockage be relieved? Push with all your might they kept saying, until the pain crashed through me and all I knew was muddled darkness. Then surfacing to hear their ululations, the sound coming as if from far away. As if the joy were coming from another house. But no, it was coming from merchant Abdelrahman's house. His wife had just given birth to another boy, and they were distributing dates all around.

She was there, Bakhita, that day helping, getting water for all these gathered women, keeping the children away from me. Afterward, she was the one who washed and changed me, wrapped my stomach tight so that it would not stay enlarged. Her touch was gentle, and I felt safe with her. She was older than me, much older. Tall and hefty, puffy cheeks, small eyes that rarely smiled as if she were locked away in memories of her own. I was intimidated by her, though I would never admit it. True to her name, she brought the house luck. Me, producing one boy after the other, my breasts full of milk enough for them and more. I could not fault Bakhita, except that I did chide her for her hearty appetite from time to time. She ate like a man. But as I said, she was well-built. I fretted about the amount she ate when we had guests. It made Abdelrahman furious to come home with a guest and not find enough food. I understood early on in my marriage that I must not let this happen. Beg or borrow, be innovative, do what I could but come up with an adequate meal for the guests. I learned to hide potatoes, eggs, and dried okra for such occasions, peanuts and sesame oil. I once hid a gourd of honey and wept when the ants got to it first. Bakhita knew her place and never criticized my hoarding. We lived as if she were a servant in the household. If my husband went privately to her, I was expected to turn a blind eye. Did he? She traveled with him to cook for him and look after the camels, so I assumed they were together then. But in our house, he did not go to her, certainly not in the early months of our marriage. Later, when I was pregnant and the weeks after I gave birth, most likely he did. I suspected that he went to her then and I didn't mind. Never was a word spoken about this, by him or her or me. She was certainly cheaper and less aggravating than him taking a second wife. I was, though, always on the lookout for her getting pregnant. That would have been the worst outcome for me, the best for her. A child for her meant manumission and a half-sibling to my children. This never happened. She was too old, as I said.

Bakhita shared nothing of her past life with me, only the local gossip. She had lots of acquaintances though and was always in and out of the neighboring houses, making herself useful. I liked it when she was out of the house. I felt I could breathe more easily, especially when my mother-in-law passed away and I took over the household. I never asked Bakhita questions when she came back. If she wanted to share anecdotes or gossip, that was her prerogative. At first, she used to go through the formality of asking my permission to leave the house. After a year, she would wrap her muslin shawl around her first and then inform me she was going out. Later, busy with the children, I would turn to find her gone. Out of all the children, Yaseen was the one she sometimes took with her. She taught him her language and he could speak it fluently. For sure that was how he spoke to that girl of his in Al-Ubayyid.

Today the ferry to Tutti was full, and I kept the basket of gifts close to me. The nosy woman sitting next to me wanted to know what I was carrying. I showed her and she said with authority that I was taking too much for a Tutti girl, especially one who was the eldest in a family of five girls. Her parents would be keen to get her married off so as to pave the way for the others; they would not be so demanding. So, I took the kohl out of the basket and hid it in my clothes. I would sell it instead. I no longer used it myself, not since I was widowed, though it does ward off eye disease there was no doubt. I did not miss all the beauty rituals I used to indulge in. Their time had passed. In winter, I needed sesame oil for my dry skin but that was all. The other things—the dukhan, the dilka, the perfumes—I don't even think of them. They belong to another version of myself. After giving birth and staying away from her husband for forty days, a woman would be decked out like a bride again. Clean and exfoliated, skin shining with oil, drenched in perfume. For the young, forty

days was a long time. A time to yearn and pine, heavy on
the heart. Now a week passed for me like a day, time as easy
as poured water. My husband never gave Bakhita gifts. He
never even glanced at her in my presence. Other men weren't
like that. They favored their concubines, pampering them
with all they could afford, then they blamed the women for
becoming jealous! Lucky for me Abdelrahman was not like
that. I never felt that my position was threatened.

Tutti was green and welcoming. So were the girl's family.
Salha—that was her name—was skin and bones, though,
when I prodded her. I protested that they must feed her up
before the wedding; I would not take her like that! A delay
for sure, it could not be helped. The girl needed at least two
months of feeding and leisure. They must not work her hard
I insisted. They were a well-off family with vast fields and
numerous slaves. Perhaps this was why she laughed at what I
said. Her teeth were excellent, and she had wide clear eyes.
"Milk," I said, "butter and sugar, mix and drink." With a
layer of fat, she would be a beauty.

"You are skinny, too, Aunty," Salha said, and I was so taken
aback at her boldness that I laughed. "I am an old woman,"
I replied. "I am not the bride. Can you dance?"

"I will learn, Aunty," she said, her eyes lively. I approved
of this answer as I did not want someone who bragged and
then failed to deliver. Yes, she must learn; that was what life
was all about. Learning.

I learned to trade only after my marriage. My father was
a weaver and I learned from him how to weave angareebs.
It was a worthy skill but one that I moved away from after
marriage. Abdelrahman was a merchant, and the women in

his family traded, too, in women's goods. Henna, kohl, perfumed oils, snacks. I discovered a knack for this, the pleasure of going to the souq laden and coming back with the light weight of money. Baby slung on my back and the older ones helping or pretending to help. I had so much milk, as I said, that I often left my wares and nursed the fretful babies of other women. Just hearing them cry would make the milk trickle from me, even before I held them in my arms. How different they all were, some sucking vigorously, others feeble, waiting for their mouths to fill before swallowing great gulps. They would grow heavy in my arms, satisfied, sleepy, their eyes rolling in their heads like drunks. These were some of the happiest times of my life. With all this breastfeeding I ended up with foster children and gave my children foster siblings. When they were older, they were forbidden to them in marriage because they nursed at the same breast. We had to search for spouses for them from afar and that was one of the reasons why Halima married in Al-Ubayyid. When my milk dried up after Yaseen was weaned, I cried. It seemed to me a sad loss. He was content to crouch next to his siblings and reach out for bits and pieces with his fingers. He did not need my lap anymore. I kept expecting to get pregnant again, but it never happened. I waited year after year and thinking that my stomach might not harden again nor my breasts fill up made my eyes fill with tears. I would hold crying babies, rock them and croon to them when all I used to do before was stuff my nipple in their mouths.

There were beggars around the Grand Mosque with their children. I started giving them one cooked meal a day. When they were older, they found out where my house was and started coming over. This was easier because it meant I no longer had to carry the food all the way. Sometimes, the meal they got from me was the only one they had in a day. One of the boys I regularly fed once took a banana from the mission garden and he was whipped mercilessly by the foreign priests. It shocked me that men of God could be so harsh. A hungry child reaching out for nourishment is not stealing. And it was from a tree, too, common property, not from someone's storeroom. From that day on I hated the missionaries, even though I had no direct dealings with them at all. The nuns had no need for my beauty products. When they fed the poor, it was because they wanted them to convert to Christianity. No one gossiped about the nuns though, only about the priests and what they did to little boys. The parents of these boys were enslaved, so they did not have protection. It was Bakhita who told me all this. She knew all sorts of things that I didn't, had contacts inside the mission. Seating Halima between her legs, oiling her hair and braiding it, she would occasionally become talkative, starting with chiding Halima, who fidgeted and squealed from all the tugging, and then moving on to other topics. I could see the two of them now as if they were in front of me. Bakhita's dress hoisted up, her long, sturdy legs spread out straight on the ground with Halima sitting between them. "Keep still, girl. No, I won't stop. Yes, this has to be done." On and on, Bakhita's voice rising as Halima's protests grew, until Bakhita would start talking to me about this, that, and the other, all of a sudden vocal and eloquent. Tears would pour down Halima's face and the two of us would ignore her. Bakhita telling me something I didn't know and me giving her my full attention.

Tomorrow, I will go to the khawaja engineer with the kohl that I didn't give Salha. He will buy it for his paintings for a higher price than any woman would. His house is far away near the boatyard because this is where he works, but it is worth the walk. At first, I didn't understand why he would render on paper what he could see in front of his face. Apparently, he intended to send them to his people back home. They had never even seen a camel. The last time I rode one was when I went on Hajj. Getting on it was easy but not dismounting. When it lurched forward on its front legs, I felt as if I was going to be pitched forward. Even though we had been eating dried bread for the whole journey, I felt I was going to be sick. So no, I do not wish to go anywhere on those beasts again. And no, I would not waste money to look at a deaf and dumb version of them etched on paper. To each his own.

Bakhita used to sing to the camels. Yaseen told me that. I heard him singing to himself, and I asked him what he was singing. He said, "It's a song for the camels. Bakhita taught me." The last time I saw her, she was high on a camel and my husband was on another one. They were heading out to the south after the rainy season as they always did. Every year they did the same thing and came back with the gum. This time when he returned, she was not with him. I was shocked of course. He said he had freed her because he had broken an oath made to another merchant! He had promised him a certain amount of gum at a certain price, and he was unable to fulfill his side of the bargain. "You gave her to him?" I said.

He shook his head. "I told you I freed her. Breaking an oath to the Almighty requires expiation. I either free her or feed ten. I chose to free her."

Men are selfish. He was speaking calmly as if my life was
not affected. True we couldn't afford to feed ten, but she was
a loss for me. "Why did she not come home with you?" Did
not freed slaves stay on as servants?

"She did not want to come back," he said. "She found her
people and wanted to stay with them."

"What nonsense!" I said. "This is her home. We are her
people."

"Freed means freed," he said.

I grumbled of course. She did not even say goodbye. She
was ungrateful. How was I meant to live without her! "Bring
her back," I told him.

This made him laugh and call me a stupid woman. I was
agitated. Who would help me now? I had to muddle along
on my own. Halima was old enough to do some chores. I
sent the boys out for errands. We were a smaller household by
then. Abdelrahman's sisters had long married and his brothers
with their families moved into houses next door. I did not
have another woman for company. I felt Bakhita's absence. I
tried to think of her in the south, where I am told it was all
green and lush, her with her people, but I could not imagine
her anywhere except with us. I was young in those days,
still sentimental. Slowly with time I understood the world
better. She had neither cared for Abdelrahman nor regarded
me as a sister. She had wanted her freedom: that was what
it was about. No one, sane and able, when offered freedom
would not take it. I would have done the same. She gave us
her youth, her labor, the strength of her body. She gave us
all this because she had no choice. We were not her kin; we
were not her people. It was something we liked to think about

ourselves, but it was not true. I did not hold a grudge against her. Her absence stung at first but bit by bit we lived our lives without her. The emptiness she left was never filled by anyone else. I started to do Halima's hair; my husband started taking our eldest boy with him when he traveled. Yaseen was much too young to go with him. He was still small and confused about Bakhita's sudden absence. He even fell ill when my husband returned alone. He had a stomachache and refused to eat. He would call out for her and cry. He was her favorite among all my children. In time they forgot her, but he always sang to the camels like she taught him.

# 8

# Robert

**Khartoum, February 1881–February 1882**

The first time he saw the confluence of the two rivers, the Blue Nile and the White, he was reminded of the drawing *Sunrise over Mars*. Waterways crisscrossing and merging, small islands of grass growing wild, the sun burning the sky even as it was rising. Robert was not on Mars, though he might as well have been. Between the shore where he was now standing and a tributary of the Blue Nile was Tutti Island. Ferries took passengers there and back every day, men in white robes, women in their colored tobes. Donkeys, chickens, baskets of potatoes and tomatoes floated on the water. A crocodile was spotted, and the passengers laughed. Along the shoreline were a convoy of private vessels, the loading of which he had been supervising. They were ready to sail tomorrow carrying four thousand pounds worth of elephant tusks, each tusk with a lump of gum the width of a palette stuck to its tip.

He could write home about this, describing in detail, never mind a sketch. Without a sketch. But they hardly ever wrote back. He was still an outcast: *Awae with ye*. Their silence also meant that they wanted nothing more from him. The money was reaching his in-laws in Aberdeen; otherwise they would have been nagging. Christina was well looked after. In the few and far between letters, they said so. The letters made no demands, expressed no interest in his new life. His in-laws, his parents, his sisters—they were a united front. No matter, he did not need aggravation from them or anyone else. In three or five years' time he would go back, a man with a modest fortune, able to support his child. He would take Christina in his arms—*wave to Granny and Granda*—he would tip his hat off to them and never be back. They would live in their own house, widower and child. He would be the best of fathers to her. It was not complicated. It could be done as long as he continued to work in the Khartoum boatyard. Eyes sharp, making sure the design specifications of the boilers and steam engines were suitably matched and of sufficient capacity for the size of each vessel. Overseeing maintenance and repairs, not reluctant to get his hands dirty, recording spare parts in ledgers, what was unloaded and what was hoisted on board, nothing ever went amiss on his watch.

*Awae with ye*, his mother had said to him when even her sympathy had run out, and it ran out much later than that of the others. When his father could no longer bear the sight of him. After the fire and the funeral, Robert had been unable to show up for work at the ship broker. That clean shirt situation, junior clerk poring over ledgers and bills of lading, safe from haar and cold, with his father a stone's throw down the docks at the shore porter's warehouse, heaving cargo and stacking heavy crates. When Robert did show up at the office disheveled and clutching a bottle of ale, he was dismissed.

With severance in full, mind. Dinnae deserve it. Good for nothing. Could not even be trusted to look after the wee one. This he knew without a doubt. Took Christina to her maternal grandparents early on, then wormed his way back to his parents' house.

To sleep by day in his childhood bed. To drink at night until his money ran out and even after his money ran out. Warm, hazy pub dissolving in other people's presence, sweet smell of tobacco, froth tripping over mugs, the hum of voices all around him, soothing until they closed, and he was pushed out in the cold drizzle, balancing himself straight to take a pish. Granite buildings looming around him in the dark, buildings he had once sketched with detail. Paintings lost in the fire. Every canvas burnt to ashes, days before he was meant to exhibit in Edinburgh. That one of Heather facing away, standing on the Brig o' Balgownie, red curls under her bonnet. Why did he think of the paintings instead of his wife? Because he could not think straight or because he could still hear her voice while the paintings were silent as if they had gone back inside him. Bleary, with eyes half-closed, he noted, in abstract, the energy it took to make something out of blankness, to put color on empty canvas. That energy did not exist in him anymore. It was gone. One night, after being thrown out of a pub, he climbed the pier of the Brig o' Balgownie, looked at the water below, and it was cold—too cold. He did not have the courage to do it. *Sway,* he told himself. *You're drunk, so act bloody drunk. You don't even have to throw yourself in, just a wee totter and a lurch.* But even that had been beyond him. How he scurried off! Like a rat. He was not brave enough to join her on the other side.

It was the constant smell of smoke that stoked the wild grief. Indoors, outdoors, in the rain, the smell of paintings on fire, the smell of wood, of mortar, and horror of horrors, her skin. The smell was on his clothes but peel them off and he could not get rid of it. The smell was in Christina's hair, and he did not want to hold her, could not hold her for long before he needed to choke. They had survived because they had been together—in a shop buying supplies—Christina clutching a brush in her hand, banter with the shopkeeper that the child would follow in his footsteps. They had survived because they had not been at home when the fire broke out, taking everything. Then the smell lodged up his nose, day after day, month after month.

His mother was the one who helped. Not his father, who despised his debilitating grief. Expected him to be tight-lipped, to get a grip. Even when he was gentle and asked, "Are ye no feared, son, to throw yer life all awae?" Robert could not listen. His friends did not know what to do with his bitter, silent company. Besides, he had done well for himself with the recognition for his art and the marrying above. Now that he had lost both, they did not know what to say to him. His mother did. *Remember youse wanting to go to foreign lands.* Did he? Vaguely. She remembered. Pictures in books she could not read, listening to his childish eager voice. *The Sphinx, Ma. The what? The Sphinx.* Aye, he had wanted to go there. Sand and colossal buildings, temples. *It's all still there, is it nae? Och, one didnae just up and go, fancy thoughts from a woman.* But the next day she put on her best hat and went to where her grandchild, Christina, was living, met the dour grandfather, who had not allowed his heart to break, who sat through the funeral service of his only daughter without shedding a tear. He was a stalwart member of the kirk, head of the city's biggest shipping company who had always believed that his daughter had married beneath her, never mind that he had given his blessing. Might have been a promising lad, but now this tragedy was revealing his true colors. Robert's mother asked him to help her son with a posting overseas. To get him out of the way was an attractive proposition. His drunken brawls were turning them all into objects of derision.

Heather's father did have connections, shipping connections, a Malcolm Ramsay employed by the Egyptian khedive, as head of his steamers in Khartoum. Ships—this was the career Robert had planned to discard in order to pursue art. Now it would be his salvation. He would go to Khartoum, wherever it was. Suddenly there was this to do and that, packing. *No Ma, I dinnae need brushes, paints, canvas. I'm done with all that. Nae even a sketchbook?* No, it was dead in him. Then the ship, Egypt (the Sphinx), another ship down the Red Sea, crossing the desert by camel, deeper into Africa— this city with the two rivers his new home.

Marine engineer in an unpopular and hence well-paid outpost. Khartoum might seem like a frontier town, all of it facing the Blue Nile. It was first built by the Ottomans, a trading crossing for goods coming from the south, soldiers coming from the north by river and by camel. There was a constant blending in Khartoum, a swirl of nationalities. Locals in flowing white robes, Blacks in more colorful ones, Arabs who were not local but came from Morocco and Libya, Austrians, Armenians, South Africans employed in the Egyptian foreign service, a Jewish community of Europeans and non-Europeans. Robert heard around him snatches of Arabic, German, Greek, Swahili, Turkish. New words to learn. It was a lot to absorb now that he was so far away from Marischal Street and Footdee, but Khartoum welcomed him with the wild cries of the birds at dawn and the verdant garden of the Roman Catholic mission full of banana and fig trees, mimosa, and jasmine bushes. Fertile land where anything could grow as long as you kept watering it, earth that could never absorb too much, would dry back to being a desert in a jiffy. Hence the waterwheels all along the riverbank, some pulled by bulls and a few mechanized. Women washing clothes, an endless stream of boys balancing water jugs on their heads. Palm trees and parakeets, sandalwood and sailing boats. A world of watercolors. Bonnie.

The man who hired him—Malcolm Ramsay, also a Scotsman—was kind and straightforward. Directing Robert without being too intrusive. "We tend to be social here, there being so little by way of entertainment. Come and visit, don't be aloof." Robert was aloof; he could not be otherwise. But soon gratitude softened him. He noted this sudden stroke of luck for a man unlucky enough to have lost his wife and best work in a house fire. He could think such a sentence now, put the horror into words. There was a time when it was a nameless tragedy, the end of the world. There was a time when it was outrageous that everyone was immersed in the business of living, eating, shitting, carriage wheels rolling on the streets, ship horns blowing, the fog rising from the North Sea. It was not that he did not think of her every day, smelling smoke where it did not exist; nor was it the case that his memories were fading. No, they were all intact. The only difference was that he was distracted now by what was novel.

When Robert first arrived and found the natives snoozing in the middle of the day, he had judged them lazy. Then he understood what they had known all along—that the best part of the day was the early morning. Wake up at dawn, before even the first layer of light; a fresh breeze, there was thank the Lord always a breeze. Here were the most productive hours of the day. Get the most exerting work done, pause for a hearty breakfast, this he took at home, and then back to continue work until the sun climbed the sky. After that in summer, the heat could well kill you. Any iron exposed to the sun burnt his hand; to go out without a hat made him dizzy. Take refuge in the shade, better to be indoors with the shutters down. There were no curtains in Khartoum and very few buildings had glass. His house was made of separate rooms facing a paved gallery that circled a yard. In the yard was a well and some palm trees with, yes, monkeys. Bad water was an issue, dysentery was a constant threat, and he appreciated the well.

Late afternoon the sun would soften, and he would go back to the boatyard. Then, at dusk, a walk along the river, heading toward the huge setting sun. Past the palace, past the civil headquarters of the city, past the Austrian consulate bearing the double-eagle arms of the Austro-Hungarian Empire, past the mission school. Looking at the birds—storks and ibis—sighting a shadow in the water, good heavens, a hippopotamus. The flow of the river was sometimes wild and at times sluggish. The river breeze soothed him; the sun bleached his soul. He carried himself like someone at the tail end of an illness, wary lest anything ruffle his convalescence. He neither confided in others nor kept a diary. The work at the Khartoum boatyards was never tedious. He was no longer just a cog in a big wheel; he need not be buried in paperwork or bureaucracy. Every day there was the chance to be innovative, to solve problems of shortages and repairs. The most challenging aspect was liaising with the suppliers of materials and spare parts; he preferred to work on his own. Malcolm Ramsay was not a difficult superior. They worked well together, and Ramsay drew out the best in him, the kind of confidence that came with acknowledging that ships were in his blood. Robert had grown up around the docks of Aberdeen, lived in a house with a view of the harbor, played on the cobbled roads of the fish market, in the shadow of the great sails that took and brought goods to Scandinavia and to the Indies via Southampton. But never mind Aberdeen and its memories or his artist self that was buried next to Heather. She had always believed in him, she an artist herself, painting mermaids and selkies. She had put all her equipment away when she became pregnant, made nauseated by the smell of paint. After she gave birth, she devoted herself to their daughter and encouraged him instead. He would not have admitted it to anyone, but her opinion was the one he had valued the most. Her criticism, the strongest impact. He drew for her and that was why he stopped after she was not there to love what he had made.

The first time he experienced a haboob, he was outdoors in what felt like the hottest, most stifling of afternoons. He stood outside his house and watched the tall brown cloud approaching from a distance. A whorl rising from the ground, orange, dark yellow, brown, whipped by its own frenzy, propelled by its own energy. The only thing moving. It approached without a sound; the only sounds were those made by the people gathering their things and fleeing out of its way. The sand column was heading toward him, expanding in width, no longer a column, diffusing, spreading in stacked clouds so that he could barely see anything beyond it. Light brown, red brown, coming closer and then he was inside its hot breath, sand in his throat and nostrils. He started to cough and found that his eyelashes, the rim of his hat, his ears, the creases in his palms, the folds of his shirt, were covered in the finest sand. And the smell of dust was all that he could smell. Dust and not smoke. Dust, breath, and nothing else.

On one of his days off, pencil in hand, the wrong paper, and an absent mind, he attempted from memory a sketch of the *Sunrise over Mars*. What a poor reproduction! It couldn't be worse. He used it to light the thick Bogie Roll he smoked once a week, as a treat, to ration his supply.

His next attempt was a sketch of a palm tree. It looked like something a novice would accomplish. The egret swooping over the Nile, much better. A novice with promise, a fair bit of talent. So much for that. The first inklings of a celebration, a jaunt in his step, jaunt would be an exaggeration, but still there was something to look forward to. Progress in increments, planning to sketch an ostrich to send to Christina. He was not satisfied with the ostrich; the one of the monkeys was better. Each day his confidence grew. At first, he had waited to hear Heather's voice, praising and commenting. Finding silence instead, he would give up and wallow, then slowly start again. The action was enough. That he was able to do it. He did not need validation. And this return not an aberration, he would not stop now. The slump was over. Who would have thought that here, of all places, he would be able to think straight and instead of losing himself, want to reach for brush and paint?

He had brought nothing with him—no canvas, easel, brushes, or paints. Starting from scratch. Not even a sketchbook even though every traveler worth his salt kept a diary and a sketchbook. So it was hours spent asking for this and that, experimenting, making do, trying the mission school, the foreign embassies, scouring the souqs for what came from Ethiopia and Morocco. Pencils and charcoal were readily available at work. Parchment, he could purchase. He made some brushes out of horsehair. Others he was able to order from Cairo through an Egyptian ship captain. At first, he used a table and his lap before he thought of fashioning an easel. Soon word got round of his needs and things came to him. But they were usually of poor quality, and he rejected them. Then, he encountered Fatimah in the souq. She understood and sniffed out his latent, unacknowledged desperation, his willingness to pay.

Colors were Fatimah's speciality—henna, indigo, kohl, crushed scarab beetles. She also brought him gum. To bind the paint, she said. He had been using egg whites, but the dryness made the colors flake and become brittle. Mixing in the gum would bring moisture to the colors, an attractive thickness. The paint would dry slower too. Fatimah usually arrived in the morning, at different times and different days of the week. He had spoken to her about this. Why not stick to every other Tuesday? Why come at ten when you know I

would have finished breakfast by then and likely to be back at
the boatyard? She was oblivious to all he said either because
she didn't understand what he was saying or didn't care. The
quality of her goods was the best, though, so he put up with
her inconsistency. She was dry and slight, with braids that
hung forlornly at the side of her face. Her tattooed lower lip
was as if born from cold blue, now a dull gray. She would
come with a soft basket called a guffa, squat on his front
porch, and wait for him to appear.

It was not easy to guess her age. Do you have any children?
His Arabic had by now improved to the extent that he could
formulate this question. Yes. How many? Reluctantly she
replied as if some things should not be counted. Four—
three sons and a daughter. The daughter was married in
Al-Ubayyid with children of her own. Two of the sons were
married and living here in Khartoum; the youngest one's
wedding was being prepared. Robert registered this piece of
information. The preparation for her son's wedding might
stop her from coming back next week. He brought extra
supplies and explained his reasoning to her. So as not to raise
expectations. He did not want to stop doing business with her.
Much of what she said to him and what he said to her was
lost in a confusion of foreign words and false presumptions.
What was he to make of her enigmatic words: "My sons don't
approve of me trading. That's why I now avoid the souq. The
youngest, especially, can be stern about such things."

She had an odd habit of looking away when she spoke,
fiddling with the edge of her white tobe or scratching her
forearm, but she could also sit in a squat position quite still
for long periods of time. Waiting for him to finish his siesta,

waiting for him to come home. She was overcharging him, even though she insisted that she wasn't. He didn't mind. His art was a sickly new infant, needing constant care, no expense spared, no luxury withheld.

He tried to sketch her one day, in profile, with her head turned away, avoiding her face, concentrating on the folds of her tobe as she squatted on the ground. At first, she did not understand that he was asking her to pose and when she did, waved her arm as if swatting a fly, stood up, and walked away. It would be a nuisance if she never showed up again! He could find another model. The next woman he tried to sketch was one of the slave girls who baked durra cakes for the sailors. These girls would sit in a group in the hatchway, crouched over a brazier, cooking all day and miraculously never setting the steamer on fire. He did not notice the antagonism he created until the Egyptian captain took him aside, tore up the sketch, and said, "Stick to the women in your home!" An argument ensued, with Robert angrier about the torn sketch than being reprimanded in public. Even Malcolm Ramsay did not take Robert's side. Because of this altercation, procurers started to seek him out. They had sniffed a need in him and could provide. Curiosity wrestled with repugnance. He had yet to take up any offers.

Instead he painted Khartoum's eucalyptus trees, birds landing on gardens that were regularly pruned, roads that were swept clean and sprinkled with water to prevent the dust from rising. A medley of clothes—Sudanese jellabiya, tarbush with European suit, traditional Turkish, traditional Egyptian, Shilluk men from the south with little more than a loincloth. Coming home from work to the shaded room in his bungalow, the smell of colors, brush in damp hand, remembering to put it down and wipe the sweat from his palm, otherwise the brush would slide through his fingers and drops of sweat would splash the canvas. The day job and the real work, two distinct spheres that kept him in balance, the precious harmony this country gifted him.

# 9

# Zamzam

There was the time before she knew that Yaseen got married and the time after it. One bit of knowledge tore away the patience that had made waiting for him a way of life. He had given his word to the governor and to her. He would want to keep his word, so he would do his best to come to release her as promised—that she was confident of, that was in keeping with his character. But it cost to get married; that was a fact too. He was bound now to be delayed. A bridegroom could not spare fifty pounds; she would have to wait. For how long? Months, years, a lifetime? Time oozed left and right, backward and heavy. Bol—no longer Bol but Ishaq—was growing away from her. He seemed to grasp now his favored position and her lowly one. She was enslaved; he was the adopted son of a respectable home. Because he no longer asked to see her, Halima did not bring him. She stopped visiting altogether. And what happened to Zamzam? What happened to her after the news of that faraway wedding in Khartoum? One that Halima traveled to attend, taking Ishaq with her and her younger daughters. Her husband, Hassan, too, and their eldest daughter, Buthaina, with her husband. A family gathering without Zamzam. She was left behind. What could possibly happen to her after she had fallen out of Nazli Hanim's favor? She took up the position Hibra had vacated.

The guest quarters were always full now that various army units were sent out against the Mahdi. A lot of comings and goings. Rooms to be swept, sheets to be washed, pitchers, basins, and chamber pots to be carried back and forth. Zamzam was kept busy, assisted by Hibra, who now stayed out of the way. Without her front teeth she was no longer the smiling, pretty sight. Lost, too, were her goat's hair extensions. Instead, she bossed Zamzam around and even gave her tips for avoiding pregnancy. "Why didn't you use them yourself?" was met with a slap for insolence. Afterward though, they kissed and made up. They could not afford to be enemies.

Zamzam's virginity was taken by a binbashi. He assumed it was a gift included in the governor's hospitality and did not pay extra. In addition to the violation, she had to endure Hibra's taunts that she was an idiot. She had failed to seize an opportunity.

The drummer who fancied her continued with his advances and got bolder. She gave in after hearing the news of her merchant's marriage. Yaseen was not hers, she reminded herself, had never been and was now not even a merchant anymore. He was Sheikh Yaseen Al-Azhari, out of her reach. Zamzam and the drummer lived in the governor's compound bound by a semiformal marriage. The drummer had freed himself, but he could not afford to free her. He was away, too, often, in the attacks against the Mahdi or the attacks against the tribes that supported the Mahdi or had sheltered him during his migration to Jebel Gadir. The government must take a firm stand against all insurgents and supporters of the false prophet. A friend of the Mahdi was an enemy of the government and as such deserved full punishment. Zamzam could repeat the official line verbatim.

In the governor's compound, there was no doubt whose was the superior force and who would win. So, knowing that the Mahdi and his army were heading toward Al-Ubayyid did not perturb Zamzam much. She was embedded in the world of the kitchen and the guest quarters, a daily routine in which her body was busy and disciplined while her heart flapped wild. Her body numb and her thoughts a restless force straining toward the unattainable, circling old encounters and memories. Never mind the news trickling in of one defeat after the other for the government, one success after the other for the rebels. Garrisons in other towns were coming under attack; the rebels were now in the tens of thousands. Her drummer soldier died in one of these battles. His death shocked her, then made her bitter but no lonelier. Perhaps life was meant to be cheap and short.

Refugees filled up Al-Ubayyid. They came with stories of torched villages, stolen livestock, and youth running off to join the uprising. A sense of unease started to grow, until it became palpable. Reinforcements were meant to come from Khartoum, but they didn't. Help was meant to come from Egypt, but Egypt had its own problems.

Soon the speculations became direct threat. The Mahdi descended with his army from Jebel Gadir and camped six miles away in Kaba. In preparation, a huge defensive trench was dug round Al-Ubayyid. Further trenches were dug around the governor's compound, the arsenal, the largest wells, and the food stores. Zaribas made of thorns were set up as walls in front of each trench. Nazli Hanim was evacuated to Khartoum. Flustered, she did not bid the staff goodbye.

One day Zamzam saw Yaseen. She was crossing the courtyard, which was full of kneeling camels from which crates of guns and ammunition were being unloaded. Piles of the spades that had been used in digging the trenches, a row of new zeer pots filled with water. He was coming out of the governor's office. Nothing about him had changed. The same look as a year ago, the same smile, the way he called out her name, her real name, her old name, the one her parents had given her. Akuany.

She stood still.

"It's all settled with the governor," he said. "Go get your things."

Just like that. He had no idea.

They stood under the burning sun. "I'm not right for you anymore," she said.

"Nonsense." He wasn't smiling anymore; he understood. "Go get your things and come with me."

"No."

He lowered his voice. "I paid the governor. It's all settled. You're free from these people. You should never have been here in the first place. Now you can leave. You won't be kept here against your will."

"It's not against my will," she said.

He was controlling anger. She could tell. She looked down at his sandals. They and the bottom of his jellabiya were covered in mud. Mud from the trench he had crossed. Crossed for her. Paid fifty pounds for a virgin as was the original agreement, got himself cheated by the governor. She was now worth much less. He did this for her. But she must not let herself believe this, sink into it. She had said what she had said and could walk away, back to whatever chore she was doing before he appeared. She couldn't now remember what it was.

"It's only been a year," he said.

"One year too late."

"It's because—"

"I know," she interrupted him. "Circumstances. I heard from Halima."

"Is that it?" he said. "You're upset."

He was giving her an entry point. A few words of reproach, a pout if she could manage it, then gathering her things in a bundle, heading off. Was that not what she had always wanted, lived for, grew up for?

He had come too late. She had been violated and spoiled, she had moved away from being the girl who a year ago had run away to be with him. He had wasted his time and his money. Endangered his life with this journey, dirtied his clothes. If he didn't understand now, he would soon. She turned to walk away and then changed her mind.

"I was upset," she said. "But I'm not anymore. I can't go back with you to Khartoum. My place is here. Someone should have told you about me, then you wouldn't have bothered."

"I don't go back on my word. Whatever rumors I heard I would still have come."

"They're not rumors; I am not suitable."

He was angry now. "I decide what suits me. You have no choice in this matter, girl. I paid for you."

Big words. Let him come and take her by force. If he dared. She turned and walked away.

Even back indoors, it was as if the force of the sun still beat down on her head. She swept one side of the guest room but not the other. Emptied only one chamber pot. It was time to eat, but she could not eat. No one asked her what the matter was. Did they know? Had they seen him? Could she continue knowing that she had given up the chance to leave? This was meant to be the happiest rescue.

By the following morning, she had convinced herself that it was all a dream. She had not seen him in the courtyard, he had not come for her. After all, she had dreamt such dreams since he first left her in Al-Ubayyid four years ago. If the governor wasn't busy, he would have asked if she had packed already and gone. If these were normal times, news would have spread around the compound that the man from Khartoum had come for Zamzam. Instead, the focus was on how some notables in Al-Ubayyid were secretly allying themselves with the Mahdi. They had gone to meet him in Kaba. Their names were whispered in the kitchen. Hadija, who knew everyone in Al-Ubayyid, loudly condemned the traitors. Going after personal gain, she repeated, no chivalry, no decency. With all this tension in the air, Zamzam's latest development did not garner interest.

At dawn on Friday, the Mahdi attacked. Zamzam, standing on the roof of the guest quarters, could at first only see clouds of dust hovering over the ground. Then a gust of wind blew to reveal the army undulating like a mirage. Thousands of men on foot and on horseback. Droplets of colors—green, red, black, blue—were their banners. It seemed as if they were swaying, not moving forward, but they were advancing for sure. Now she could hear the dull roar of gallop, stomp, war drum, and chant. The sound got louder, the flags and patches on their clothes more visible. So many of them. The garrison in Al-Ubayyid was outnumbered.

Zamzam did not remain long in the compound. Everyone who could stand on two feet was roused out to the front lines. Free and enslaved, men and women, defending the town. In the trenches, the government soldiers waited and with them were selected civilians who had been given arms. They waited until the rebels came near, the thud of their feet louder, their cries distinguishable words. They waited until they could see their spears rising, clustered together, silver bolts, before the order came for firing the cannons. Blast after blast and they died with cries and blood, their bodies falling into the trenches. And they were followed by others. Waves upon waves of the Mahdi's faithful fighters carrying spears, sometimes throwing corn stalks into the trenches to fill them up and cross over, rushing headlong toward the muzzles aimed at them, fearless.

It went on. The day progressed and the heat became intense. Rags needed to be placed in water and wrapped around hands so that they could hold rifles and fire cannons without getting scalded. Zamzam carried pails of water, and around her the women were trilling the zaghrouta, clapping and beating drums, singing songs to raise the morale of the men. Ululations as if they were at a bridegroom's procession.

Women smiling in approval, in enthusiasm, to show that they were not frightened, to prove that they had complete trust in their men. Young girls from conservative families who rarely allowed them out in public, sang side by side with middle-aged women who brewed merissa, stood with the maimed and the fit, refugees and town dwellers, professional soldiers and those who had never held a gun. The women chanted, "Gallant men of Al-Ubayyid, don't let these wild intruders into your homes. Hearts of gravel, protect your women and your town, don't let your enemy take your child." Sometimes the chants addressed the enemy. "Look, you rogues, here are brave warriors, men of destiny offering you a certain death."

Zamzam felt a surge of belonging. There was Hadija, standing tall, bald head glistening in the sun, crowned with her yellow beads, shouting curses at the enemy. There was Hibra, launching into one ululation after the other, her smile broad, as if her former beauty were restored. Yes, indeed, Al-Ubayyid was home, and they were her sisters. Bol, too, was in this town, her own flesh and blood. She missed him suddenly. In the middle of this hot, deafening battle, she longed to hug him and know that he was safe.

In the toing and froing with buckets of water, she bumped into Yaseen. She did not recognize him at first in civilian clothes without his turban and robe, a gun in his hand. He seemed to her younger and vulnerable. He was still in town; he had not left. Next to him were three of the Mahdi's men killed by gunshot and a government soldier speared to death. It could have been him. That spear could have killed him instead. When a wave of ululations rose from the women and reached her, she found herself joining in. She had never been able to do that before. In every wedding and every party, the zaghrouta had evaded her. Now, it released the relief she felt, was born from genuine joy. He smiled and reached for her hand. She averted her eyes from the dead bodies and crouched down in the trench next to him. Surrounded by death, the pulse in them was bright and intense. She gave him water to drink and started soaking rags to hand around.

She stayed with him until the sky clouded over as if the rainy season had returned. She stayed so that he would not get killed and because she could not leave him to lose him again. The heat was severe in the trench, and she sprinkled water on his face and on hers. When the cannons were fired, the sound entered her womb, numbing her ears even though she held her hands over them. Only the sky was as it should be, heavenly for those bleeding to death, serene over the mayhem and the ugliness down below. Rumors circulated that in the eastern side of the city, the enemy had penetrated the zariba of thorns and surged in. The Mahdi's uncle was already sitting on a chair inside the city! But no, before morale fell, they heard that this was not true. The tide of battle was in their favor. Indeed, a group of attackers had charged in, but a trap set by the governor awaited them and they were all killed. The fighting continued until sunset when the bugle was blown announcing the cease-fire.

Later that night, Zamzam grabbed her belongings and headed to Halima's house. She did not bid anyone goodbye. She groped her way through the dark night, the waning crescent obscured by clouds, as were the stars. The bodies she stepped over were not dead but asleep in exhaustion. It had been a victory for the Al-Ubayyid garrison. Two hundred and eighty-eight dead while on the other side, thousands of rebels were killed or wounded. The city had not been invaded. It had eluded the Mahdi. Al-Ubayyid was safe and Yaseen was safe. She knew where she would find him. To be with him. To make sure that Bol was alright. To leave the governor's compound, where she no longer belonged.

The house was dark, the door half-open; she did not need to knock. She stepped in and instead of the sprawling family—Halima and Hassan, her pretty daughter Buthaina and her husband, the other daughters, Bol—there was only Yaseen. He was sitting on the ground, on a sheepskin mat, as if he had finished praying. As he had done this afternoon in the trench, he said her name and reached out for her. She knelt and held him tight. "Where is Bol? Is he alright? Where are the others?"

"I don't know," he said. "They should be alright, don't worry. Perhaps they felt safer at Buthaina's husband's house or with one of the neighbors. I was at the governor's compound just now. We need to pursue them, go on the attack—"

She drew away from him. "You were there!"

He smiled and said, "It did not seem right to ask for you."

She did not reply. Her presence here was enough. She would never leave him again.

He said, "There were a number of us telling the governor that going after them would be the best strategy. We should not lose momentum. They're weak and we can finish them once and for all. But the governor said he would not push the men further, they must rest. He said if we go out, we leave the town defenseless, and it would be best to await reinforcements from Khartoum."

She got up to find them something to eat. She knew her way about the roofed corner of the hoash where Halima kept the food. To her surprise, there was nothing but the cooked remains of breakfast, a bowl of beans, and scraps of kisra. All the stores were gone, no lentils, no dates, no dried okra or millet. Why would Halima have taken all that food with her?

The answer was revealed to them the next day when they went out for news. Halima and all her children, including Ishaq, had defected to the enemy. The only one left behind was Halima's shocked husband, Hassan, still loyal to the governor who employed him. Zamzam was anxious about Ishaq, Yaseen incensed at his sister's behavior. The two of them swapped conjecture and the little that they knew.

Zamzam said that Halima had never given up hope of giving birth to a son. She was chasing a miracle from the holy man whose power was bringing the government to its knees. Yaseen said that Buthaina's father-in-law, one of the dignitaries of Al-Ubayyid, had been back and forth in secret talks with the Mahdi and had decided at the last minute to throw in his lot with the rebels. It followed therefore that his son would go with him, bringing his wife and her family.

"But we won," she said. "Will they now move back?"

He had been lying with his head on her lap and he sat up. "We won, but the rebels aren't acting as if they've lost. They didn't retreat to Kaba like everyone thought they would. They are holding Al-Ubayyid under siege. Showing that they are steadfast even though they lost thousands and Muhammad Ahmed lost two brothers and a cousin."

It amused her that he still refused to say "the Mahdi" and referred to him by his name. Everyone else now did, whether they believed he was the Expected One or not. Some people called him the Mutamahdi—the one pretending to be the Mahdi. To Zamzam he was the enemy, whether true or false. And Bol was there with him.

In the souq, food prices were starting to rise, but cloth was available, as was perfume. Zamzam went to Hadija and Hibra to show off. She sauntered into the kitchen as if she were a bride coming from her new husband's house to visit her family. She sat and they offered her hospitality, laughed at her happiness, made all the bawdy remarks she expected them to make. They admired the jewelry she was wearing. Tiny beads around her wrists, larger ones in a long necklace, silver earrings. "They are all my mother's," she said. "I found them buried in the house where I had left them all those years ago. Only Halima knew where they were."

"Honest folk," said Hadija. "They could have easily taken them." Hadija looked tired, as if she had not recovered from that day of the battle. Instead of sitting under the guava tree, she was lying down propped up on one arm, smoking her pipe. After some coaxing, she gathered her energy to braid Zamzam's hair in a special elaborate design befitting her new circumstances.

Often Yaseen and Zamzam wondered about Halima and Bol, fretted about their fate. One day Hassan rushed in distraught and almost incoherent. Although this was his home, he was permanently stationed with his men at the fortifications. Even his laundry was done there. Hassan was clutching a piece of paper and waving it in front of Yaseen's face. "Tell me if this is legal?" he shouted. "This can't be. It can't be."

When he sat and caught his breath, he managed to tell them the contents of the letter. It had been written by his son-in-law and smuggled into the town. In it was a pronouncement from Muhammad Ahmed, the Expected Mahdi. If a married woman joined his cause while her husband remained serving the Turks, their marriage was abrogated. This was because a man fighting on the side of the Turks against the Mahdi was, like his masters, an infidel. An infidel could not be married to a Muslim woman. And so, whether she wanted it or not, and whether Hassan liked it or not, Halima was no longer his wife.

Yaseen reassured Hassan that the Mahdi did not have any legal power. It was the grand mufti in Khartoum who made rulings, and he would never ever make such a pronouncement. It was preposterous that Hassan could be branded an infidel. "We have to be patient," Yaseen said. "Egypt will not forsake us. Look how we defeated him at the Friday battle. He is not invincible. Believe me, sooner or later a successful expedition will be mounted against him and that will be the end."

Zamzam could see that Hassan was not being reassured. He was like a man condemned. "I must go to her," he said. "I must bring her back." Despite Yaseen's pleas, he bolted out of the house.

They did not know what happened. Whether he did try to go to Halima or not. Whether for her sake, he threw in his lot with the Mahdists. Whether he reached her in time. "She could well be married now to someone else!" Zamzam blurted out and regretted saying this when she saw the anger in Yaseen's eyes. It spelled chaos for him that sacred law could be trampled upon. It wounded him that his sister could have so little regard for his theological opinion. That she could possibly marry without his consultation or knowledge was insulting. When he spoke, he sounded stern, as if this were the voice he used for work. "In this situation it would be best if Hassan divorces her. To save her from the sin of being married to two men at one time!"

Day by day as the siege intensified, more people slipped away, squeezing themselves and their families through the zariba fortifications. The governor responded by confiscating their properties, and one of the deserters, a merchant, blew up his store of grain before running out at night to join the rebels. Food was getting scarce. What had cost ten before the siege now cost thirty, then fifty, then seventy-five. One could not get this, and one could not get that. Power was shifting to the rebels. When the people of Al-Ubayyid were forced to eat horses and donkeys, when the price of corn kept soaring, they defected to the Mahdi. There was food on the other side and to the food they took their families.

Zamzam was now used to Yaseen's habit of reading at night. When he could no longer find kerosene, he would light tarred sticks. He would read until, laughing, she snatched the torch and plunged it into the ground. The way the smoke rose from the sand as she settled herself astride his lap, as if the smoke were incense and perfume. When he got up to wash and pray before dawn, he did so in the darkness, and she was not disturbed. One night he woke her up and said, "Look." She saw in the sky a bright star with a long burning tail streaking across the horizon. "How beautiful," she murmured and fell asleep again to the sound of his laughter at how sleepy she was. The next day in the souq, buying milk to make cheese, all she heard was talk of the star. How it was an omen of great change, how it could only mean one thing—that Al-Ubayyid would fall to the rebels.

The star appeared the following night and the one after it. Zamzam and Yaseen would lie looking up and wonder, *Has it moved or not?* It blazed in the clear sky, yellow white, fire-colored while its tail was pink and yellow. Next to it, the other stars were small and pale, as was the crescent. Only the rising sun burnt it away, little by little until it was invisible in the cloudless morning. Then late at night it would shine again. She asked him how something so pretty could be a bad omen.

He said that it was a comet, one of Allah's creations, and that it meant neither good nor bad luck. He told her that the Prophet Muhammad once had a son whom he named Ibrahim. When Ibrahim was two, he fell ill and died, and his parents were heartbroken. On the night of his death, there was a solar eclipse, and the people of Medina assumed the eclipse to be connected to the baby's death. The Prophet explained to them that the sun and the moon were signs of Allah's creation, and an eclipse is not related to anyone's birth or death. "Superstition has no place in true religion," Yaseen said. "Islam would not have survived if it followed people's whim. It spread because it is pragmatic, because it gives stability to faith."

She believed him, but even if the comet weren't a sign, the mood in Al-Ubayyid was moving toward despair. Week after week, even after the comet disappeared and one new crescent after another moved to full moons. The end was near but instead of being anxious, she thrummed with life. He left her each day to pray at the mosque, to get news, to doggedly help others, and then he returned with obvious relief to her consistent love. She was happiest when she was alone with him, and she could pretend that nothing else mattered. Neither their hunger nor the future, nor the wife waiting for him in Khartoum. The present, the present, and she presided over the present. With him she was safe and blissful, so what else mattered? Without a tomorrow, the here and now was potent and lengthy. He was hers, so she was rich. There was nowhere else she wanted to be, so she was free. Because he remembered her as a child, she felt rooted. Because he desired her as a woman, she was the most beautiful one in the world. Because she had come to him by choice, she was strong. Because they had traveled, were separated, and reconciled, their history provided hours of banter and reminiscence.

It should be a bad thing, being under siege. It was, but it did not feel that way. The house all to themselves, long days and the full sky at night. Forehead pressed against forehead, her nose ring grazing his shoulder, the beat of his heart against her stomach, pulling the angareeb indoors when the nights got colder. Lightheaded with hunger, they became uninhibited, speaking in reckless rambling words, she of how much she had pined for him, he of her body. This minute, these days, the sun softening, torch plunged into the ground, and his laughter—she convinced herself she was like honey, safe and sticky, dewy and shaded in a strong earthenware pot.

# 10

# Musa

**Al-Ubayyid, September 1882–January 1883**

When we came down from the Nuba Mountains, we went from safety to war. We left the summits of shade and wild fig, the granite home of the panther; we gave our backs to land crisscrossed by streams and tributaries, and we marched straight into the desert. We would never again be the small community of faithful, simple people, close to our beloved leader, the memory of the miracle of Aba binding us, Rabiha of Kinana's warning comforting us. Instead, we would swell in numbers, thousands upon thousands of Baggara tribesmen, of disaffected villagers. Up and down the Nile, news of the Expected One had spread. In Kaba where we camped—Al-Ubayyid merely six miles away—I would ride my horse and keep going past tents and clusters before reaching the end of the whole army. I would speak to men who had never seen the Mahdi from up close, for whom he was as remote as the moon, and they were content to receive his light from afar. They would tell of his miracles—how government bullets turned to water—and they would repeat his words. The first letter of the word for Paradise (jannah) is the same as that of hunger. I would come across slaves who were ready to fight because their masters had, for political reasons, joined the cause. And there were others, hundreds of them, who were more motivated by the spoils of war. They needed to be educated. Different tribes, different temperaments, varying degrees of faith, but we were all fighting under one leadership, against the same enemy.

It was these wayward elements that let us down at the Friday battle. Instead of following orders, they charged into Al-Ubayyid in search of booty. Choosing their entry point accordingly, not paying heed to the strategy that was laid. The result was chaos and death. A wretched day, and then the keening of the women. On first hearing news of the death of their menfolk, they tore their hair and rolled on the ground, poured dust on their heads, wept, and wailed. Then until dawn broke they sang the dirge for their lost ones. They lamented those felled by shots coming from the governor's rooftop. These high positions our spears couldn't reach. It was our first defeat, and it was a turning point. All could have been lost. Instead, we were determined to rise again more ferocious than ever. We learned from our mistakes. Instead of backing away, we shifted closer to the town and squeezed it.

By that time, the inhabitants of Al-Ubayyid were coming out to join our cause, and this decision was in their favor. Al-Ubayyid, too, was my hometown, but I no longer had much sentiment toward it. The Mahdi was now my family and my home; I lived for him and no one else. My wife and newborn daughter were indeed my responsibility, but they did not distract me from him. He, bless him, was the one who asked about my family in Al-Ubayyid. I wished that, like others, I could bring him hundreds of followers. But my family were small, my influence insignificant—all this a reflection of my humble background. I need not have felt ashamed. Even as he referred to my parents and siblings, they grew in stature before my eyes, as if they multiplied and became significant. "Bring them over," he said. "Your father and stepmother, your flesh and blood, they belong here with us."

When they came, they were impressed by my new position. How high I had risen, how well known I was among the emirs and the Mahdi's closest advisers. They were pleased to meet their new grandchild and daughter-in-law. We offered them food, but at first they were too hungry to eat. Starvation could do that to people. There were instances of people dying from eating too much after a prolonged period of severe hunger. Fortunately, this did not happen to them. My father's profession as a blacksmith was in great demand. When he recovered his strength, he set to task on making new spears. We could not have enough.

One night before dawn, a star appeared in the sky with a tail that curved like the mast of a boat. Throughout the camp, I could see the shadowy figures of people standing up to scan the sky. What a powerful omen! A calamity for sure was going to befall the people of Al-Ubayyid. The star was certainly a sign that the town would fall. Morale rose especially when the Mahdi did not dispute this assumption. Many of us would be asleep when the star appeared on the horizon. We would only catch it when we rose for the dawn prayer. Some of us waited up at night to see it. I held up my baby daughter under its light. On another night a woman let out a piercing ululation at the first sight of it, and I and the other men who were also on patrol laughed out loud. We were not immune to these signs of grace. How at times in the dark, our spearheads would glow. And how the meat of a female camel, taken as booty, would shine in children's mouths.

I was always afraid that the Turks would assassinate the one who was dearest to me. It would be the sort of thing they would do. Twice they had killed our messengers. Once in Fashoda and recently here in Al-Ubayyid. What kind of people do that? Two unarmed men delivering a message from their leader, ambassadors to be treated as guests at best or at the least to be granted safe conduct. Was this not law and tradition since the beginning of time? Instead, the Turkish governor became incensed by their attitude, their confidence in the Mahdi's power, the way they stood and the way they talked, he said, was insular and deserving of punishment. He had them hanged. Not where they usually hang prisoners but at the outskirts of the town, so that their limp bodies could be seen by us. I spoke to the Mahdi about this, almost in tears, for in the case of Al-Ubayyid, I was meant to be one of the ambassadors and at the last minute I was replaced. This left me with conflicted feelings, relief that I was still alive, able to continue and to serve, jealousy that I was not martyred, and then anger at the injustice of it all. He listened to me and said, "Arrogance and love of the self made that governor tyrannical. Casting aside the law and all decency. The governor lost his temper with our ambassadors; they were not subservient enough, not cowed by his presence, steadfast in their demands. He gave the order without consideration. That is the kind of people they are. Where they want us to be is under their feet. But we will not bow our heads to them nor to any other foreigner. We were not created to be lowly."

When he addressed the people, he spoke to them in simple words. Words that went straight to their hearts and affixed themselves. They would be rapt with wonder when he spoke, gazing at him with love and awe. More and more inhabitants from the town came out to join us, driven by hunger. At first, they spoke of inflation and then people reduced to making soup out of gum and the ropes of their angareebs, women frying cockroaches to feed their children.

Strange that in all this time, I had no knowledge that Buthaina, the girl who had rejected me, was here among us. Her father, an officer in the governor's army, and her husband, the son of a local dignitary, did not make her family likely candidates for defection. Whenever I thought of Buthaina, and I did so occasionally, I thought of her in Al-Ubayyid. I planned to rescue her when we took over the town. I would take her away from her infidel husband and she would be mine.

Perhaps another reason that I did not know of her presence in the camp was that I was away part of the time. I was sent on an important mission. It filled me with pride that the Mahdi trusted me, that among the ones closest to him I was considered discreet and reliable. The setback in the Friday Battle—it was not a defeat; we must not consider it a defeat— had led him to reconsider his ban on our use of firepower. He explained to me that such reversals could confuse the people and cause them to waver. This was why going back to Jebel Gadir to retrieve the rifles we had collected in Jazira Aba and from Rashid's troops was a sensitive issue. We had left them there with the infirm of our community, those who had not been able to travel—the maimed, elderly, and heavily pregnant women. I traveled with a handful of my men. "My men"—I, who in recent memory had nothing.

I did indeed return after a fortnight of constant travel, and I was successful in bringing the rifles and ammunition. The sight of the camp as I descended the mountains was heartening. The flags of the khalifas and their emirs, posted outside their large white tents, were lifted by the breeze. Each emir was surrounded by his followers, who had set up makeshift huts to shield them from the sun. I reined in my horse and observed this great sight. Strength in numbers spread out over the dusty plains from the base of the mountain to the pond, which was still full after the rainy season. From afar, the patches on men's clothes were like colored dots. Smoke rose from the cooking fires; dust rose from the horse riders patrolling the outskirts of the town. Humps of camels on the ground, horses saddled and ready, spears stacked, and if I listened intently, I could hear the thud of the war drums.

Three months later, when the weather turned cool, Al-Ubayyid was brought low. Soldiers dying at their posts and scurvy spreading throughout the trenches. Carrion feasted on these corpses, and when the birds became too fat to fly, the soldiers would seize them to slaughter and devour them. The Mahdi sent the governor a gentle letter, promising the leaders of the city free passage. His offer was accepted, and Al-Ubayyid fell into our hands without even a skirmish.

We entered my hometown victorious and prayed behind the Mahdi at Al-Ubayyid's main mosque. After settling my wife and parents in their house, I went in search of my prize. The household that had previously rejected me would now greet me with the respect I deserved. Buthaina's marriage would be annulled under the Mahdi's new laws, and she would be mine. I entered the house and there was her uncle and a girl. It was he who told me that Buthaina had been physically nearer to me than I had thought and how she was out of reach. Her husband had joined us, their marriage was intact, and therefore I would not be able to have her.

In my disappointment I lost my temper, abused the man, and claimed the girl. I wanted compensation. I would not walk out of this house empty-handed. Not again. I would not walk out of this house denied, not for a second time. He fought me when I grabbed the girl. Not with any discernible skill but with passion. And she fought me, too, shielding herself behind him. I could tell that she had been pampered and favored. It was a cold morning, and she was huddled in his robe—the special one worn by the Al-Azhar graduates. I snatched it off her. Better to warm with it three destitute children than the shoulders of a concubine. He shouted at me that his family and property were inviolable. I could have killed him but remembered how the Mahdi valued the learned scholars and urged us to treat them leniently, how he yearned for them to see the truth of his mission. Our scuffle must have been heard by some of the fighters outside because they hurried to my assistance. I gave the order to imprison him and dragged the girl kicking and screaming to my house.

She would not submit to me, daring to say that no man may touch her. She even had the audacity to grab my dagger and threaten to kill herself. I left her with my family. Time would knock sense into her. I could not bear to be long in one place, roaming the streets, nursing my hurt. To see Buthaina's husband, one of the notables of the city, conversing with the Mahdi was a personal affront. So often I had fantasized about him being an infidel on the side of the Turks. Instead, he was one of us. And not only one of us but set for a high position in the new Al-Ubayyid. True, his father had always held one but now as allies of the Mahdi, the ones who left their homes and stood by him—that was a special station indeed.

Al-Ubayyid was a rich prize. After swearing that he possessed nothing, the general was betrayed by one of his slaves. She revealed the hiding place of his wealth, an alcove in the wall of his house that revealed thousands and thousands of gold coins. The Turkish generals were made to dress as we dress, in patched jellabiyas, and they were to be reformed. We were to treat them well in the hope that they would join our side.

It was moving to see the blessed Mahdi talking gently to one of these generals, chiding him for killing his brothers, urging him to repent and acknowledge him as a leader. Once after the Friday prayer, he was preaching to us, and we were rapt. The Turkish general—whom he had seated near him, such was his magnanimity and capacity for forgiveness—was looking away, bored, his chin in his hand. With his blessed fingers, he reached out and peeled the former general's fingers away from his face. Addressing him by his first name, he said, "Here I am speaking to you of the hereafter and my position as Mahdi. Here I am telling you the most important things you need to hear while your mind wanders, and your heart is occupied. Stay mindful."

Instead of apologizing or sitting up straight at the very least, the man stood up in a huff of supreme impatience and strode off. I was on my feet in a minute, sword drawn ready to finish him off for his insolence.

"Leave him, Musa," my beloved said. "He was in a grand position and now he is in a lowly, defeated one. For such a person, for whom love of this world is paramount and fixed in his heart, this is indeed unbearable. Give him time."

We gave him time, but he continued in his disdain, snorts of disgust, and saying "oof, oof" to everything. We challenged him to proclaim his faith and loyalty to the Mahdi; he refused. Councils were held to discuss what to do with him. At the end, the Mahdi handed him over to one of his emirs, who immediately had him beheaded.

He was not a great loss. Every day more leaders flocked to join our cause. They brought with them whole tribes. And even outside Sudan, the Mahdi's miraculous victories were capturing people's attention. Delegations came from Tunis and Fes and even from as far away as India. These were heady days indeed.

I reveled in my new position and how my family now held me in awe. I walked with my head held high. As for that slave girl from Buthaina's house, nothing seemed to work with her. Neither kindness nor severity, neither attention nor neglect— she remained untamed. This, at a time when women—virgins freeborn offered by their fathers to the victors—were aplenty and we were spoiled for choice! I ended up selling her.

# 11
# Yaseen

I am a prisoner of the false Mahdi, chained until I swear
allegiance to him. I could not protect her. I did not save her.
All through the night we are kept in a dungeon, chained
together feet and hands. At dawn, we are unchained and let
out in the open-air yard. Breath after the suffocating stench
of the night. There are cracks in the walls, we can see out,
but they are too high to climb over. The fajr prayer is a brief
respite before we are chain-ganged and made to walk into
the desert. Under the supervision of the guards, we collect
rocks to block up the wells surrounding the city. The slightest
resistance is met with blows, attempts at escape by death. Back
in the prison, there is never enough to eat. In groups we are
compelled to shove and squabble over a single basin of kisra
with lentils or beans, overcooked or undercooked, never tasty.
The prison is filthy and full of wounded men, many ill with
scurvy and dysentery. They are dying and after they die, we,
the other prisoners, are responsible for burying them. At times
it is as if I have been forgotten. All is upheaval outside, one

order shattering, another settling in its place. Those caught in between rushing to recant, to fall over themselves in promises of fidelity, to denounce others and distance themselves from the "infidel Turks," a definition getting vaguer and vaguer and now meaning anyone of whatever faith or nationality who wears the tarbush! News pours in from the guards and from those joining us for the first time, shoved in or chained. There is no easy way out of the Al-Ubayyid prison. The Turks did fortify it well. Zamzam used to live nearby in the governor's compound. The governor had been beheaded they say, and I was unable to save her. I did not protect her.

When the full moon marks a month spent in captivity, I am dragged to meet the man himself. He has taken over the district office, apt enough now that he is occupying the seat of power. The place is almost unrecognizable—all the furniture gone because we are in austerity. There used to be armchairs with cushions, a high brass inkstand; the governor had, I remember, a magnificent penknife. No more and we are on the floor.

I am thrown at the feet of the Mahdi. No, I will not call him that, not even if he is the de facto one. I will call him by his true name, Muhammad Ahmed. I am thrown down in a heap to easily kiss his feet, to beseech for my life and profess my undying faith. When I make no move to do so, I am dragged to the side, cast out of the illustrious gathering. He is surrounded by his emirs, some familiar from the time I saw them in the cave at Jazira Aba. They are better dressed now, still the jellabiyas with the patches, but the material is brand-new, and the patches are fine silk from the looted monastery in Fashoda and what looks like the curtains of the governor's residence. The intended effect of poverty and austerity is not achieved; instead the patches have become a style, a fashionable uniform. Shining spears are laid aside, skins well oiled, the fatigue of warfare and travel gone. A bit more flesh on the bones. It is said that now all his sermons are exhortations against love of riches, against wife snatching, against disputes over captured loot, against the distractions of the world. These are the challenges of Mahdist rule. Let him moralize. Let him flog those who smoke, drink, and fornicate—and keep flogging them. Fanatics can never draw out the good in people. They will go to war I predict. They will raise armies, invade, and pillage because it is only aggression that will keep their cause alive. Fighting an enemy is always easier than governing human complexity.

The notables of the city come to pay homage. Beyond us, out in the hoash closer to the street, are the praise singers. With soft beats of the drums, they chant the virtues of their leader, his miracles and blessings, his exploits in battle, the amount of love he evokes. They sing, "You are the eye of life itself/For people everywhere." Enslaved men bring in waterpots from the wells, merchants come and go, tribal chiefs swear allegiance. I am shoved to the side, in this lowly spot as a sign of my disfavor, an outcast until I repent. This is the reason I have been brought here. I did not save her. I did not protect her. I then see him come in. I remember his name—Musa. His story, that he wanted to marry my niece Buthaina and was rejected. I measure his pettiness. He, vile, catches my eye and pounces on me, drags me to the center of the circle, so that I am on my hands and knees. Standing above us all, he lifts his sword.

"This hand," he addresses the gathering and in particular Muhammad Ahmed. "This hand wrote lies about the blessed, victorious one. Here he is, one of the ulema of evil, who sup at the sultan's table, who deny you. The blind sheikh Amin Al-Darir, sitting in Khartoum, does not pen his own fatwas. But here is his right hand and I will cut it off."

I look at my hand and note that it is grubby. I look at it and think I will lose it like I lost her, unable to protect her, what my right hand possesses, rightly possesses. "No," says Muhammad Ahmed, raising his arm up toward Musa. "Leave him."

"Give me your hand." He reaches out to me.

I sit back on my heels and place my hand in both his palms. He studies it, turns it around to look at the palm. Around me, a miracle is expected. Will he cause it to wither on its own, to freeze, to spasm? I feel it heavy in his warm hands. He smiles, and I remember that smile from the cave in Aba. His heavy hypnotic presence. The way his eyes do not meet my eyes and yet he knows things. Guesses them or is a magician. He has delved in mysticism, seen what others haven't, been privy to secrets. But this is neither here nor there; it does not make him the Expected One. The hand he holds in his palms wrote in ink and quill, on headed official paper. A treatise, a proclamation: *For Those Who Seek Guidance on the Clarification of the Mahdi and the False Mahdi . . . the imposter, fake, a rebel . . . Anarchy is not part of our religion, he is causing chaos in the land, fermenting war, the killing of Muslims, dishonoring women, plundering property . . . he does not meet the requirements of the Expected Mahdi . . . His claim is thus refuted for the following reasons—physical attributes, lineage, place of birth and manifestation, the contemporary background from which the Mahdi would be expected to emerge, in a time of chaos and calamity, at a time when Muslims are lacking a Khalifa . . . but now the Muslim world does have a Khalifa, the Ottoman sultan Abdul Hamid II in Constantinople is the legitimate defender of the Muslim world, our rightful ruler.*

He reads my mind. Presses my hand and says, "But the Prophet himself told me I was the Mahdi. I, a simple man, did not seek this. I, a sinner, do not deserve this honor. You know because you are well schooled that the devil cannot take the form of the Prophet in a dream. Whoever sees him has truly seen him. Whoever hears him has truly heard him."

Dreams, even true visions, cannot be taken as proof. They do not abrogate law.

His voice is low. He does not need to justify himself to me. He knows this and says his words with obvious generosity. *Look*, he is telling his followers, *I have time for the undeserving. I am ready to forgive those who slander me.* My hand is heavy in his palms. Heavier, until he lets go and it falls like a dead weight onto the ground. Chuckles and indrawn breaths all around. Instead of moving it, I find myself participating in the charade. I use my left hand to lift it off the ground, I clasp it, cradle it to my chest as if it were wounded. Back in prison I move it and rub it. It is colder than normal, the muscles all the way to my neck locked in a spasm. I wriggle my fingers and want to write with it again.

I manage, through a guard who had previously worked under Hassan, to get word out to my sister. Halima is back in her home now, and no matter how much she believes in this imposter, I am still her brother. The next week I fall ill, collapsing under the sun, my gums bleeding. I am unfit for labor and spend days lying down. It is scurvy and, through the guard, Halima sends medicine and food. I wait to hear from her. Children sometimes come into the prison, bringing food to their relatives, selling snacks to the guards, wandering in the company of other children. The guards allow them to come and go as they wish. One day it is Ishaq who comes to see me. I am delighted with how much he has grown; he is already eight years old. I am relieved to see a familiar face, a connection to my life. He is reticent, but he had always been a quiet child. He does not have a letter for me; letters are dangerous. Instead, a bag of dates and some guava. When I ask for news, he whispers the name of Halima's new husband. I am dismayed. Poor Hassan, now serving the new administration and no longer deemed an "infidel Turk," has been trying to claim his true wife back. Ishaq shakes his head. There is no hope. I can imagine Hassan devastated by this. I ask about Zamzam. Does he have any news?

I do not sleep that night nor the next. By day the sun burns my head; I earn lashes for not pulling my weight. I deserve this because I did not protect her, did not save her. It is such a hot day, and the physical work is grueling. When a visitor is announced, I tell myself I am hallucinating. It is my dear friend Sheikh Isma'il, and I break down in his arms.

His voice is full of sympathy. He says, "I can't bear to see you like this. We must get you out of here." I note then that he is not wearing his tarbush, but of course. It is banned now, the fashion of the "infidel Turks." Still, he has his robe on, the one that marks him as an Azhar graduate. I had wrapped mine around her to keep her warm and Musa snatched it off. I could not protect her, keep her warm. I did not.

Isma'il says, "Don't cry my friend. I am here to help you. You helped me when I was destitute in Cairo. I will not forsake you. The prospects are not as bleak as you think."

I croak. It is a laugh of derision. "Oh yes," I tell him. "Insanity reigns . . ."

"Shush," he says. "Don't talk like that. Sit down and listen to me. There is a way out."

We sit on the ground, our backs against the wall, the rays of the setting sun soft upon us. He talks in a low voice, his logical self. He outlines a plan. Expedience, he says, pragmatism. "They need you. Are willing to offer you the position of a judge. A house, your girl. It might not be too late to retrieve her. Consider."

At first, I struggle to understand what he is saying. It sounds like a foreign language. "Would you believe it," he says. "They were all set to execute that Austrian priest they kidnapped from the monastery in Fashoda. And a bunch of nuns, all for not renouncing Christianity and accepting the Mahdi. They had them all lined up, then a village sheikh wakes up from his siesta and casually says, 'Oh no, no, according to the sharia, unarmed peaceful men of religion are not to be executed.' So, they leave them be. It shows you the chaos and lack of legal structure they are operating with. The Mahdi is highly learned. He has studied with the best teachers this country can offer, but he doesn't know the nuances of jurisprudence, and he is surrounded by clueless illiterates. That's why they need Al-Azhar graduates, they need trained jurists, and the Mahdi has taken a liking to you."

He is calling him the Mahdi. The reality of what he is suggesting sinks in. The reality of who he is becoming. "You swore allegiance to him, Isma'il." There is no anger in my voice, no reproach, just a dull surprise. "You did, didn't you, and yet after we met him in Aba, you were the first one to say that he is not who he claimed to be?"

"This is not the point."

"This is the point."

"He is pious."

"I don't disagree with that."

"He intends to establish justice."

"By killing the innocent?"

He frowns. "Think of the bigger view. The Ottoman Empire is shrinking. Bosnia, Bulgaria, Cyprus, Tunisia. All lost. Gone! Egypt will be next."

"Shrinking but it still exists. We have a commander of the faithful in Constantinople; he is not here in Al-Ubayyid."

"You saw for yourself. Spears against gunfire. The Mahdi's victories are spectacular."

"For how long? Do you not think that as we speak armies are being raised against him? Do you think Egypt is just going to give up Sudan?"

He softens and puts his hand on my shoulder. "You are relying on the Egyptian army? After they were bombarded by the British in Alexandria, then in Tel El Kabir? There is no Egyptian army left. The army supported Urabi in his nationalism and now Urabi is finished. Sentenced to exile."

All this had happened before Al-Ubayyid fell. It is not news to me. Egypt is under British occupation. Its army defeated, its pride Urabi Pasha, the former minister of war and head of the nationalist movement, rendered powerless. The khedive is deep in debt, under the control of the British and the French. They make political decisions dictated by the needs of the creditors. And the Sudan, expensive to run, had been one of the reasons for Egypt's financial problems.

Isma'il says, "The only army now in Egypt is the British army. You think they will come here to liberate Al-Ubayyid? Britain announced that its occupation in Egypt was temporary. How can it now dig farther into Sudan without losing credibility? I can tell you that the telegrams sent from Khartoum to Cairo are left unanswered. Don't back the wrong side, my friend."

"The wrong side is the side of the imposter," I say.

He covers my mouth with his hand. "Don't be rash. Think about what I've said. What they are offering. I will repeat it. The position of a judge here in Al-Ubayyid. Consider."

He gets up to leave, and I want to leave with him. It seems to me impossible to sustain this imprisonment. I will attempt to escape and get myself killed in the process. He is offering me a way out. Deceitful but one can argue—I can argue to myself—that I am under duress. It is permissible to lie if one fears for his life. Swear allegiance without meaning it. Say I believe in the imposter when I know he is deluded. Live with the guilt but at least live. Then I can get Zamzam back, save her, protect her.

I practice the oath of allegiance. Force my tongue to form the lie, I try again, and the words are stones in my mouth. I sink down so that my head is on the floor. I pray for strength. I pray for strength and in the morning, there is news. Muhammad Ahmed announces the abolition of the four schools of Islamic law. No more madhabs—we are all one under his guardianship. No Maliki school for the Sudanese, Shafi'i for the Egyptians, Hanbali or Hanafi—they are made obsolete. Centuries of Islamic scholarship chucked to one side. Thousands of volumes, years of academic research, realms of debate—all jettisoned in favor of unity. Outrageous. The Muslim world will never accept this; here in the Sudan the Sufi tariqas—the Khatmia, the Tijania, the Qadiria, the Shazilia—will know him to be fake. And sure enough, to preempt this, he bans them too. No more plurality, no more diversity of practice and interpretation—only one arbiter and a "pure religion." I laugh out loud. There is now no iota of doubt in me. He can win as many battles as he can, rule the whole world—but he will ultimately be doomed because he is not the true Mahdi, and I denounce him. His way is not my way, and his enemies are my allies.

Imprisonment is easy after this. If they execute me for refusing the offer, then these are the last days of my life. I will live them well. Each new sliver of a crescent marking the start of another month. I use every minute. Every day I recite three parts of the Qur'an, complete it in ten days and start again. I wake up for the night prayer, standing until dawn. I fast Mondays, Thursdays, and the three white nights of the full moon. I fast the whole of Rajab and the first two weeks of Sha'ban. We dig trenches in the sun and carry heavy loads. I am frustrated that my friend Isma'il has not been able to at least improve the conditions I live under; I am disappointed that my sister, Halima, does not send me food more frequently. Then Ramadan comes bringing its own stillness and everyone every day is fasting. It is easier to be patient then, to fret less and bear more easily the wretchedness around me. When I pray, I find that more and more have joined me, even the guards. The reading lessons I have been giving start to yield fruit. I listen to the life stories of criminals and others, like myself, who cannot be part of this new regime. In my mind, I turn over the pages of books. I read them as if they are in front of me; I savor the words. Ibn Battuta's travels, the chapter in which he visited Baghdad—its sumptuous baths, its magnificent bazaars, its famous university, where each of the four madhabs has a separate wing with its own mosque and lecture hall. Ibn Battuta's journeys to the Maldives, to Ceylon, and to Bengal. His descriptions of the women in Mali. I am so sorry I could not protect you; forgive me I did not save you.

Then hope bounces into the prison. It comes with the falling rain, with the thick clouds and puddles in the prison yard. A great army from Egypt is coming to save us. I catch malaria and in feverish dreams see Egyptian soldiers led by a British general. His name is whispered among the prisoners, among the inhabitants of the city who only accepted the Mahdi under duress. General Hicks is leading thousands of men; he is marching toward us. No one can stand in his way. He will liberate Al-Ubayyid. I breathe optimism in the air. It has been a year since I left Khartoum and came to Al-Ubayyid. A whole year since I saw my wife, my mother, my brothers. A year away from my work. Sometimes it feels longer, sometimes it feels short. Perhaps my ordeal is coming to an end.

Tension among the Mahdists. Intense preparations for a defense. Until—and this is the report that reaches us from the guards—a horseman races into town demanding a meeting with the Mahdi. A defector? No, he is a guide, an expert on the terrain, seasonal watercourses, and wells. He had been employed by Hicks to advise the army in navigating the desert, to make sure they go from one watering place to the next. He says, "I tricked Hicks and his infidel army and led them to the middle of Sheikan. They've been now three days without water! Such is their thirst that they've taken to slashing open the bellies of camels for a drop to drink."

Immediately the war drums start to beat. It is the sacred month of Muharram, but no law restrains these people! They cry out for war. Tap, tap goes the drum. I feel the sickness of it in my stomach. The Mahdist armies gather. Their leader promises tidings of victories and abundant booty. They set out on foot and on horses. A hush descends on the town until we hear the cannons blast. That great army, that great army. But could it be, could it be?

The next morning, early, I spot through the cracks in the wall the first of the soldiers returning. They are carrying the bloodied uniforms of Hicks's soldiers.

# 12

# Zamzam

Warm in his robe, she had showed him the precious ointment kept safe from their own hunger. It was made of bone marrow and clove oil, with sandalwood to muffle the smell of the marrow. He rubbed it on her arm. Winter made the skin dry. His, too, but he didn't matter, he said. Beauty was made for her. He was restless, anxious about the Al-Ubayyid surrender. Today they must stay indoors, he said, not even talk to the neighbors across the wall, not answer the knock on the door, unless it was Halima returning home. That was something that made Zamzam happy, that she would be with Bol again and that they would all be together as a family. But the soldier broke in and she screamed. Then it was loudness and jagged pieces, lashing out and being dragged—Yaseen fighting to keep ahold of her, his robe snatched away and all her mother's jewelry. For the next few days in the soldier's home, she was expected to be tamed, but how could he even imagine she would give in to him.

It was a kind of victory when he gave her up, though she was afraid of where he took her. An enclosure, a pen encircled with walls of thorns full of women, men, and children. But there was a familiar, loving face. Dear Hadija. The elderly woman looked dazed, weakened by the siege and the capture, but she was still herself. Ranting about Hibra, who had betrayed the governor by revealing the hiding place of his gold. She had told the Mahdists where he kept it in the wall after he had sworn he had nothing. The result was that he would get executed, and as for the accursed Hibra, she had now been rewarded—granted freedom and a servant position in the Mahdi's household. *Disloyal, ungrateful whore*, Hadija grumbled. Then, on hearing the azan, she stood up to hitch her dress over her head, and in her pantaloons, pray facing Mecca.

They, now deemed a surplus, were to join the slave caravan heading for Khartoum. Get up, line up—men to be shackled in chains, women walking in front carrying baggage and children. Hadija stood up, but she did not join the others. "I will not be enslaved," she shouted. "I'm a Muslim. I go where I please. I went to Mecca on the Hajj."

The guards pushed her forward to join the others. Zamzam held her to protect her. A whiplash aimed at Hadija stung her shoulder. "Damn you," Hadija shouted at the guards. "Damn you and your false Mahdi. The imposter has brought calamity on Al-Ubayyid."

One of the guards held her throat. "Don't you dare! I could kill you for this, woman. Shut up for your own good." She was loose skin over fine bones, eyes flashing. She spat in his face.

He hit her with the back of his hand, and she fell to the floor. He gave her a tirade on the miracles of the Mahdi and his rightful position. "Lies," Hadija shouted, waving her arms, which the guard struck again with his whip. Zamzam cradled her and another lash of the whip landed over the first wound. She screamed, and Hadija lifted her head. She was angular and light, bald scalp, slack chin, grayish skin; she was almost androgynous. "Look at my lips," she shouted at the guard, voice hoarse. Her lips were bleeding, her words slurred but still clear. "These lips kissed the black stone in Mecca; they will never swear allegiance to your false Mahdi."

He lost his temper and stomped on her stomach. She did not survive. Zamzam wept over her, wailed with a straightforward wildness that went on and on.

She could barely see through the tears. They were made to walk, to leave reddish Al-Ubayyid and head north over sand and stones. Zamzam's hand tied to another woman, a stranger wrapped in her own story, in her own knotted pain. Zamzam hummed a blurred song. No tune that she could remember, just the cadence of elegy. *Hadija, my mother, Hadija, my beloved friend. I am orphaned without you. Flash, light, you are a lamp that has been extinguished. Made the world depleted. You were a generous woman . . . true you are. When asked for help, you said yes. Hadija, full of common sense. Blessed Hadija, where are you now? Who will give you the burial you deserve? Are you already in Paradise, living forever?*

Everything around her mirrored her grief. She saw now how the men were yoked together, the wooden beam heavy on their shoulders, feet shuffling in chains. Young girls, terrified, clinging to each other, urged to keep pace and barely catching up. The town faded away; there was now only the scrubby unknown desert. For them to walk hour after hour. At sunset, exhausted, they were allowed to rest, the yoke and baggage laid aside, feet tied together instead of hands. Groans and sobs. If a guard lost his temper, there would be random whipping, and as for escape, how far could one go, which direction? A couple—brother and sister—tried but were caught. The girl raped, the boy whipped with such violence that he had to be carried by the others the next day.

Bringing the caravan to a halt, a pregnant woman sank on her hands and knees by the roadside and gave birth. Zamzam hadn't even know that she was pregnant as her stomach was hardly showing, and she had been walking as fast as everyone else. The baby died minutes later. No one had the energy to bury him. Eventually, the mother herself started poking the earth with her fingers. She did this in a distracted, half-hearted manner, and Zamzam took over the task. Without shedding a single tear, the mother continued to walk when they were again all ordered to march, trailing a thin line of blood after her.

One afternoon a young man with bright eyes started lashing out, foaming at the mouth, and the guards abandoned him, tying him to a post by the side of the road. Zamzam kept her head down. She did not want to see, did not want to hear. She did not want to bear witness to the suffering of others. She did not want to think that this was what had happened to her cousins and neighbors when her village was attacked all those years ago. If Yaseen hadn't rescued her and Bol! She must not think of Yaseen. Not remember love and life, not be who she was, laughing because he was too serious, joyful because he was intense, smug because she had known about them before he did even though he was older than her. He thought he had rescued her, taken her to a better place—for Bol, so far, maybe—but here she was now, going through it all as if it were always meant to be. Day after real day of moving, of being alone and not alone, of others pressed against her. Of cracked heels, of wrists sore from being tied, of flies buzzing over the pus from the cut on her shoulder that refused to heal. Of fear of the guards. She made sure she did not meet their eyes, did not provoke or rouse their interest.

Walk, walk, stop, shuffle together with whichever woman she was tied to that day, to relieve themselves behind a bush if they could find one, under shadow of darkness, hold everything in when neither shelter was available. At sunset, swallow whatever was tossed in the dish, not enough for the ten gathered around it. Shove others aside for her portion, because if she held back out of politeness, she would faint, she would starve, and every day they must keep walking. Even the water was rationed until they came to a well or stream. At night lie on the hard ground, look up at the sky, beg for oblivion. Sometimes when they passed through villages or crossed paths with nomadic tribes, kind souls would give them food. Or children would laugh at them and throw stones. Occasionally sporadic sales would be made and one or two of them would be left behind. The big market was Khartoum, gateway to the East African slave trade, the unfaltering demand in the metropoles of Cairo and Constantinople. Even though the trade was officially outlawed, it continued to flourish. Usually, this route was patrolled and dangerous to the slave traders, but the government was cowed now by the Mahdists. Did not the Mahdi now control the whole of Kordofan? Now government soldiers kept themselves well out of west Sudan.

At the outskirts of Khartoum, there was a change. Zamzam saw the river; she had not seen it for years. Old friend. Appearing like a savior in her hour of need. The captives were commanded to bathe, and she did not need any encouragement. She could stay in the water forever, becoming clean, losing her thirst, desperate to lose her weakness, too, and all the bad memories. How familiar the water was, its flow and color. She understood it, could speak to it and marvel that the river had flowed all this time, all the years she had been away from it. Her very same river—the White Nile. This was her habitat, this mellow moving water. And it could fill her ears and leave no space for anything else, carry all anxiety with the breeze, the unknown hideous tomorrows. The woman who had given birth on the route was wading deeper and deeper until she couldn't walk, giving herself up to the water, not wanting the shore ever again. The guards caught her in time before she drowned. Having come that far, she was too precious to lose. They dragged her to the shore where she spluttered and vomited, cursed and breathed against her will.

In a holding nearby, the women were separated from the men. Handed over to older women who expected to be obeyed. Food, tasty and in decent amounts. Ointment for infections, treatment for rashes and itches. Oil for parched skin and cracked heels. New clean clothes. Rest. Sleep, sleep, and only to be disturbed by the snores and nightmares of others. This was no hospitality, though some could get fooled.

Zamzam knew better. Why would suddenly the cut on her shoulder receive treatment? Why would her skin be oiled, time and again, the oil high quality? Her hair worthy of treatment by a professional, plaited in an elaborate design, parted in the center, coiled over her ears. "Look at you," the hairdresser said. "Not the prettiest I have ever seen. Not even in this group. But still, you're something special. I wonder where you will end up." The hairdresser had a friend with her, a woman called Hawa who said she was here looking for a young lad. She did not have enough money to compete for the best; she must make do with what she could find, what she could afford. That's why she spent hours helping her hairdresser friend and chatting. Her voice soothed Zamzam, sharp, ironic stories—she and her husband owned a fruit garden, but it was far away from the river. She needed a strong lad to fetch water from the river.

Ten years ago, the enslaved would have been on prime show in the middle of the Khartoum market. Now a low profile must be maintained. Those who wanted them must come out of the city to get them. They came, the wealthy and not so wealthy. They came for the children, adopting them at a young age to ensure unstinting loyalty and obedience for years to come. They came for the healthy young men who would carry heavy loads and till the fields. They came for the women, for domestic services and for sexual bondage.

From all the stories Zamzam had heard from Hadija, she knew that there could be much worse fates than the governor's household. Heavy work in the fields, toiling day and night until all her youth was sucked away. Merissa brewing in a shop, working in the brothel at the back. Squatting over the fire, cooking one meal after the other for people she did not love. Middle-aged women who would treat her as a daughter and then send her in to one teenage son after the other so that he could learn. Her imagination could run wild and when it did, as the days passed and she watched her companions slide away toward such fates, she began to be gripped by anxiety. Why was she one of the last ones to go? Was that a bad thing? Was it because of the cut on her shoulder? She had been instructed to cover it with a veil. Did this delay mean anything, or did it mean nothing? To be wanted or unwanted, wanted for the wrong thing, priced, overpriced, undervalued.

The man who took an interest in her could not make up his mind. He came and went. He haggled and dithered. Spoiling her chances with others, the hairdresser and Hawa noted; that khawaja was unsettling the atmosphere. He was viewed with wariness. Were not the Europeans keen on abolishing slavery? The former governor, Gordon, and his laws were remembered. The times they were enforced and the times they were overlooked. The missionaries finding it difficult to convert Muslims bought slaves to free and by doing so, build up their adherents. Priests and nuns would come to such a gathering, pumped with disapproval and yet wholeheartedly ready to participate. Perhaps this man was one of them.

One day, he stood staring at Zamzam for almost an hour, all the time scribbling on paper. The dealer got angry and demanded a payment. Words were exchanged. The khawaja's accent was difficult to understand but the dealer's verdict was clear. You either take her or leave her for someone else. Go and find yourself an agent to negotiate on your behalf if you don't know our ways. No, you can't draw her for free.

So, he had been drawing her. It made Zamzam anxious, as if he were scraping bits of herself. No one had ever drawn her before. It did not seem natural; it did not seem right. She begged Hawa to take her. "I can fetch water from the river," she said. "I am strong enough. I can clean and I can cook for you too. I served in the kitchen of the governor of Al-Ubayyid."

"Oh no," Hawa said. "I don't want fancy Turkish cooking. You'll be too high and mighty for me. I said heavy garden work."

She kept pleading. "I am strong enough. I can carry water pitchers on my head, easy. I will do everything you say. Please."

# 13

# Robert

**Khartoum, September 1883**

In the past year, he had sold five watercolors. One of them—
*Felucca on the Blue Nile*—was already hanging in the Grosve-
nor Gallery in London. Two in private ownership. *The Fort
at Khartoum* soon to be displayed in the gallery in Bath Street.
Another, still unsold, was on the wall of the Art Club in Edinburgh awaiting the verdict of the Fine Art Committee. Still
others were with his agent, as were sixty charcoal sketches,
not for sale because he planned to develop them into oil on
his return to Scotland. When he had sent the first painting
to his agent, his accompanying letter was terse and tentative.
He did not want to attach to the gesture much hope. It
was easy to imagine the parcel lost or damaged on the way.
Then came the enthusiastic response, the request for more.
His agent also mentioned the possibility of negotiating for
him a commission from the *Glasgow Herald*. In case of action
against the Mahdi, Robert could accompany the troops, his
illustrations accompanying the news articles written by the
paper's war correspondents.

Such an incentive to work, to keep going now that he had without a doubt turned a corner, and there was evidence that not only was he excelling, but there was also a demand for what he could produce. He worked late at night, insects gathering around the lantern, the breeze barely wafting through the window. He had become unfazed by these physical discomforts, the horrendous heat, having to constantly wipe his sweaty palms with a handkerchief. More challenging was looking after the canvas during the process and after completion. Protecting it from the dust that was everywhere, even beyond the haboob season and even with the shutters down and the windows sealed, it would come again, a film of dust covering every surface.

His paintings needed to be wrapped in layers of cloth. Twice, paintings in progress, perched on the easel (he did now possess an easel, made under his supervision by a local carpenter), were ruined by a haboob because he'd been unable to run home in time to save them. He was forced to start fresh, resentful of what he had lost, shouting orders for the room to be cleared of dust. He shared servants with his boss, Ramsay, a man and a woman who came round to his place whenever they could be spared. So "shared" was not exactly accurate; he made do with the surplus of their time. This was a haphazard arrangement, and he was considering having his own staff. Now that he was more social and outgoing, though not to the extent of having people over, unsolicited advice to do so often came his way. He was, to his surprise, considered by some as an eligible widower and though the number of suitable young women was low, he did find himself with admirers. It was the mothers of these young women who gave him domestic advice. You must never drink milk without boiling it first. Always sleep under a mosquito net. Of course, a gentleman in your position needs his own staff.

It seemed to Robert misleading, to encourage any prospects of matrimony. However, he came to this conclusion long after he had spread false hope, so it became difficult to extricate himself. In this climate, the flimsiest of flirtations bloomed into passion, the slightest interest expanded into speculation and gossip. Scarcity was the cause. Prospects rare and therefore highly prized. Two English girls, a few Austrians, a handful of other Europeans, Greeks and Armenians— though they were slightly too foreign. Seasoned colonials, the European young women who orbited him were aspiring to move to more comfortable destinations—Rhodesia, Ceylon, or India. These were not Robert's ambitions. His target was the triumphant homecoming, recognition of his talents in the right circles. There was a daughter waiting for him in Aberdeen, galleries in Edinburgh, membership of the Royal Society, a knighthood like David Wilkie, far-fetched but no harm in aiming high. He would rather, thank you very much, return home alone.

He need not have worried too much about breaking any hearts. Europeans were leaving Khartoum in droves. After the fall of Al-Ubayyid to the Mahdi and the execution of its governor, the dreadful treatment of the priests and nuns—forced to marry each other despite their vows of celibacy—Europeans became jittery. The Mahdi was plotting to take over Khartoum, and though everyone reassured each other that he could not possibly do that, it was prudent to be safe rather than sorry. Besides, the whole country was liable to rise. And then what? The two routes out—north by river to Egypt and east by camel to the port of Suakin to board a Red Sea ship—could become blocked. Better leave while they could. There were hasty goodbye parties, intense kisses, breathless promises, and all was peaceful again. He continued to paint.

No more distractions until he found the city swelling in preparation for war. Finally, Khartoum's pleas had been answered. The army that would destroy the Mahdi once and for all was now gathering under the command of the British general Hicks. Made up of Egyptian soldiers, the one who had mutinied under Urabi Pasha, the army was large and well equipped. The plan was to lure the Mahdi outside Al-Ubayyid and finish him off.

Robert was eager to join the expedition in the role of artist for the *Glasgow Herald*. After much persuasion, Ramsay had agreed to grant him leave. He could not spare him at the boatyard and would cut his wages. He was also worried that it would be a dangerous mission. But Robert insisted that medics, journalists, and artists would be well protected by the mighty British square; they, along with the equipment, would remain in the center of the unbreakable formation of soldiers. He was excited about the prospect. The opportunity it gave him to travel and sketch. To see places he would not normally see. Two days before he left, he was down by the river sketching the men and women who were filling their waterpots. He saw her again. The girl he had seen six months ago, the one he had almost purchased and then at the end didn't, feeling it was beneath him to do so. He had often looked at the sketches he made of her that day. Her special beauty, only oil could do justice to her blue-black skin, the contrast of the white cloth against it—not only white but any color would sing. Her brooding eyes—the longing in them when she turned away to look at the river. On returning home that day, he was struck by a brilliant idea. He could free her once he was done with her. This would assuage his troubled conscious. He returned the following morning to that compound near the White Nile forest but found her already gone. *There are others*, the dealer said. *Plenty, come look.* But Robert was not interested.

And today here she was again. Surely it was her, in clothes that were tattered, hairstyle simple. Not like that day when she was on show—skin sleek with oil and intricate plaits coiled over her ears, but it was her for sure. She recognized him too; perhaps the sketchbook in hand was the giveaway. She stopped chatting to her friends and hurried away, balancing the waterpot on her head. He stalked.

He followed her until she reached her destination. There he offered the owner of the orchard what could not be refused. He waited because patience indeed was a virtue. He allowed the inevitable drama to subside. The exact words might have been beyond him, but it was clear that she was berating those who were letting her go, they in return admonishing her to behave herself and count her blessings. It could have been worse; no blows were struck and following him home she cried quietly without screeching and wailing. Screeching and wailing would have been intolerable.

From the moment she entered his house to the time he left with the Hicks expedition, forty-eight hours later, Robert worked like he had never worked in his life. Hour after hour, barely stopping to eat and sleep. He did not want to be cruel to her, he did not want to hurt her, but when she would not sit still as he wanted her to sit, he tied her to a chair, apologizing. *Dinnae fash.* She stopped wriggling but started cursing him in her language, long incantations that meant nothing to him. He could work through her voice. Sometimes it sounded as if she were singing: *Hadija, Hadija.* No matter, as long as she was not moving. The way color reflected on her skin. The raised tribal scars on her stomach, muscular, almost boyish arms. Nose ring—tricky to draw. When he showed her what he had done, expecting her to appreciate and understand, to share in this venture, to be part of this endeavor, she spat on the canvas. He slapped her—he could not help it—and started again.

Ungrateful, did she not understand what was at stake. He disliked her for bringing out the worst in him. He was not a cruel person, but she must understand the necessity of all this. She must not sabotage his efforts. *Keep still, girl. Dinnae get het up. Nae slumping, nae keening.* Could it be that she had no inkling of what he was doing? Could it be that she had never seen herself in a mirror? Did not even know what she looked like? Primitives believed photography stole their souls. Was that what she was fighting for? Instead, through him, she could end up like the *Women of Algiers* in their bloody apartments. Did they complain? Up in the Louvre? No, they bloody well didnae complain, didnae make a fuss. What a carry on! True these were blocks of color, still vague but wi'oot a doot this was going to be art, nothing less. Pull yourself together, lassie. To think she was being snatched from anything better. He had seen where she started from—the slave market. Carrying on as if he were a cannibal or a rapist. He wiped the sweat from his brow, reached for another handkerchief for his palms. Tomorrow, he explained to her, he was leaving with the expedition, and nothing would be required of her. Weeks of idleness. Could she then not get a grip for a couple more hours? But she wouldn't listen, didn't seem to understand. When the tears started falling down her face, he remembered her looking at the river. At the break of dawn, he untied her and dragged her to the waterfront.

The dawn blue sky was getting lighter by the minute. The occasional bird, a few rustling in the trees. Breeze through the palms, fresh heavy smell of lime trees and guava, the run of the river, its ripples becoming visible now—all of this, after the stifling room reeking of paint and sweat, had a calming effect on them both. She became more willing to do as he said, sit and gaze at the river, remove her wrapper and wade. Rise up from the water. Slowly. Slowly, rise up from the water. He was full of the beauty around him, the scents of water and grass, aware of the light and the shades of green. *The Turkish Bath*. The privilege of seeing all this was almost an ache, grace beginning to expand, but the artist in him knew that awe would freeze him; it must be held back, kept under control. It did not matter how he felt; the canvas came first. Its execution. What was on it, what others would be made to see. He wanted them to feel what he was feeling now, to know what it was like to be here in this place. The exact atmosphere, how wild it was and sweetly exotic. All the effort to render it on canvas, desperate to pin it down, enclose it in three dimensions, kill it and through skill and color bring it back to life.

He made steady progress. A fruitful two days except that there was no time to arrange for the sending of these paintings and sketches to London. They would have to wait until his return. The girl would be under the watchful eyes of Ramsay's servants. He hoped that when he returned, she would be more cooperative. She still seemed not to understand him. Never mind. The venture had been a success. He was satisfied with his work, intoxicated by what he could further achieve. A body of work that would possess more than charm. As good as anything by the Glasgow Boys—those children of shipping magnates who could afford to study in Paris, enroll in ateliers, sons of the manse propped up by financial support. All the formal education Robert ever had in Scotland was from the school of art, especially set up for workingmen unable to study full-time. Every day except Sunday, he would rise before dawn to attend lessons before putting in a full day at the ship brokers. An oil portrait of the girl—Akuany or Zamzam, he had been given two names and she was responding to neither—could end up as masterful as Jean-Léon Gérôme's *Bashi-Bazouk*. Not as lavish, certainly starker, but still in its own way gorgeous. His conception of it was so strong it was palpable; he was confident that he could pull it off once he got back home and had the space and materials for a large oil canvas. In the meantime, his technique and subject matter were on a par with David Roberts's, his watercolors comparable to Arthur Melville's, dare he say, work that Owen Jones, had he still been alive, would have approved of. In a year, he could make his mark in the world of Scottish art. His name listed among the artists in a catalog. His name linked to the painters who depicted the Orient. His own atelier. Each painting selling for thirty pounds, forty, sixty. He would never have to work with ships again. Here now in these hours was the sweaty adventure, the toil and the baptism. Beyond that, waiting for him was the charmed inner circle, the reward of becoming one of Scotland's establishment figures.

His departure from Khartoum felt sudden. He never did get around to finishing all the preparations for the journey. Drained and distracted, overworked and in need of sleep, he set out with the expedition to destroy the Mahdi.

They marched from Omdurman, heading south, parallel to the White Nile. Nine thousand men, six thousand camels, twenty mountain guns, two rocket batteries. Heat, heat, the sun beating down on his helmet. Perched on his camel six hours a day. He was not the only civilian. There were artists and correspondents for the *Times*, the *Daily News*, and the *Illustrated London News*—men who had arrived a month ago in Khartoum. He had given them a wide berth, wary lest they impose on his free time and expect him to act as a host, showing them around and pointing out how they could entertain themselves. Now, when camp was set up at the end of the day, he could be more sociable, listening to their opinions, the news from London. Gladstone, the prime minister, had advocated giving up the area west of the White Nile, focusing on holding on to Khartoum and the east. But it was the Egyptian government that was insisting and financing. So here they were and with them, a whole administrative body, the usual mix of locals, Egyptians, and Turks, who would govern Al-Ubayyid once it was liberated. This was a mark of confidence. After all, their leader, General Hicks, was a seasoned military man with significant successes behind him. He had been decorated after the Indian Mutiny and the Abyssinian campaigns, surely a Sudanese holy man would be well within his capabilities. Hicks had been planning this campaign for months and already led several successful sorties against the rebels.

Into the desert, leaving the river behind them, the land turning reddish the farther they went. Dry flat plains, sometimes a bush, sometimes a thorn tree, mirage shimmering after mirage. Robert made sketches of the cavalry, the soldiers heading out, a precious well. Water was in scarce amount, rationed. The thirst gave him headaches and he noticed that he was sweating less than he usually did. Moving from one water source to the next, the strategy was to set up camp only near water. But the wells and creeks were guarded by the Mahdi's men, if not already poisoned or blocked. Often a well must be fought for. The camels could go up to three days without water but only if they had first drunk their fill. There was foliage all around but still they weakened and fell, were slaughtered before they died and then cooked. Such a large army, at night there would be campfire after campfire, spread out over the desert under the black sky, lanterns in the officers' tents. All of this—artillery, tents, equipment, horses, and camels—must be surrounded by a square zeriba of high, thick thorns, constructed by hundreds of soldiers after chopping down one mimosa tree after the other. Outside the zeriba, the ground would be strewn with caltrops. Like someone withholding a secret, Robert moved slowly. Caught up in the watercolors he had left in Khartoum, it was sometimes an effort to focus on his new surroundings. He was drugged by memories of the girl, the rendering of her on canvas; he could not put her behind him. An irritation started to spread through his body, all day the urge to itch. The doctor said it was Nile water rash and gave him an ointment.

They were constantly harassed by the enemy. The Mahdi's men were all over the desert, his proclamations pinned to every tree and telegraph post. His riflemen were continuously sniping at them to the extent that a bullet tore through Major General Hick's tent and dented the chair he was sitting on. One afternoon accompanying a small patrol and then left on his own near a thorn tree, Robert had his first close sight of one of them. He heard the neigh of a horse and, belly pressed to the ground over a raised sand dune, binoculars in hand, the horseman came into full view. Turban, short, patched garment, muscular calves, sandals in the stirrups. His eyes scanned the area, caught sight of Robert, raised his spear, and charged straight toward him. Robert reached for his revolver, but the rider was distracted by three mounted government soldiers. The fighter turned and galloped away. They pursued. Robert's heart was racing. He took off his helmet; his clothes felt bulky—long boots, white tunic, and necktie—oppressive in this heat. The sky was huge, pressing down on the dunes and the scrubs. The sky was king of the desert, just like the river was traipsing queen of the city. Such a close encounter! Back at the camp, he made a sketch of the warrior. Taut reins, one sinewy arm pulled back sharp, the other straight up in the air holding the spear. On paper the man's teeth were bared in a snarl, even though in real life his expression had been calm, his manner composed.

After seeing his enemy in flesh and blood, Robert started warming to his compatriots. He felt a kinship with the other Europeans, no matter their background. Speaking the same language, suffering the same heat, he saw himself in them. Their wry observations, the truncated ways they could understand each other. A story circulated about how a deserter from the Mahdi's side was caught telling the soldiers about the Mahdi's miracles—how daggers turned limp when they were thrust into his body, how he rendered his enemies helpless. That same man made off back to the Mahdi's force taking with him two uniforms, a camel, one Remington rifle, and ten bullets. Clever fellow! At first entertaining but then worrying was the endless bickering between Hicks and the Turkish governor of Khartoum—petty squabbles, real differences in strategic approach, leadership rivalry. For twelve days, the camels hadn't been fed or watered. Whose fault was that? Was it wise that they were now cut off from their supplies at Dueim, plunging farther into the desert? Were the guides misleading them on purpose? Eejits was Robert's verdict. The alternative was unthinkable. It was important to stay upbeat. The correspondents all liked Hicks, his decency and somewhat endearing pedantry. They liked, too, that their illustrations and reports were almost guaranteed front-page coverage. It helped them supress their misgivings, how slow the army was progressing, lumbering, losing livestock on a persistent basis. How unmotivated the Egyptian soldiers were—their nationalist hopes dashed after the failed Urabi revolt, their country occupied by Britain, and now here they were, led by a British general, at the service of a puppet khedive, risking their lives to supress another rebellion against the Ottoman Empire. Surely a deliberate humiliation.

A tree without a single leaf stood gnarled and hideous, desolate as if this were a deep, dark winter. Instead, Robert's temperature was soaring. Sudden cramps in his stomach so that most of the time on his camel was spent fighting the need to relieve himself. Then unable to fight anymore, having to dismount, stagger behind a bush, mount again. Then the fever taking over until he could not hold himself up in the saddle. It was dysentery, and he was so weak with it that it was necessary to send him back. He agreed with reluctance and had to endure a horrendous ride to Dueim, tied to the seat of a gun carriage, pulled by eight horses, trundling over cacti, jolted over rocks and dry waterways. He arrived in Dueim feeling more dead than alive. A relief to be put at last on the *Bordein*, one of the steamers he had worked on. Aboard, he was tended to with great care by a Syrian doctor, who pulled him out of the worst of it. It took three days to reach Khartoum.

The girl was there in his house; she had not absconded. She could now nurse him, the doctors in Khartoum giving her instructions. Robert was even weaker now than he had been on the journey. He floated in and out of consciousness. Never a deep, healing sleep but instead what seemed like waking dreams. His father mocking him, *Tried to get yer jacket off and do some real work, did ye?* Walking through the wynds of Aberdeen, losing his way and then finding it again. Heather. Heather holding Christine. Safe with Heather—nothing could be more pleasing than this cold bracing breeze, nothing could feel more right—and then realizing that it couldn't be real, that she was lost to him, and the grief sloshed fresh and pressing. Through tears, to sink and dream of her again, this time aware that he was dreaming, the encounter soaked with nostalgia, iridescent with sweetness, holding on because it would all shatter; he knew that and he was back again in the backyard of his house, in a stifling night, the girl soaking rags to wipe his brow. He blamed her for waking him up, loathed her for being who she was.

Indoor, middle of the day, shutters down. She was holding one of his paintings, the sketch he had made of her. "Git yer dirty paws aff it." He lunged at her, and with the effort passed out, though she grabbed hold of him before he hit the ground. Was that a dream or was it real? It could be real though he had hidden all his work away before he left. She could have gotten ahold of it. Maybe not. In another dream, the elderly woman Fatimah was bringing him pigeon feathers. She was insisting that as brushes, they would be superior to the horsehair he had been using. *But it wus ye, ye got me the horsehair,* he said to her, and it seemed to him comic, something to laugh about. He would try the pigeon feathers he told her, and then she claimed that the girl was her daughter. She would take her home. Too bizarre to be real, surely a dream.

When the fever abated, he became aware of how weak he was, how much weight he had lost. In the mirror, his face gaunt, beard long, hollows under his eyes. But his appetite was back and when he slept, he dissolved into long, dreamless sleep. The nights were becoming cooler too. Pleasant evenings and dawns. He enjoyed looking at black ants on the ground, the taste of the Crosse and Blackwell's jam Ramsay gave him as a gift. Another gift of a hundred fresh limes came from the Austro-Hungarian ambassador, grown in the consulate's garden. The girl made him lemonade, which was refreshing. She also made tasty broth. He could not remember her name, then he recalled that she had more than one name and, besides, he could call her whatever the hell he liked.

News trickled in from the expedition. All rumors and speculation because the Mahdi had cut off the telegraph lines. First a cold denial, then the pieces of a devastating defeat were assembled. A story of shambles and murderous thirst. Soldiers wandering off from the protection of the zariba in search of water, officers losing control. Men and camels dying. Poisoned wells, others blocked with rocks, one dry watercourse after the other—until they reached the final attack that awaited them in Sheikan, near Al-Ubayyid.

The Mahdi's fighters attacked the army from the front. Seven thousand government soldiers were killed, the others surrendering to the enemy. All the European and Turkish officers were killed. Fighting on their horses and when losing their mounts, taking out their swords and fighting until they fell. Every single European Robert had made friends with had died. Absolutely rotten luck. Beastly for their families back home. Yet he could not help being flooded by an all-encompassing relief. Dysentery had saved his life. Illness had saved his life.

It could have been him who had died in the desert, but he was spared. The reason for this was crystal clear: success awaited him in Scotland. Art was his destiny. Time spooled out in front of him, radiant with possibilities, rich with creativity. Able to walk to the waterfront, Khartoum had never looked more picturesque. The winter breeze carried the smell of eucalyptus leaves, the Nile striking as ever, birds showed off their brilliant feathers. Still too weak to paint, he used the time to absorb and study. Looking at the flow of water, it was hard to believe that far west in Sheikan the bones of his comrades were bare under the desert sun. Harder still to believe that the city was under threat or that officials in Cairo and London were pressed to find an immediate solution.

He sensed a change in himself. A new feeling of urgency. Perhaps he should not delay his oil painting of the girl until his return to Scotland. With a bit of effort, he could still paint in oil here. Turpentine was available, as was linseed oil. The challenge would be in preventing cracking as the paint dried, especially with the climate so dry. He mulled over this but remained determined. As soon as his strength returned, he would paint what was sure to be his masterpiece. He could already see the luster of her skin on the canvas, the glow of light on her torso as she turned to face his gaze.

# 14

# Fatimah

She said my son's name. Not any of my sons but the youngest who was imprisoned in Al-Ubayyid and could at any time be killed. It was him she was talking about and not any other Yaseen. It was him because of all the other names and details—his sister, Halima, his Al-Azhar education, and the names of my nieces. Holding on to the art supplies that Robert had ordered, I sat in silence. I did not say anything. I did not tell her who I was. She was a pretty girl but not exceedingly so; one would not look at her twice. Wide child-bearing hips, though she was slim and still young, soulful eyes, a vehemence in her speech. "I belong to Yaseen and no one else," she said.

"No you don't, girl," I said to her. "You belong to Robert whether you like it or not."

She stuck her lower lip out and didn't want to talk to me anymore. Indoors, Robert was with a visitor, another khawaja, someone important judging by the horse and the standard of the carriage he had left at the gate. Their voices reached us, and I could make out certain words even though I could not understand everything. Any familiar word relating to the expedition or the Mahdi would be helpful. Afterward, when the visitor left, I could repeat that word and while looking at what I had got him, Robert might reveal useful information that I could then pass on. Zamzam and I were sitting in the backyard. The sounds of the garden felt shrill—the monkeys jabbering, the usual birds. It was not my first time to meet her. I had come once before when Robert was away, the day I took the papers from his room. She was not forthcoming then, wretched and withdrawn. Today, she looked rested and more talkative. She shared her story, and I listened to her mention Halima and Halima's girls. I figured out who she was. Would it be any use to tell her about myself? I could not trust her reaction and the situation was sensitive. I was doing my best to secure Yaseen's release.

This then was the girl my son was so attached to that he left his wife and went to Al-Ubayyid even with the Mahdi camped nearby. I could not see anything special about her. She would not be able to compete with Salha, who was educated and highborn. I had seen him look at Salha with admiration, listen attentively to what she had to say, exert himself to impress her. I doubted this was how he was with Zamzam. Probably he was more relaxed, less talkative. But some matters of the heart were mysterious; they defied easy explanations. The world had rent them apart. Insha'Allah, when he came home, would he still want her now that she belonged to the khawaja? She kept repeating that no man had touched her since Yaseen. I looked at Robert, thin and straining with the effort to entertain his guest. He was still too weak to work on his paintings, and that would be the first thing he would do if he could.

When I finally left the house, I felt dizzy and sat by the side of the road. A part of me was in a prison in Al-Ubayyid. Always there, always with my son. Zamzam had brought him near, I could see him before me, I could hear his voice. His laugh. All the years I had known him, how he walked and his moods. Listening to her talk about him, I could listen forever. It was as if he were with me. She knew him. That was why; she knew who he was. She did not know where his house was in Khartoum, she did not know his brothers or their shop, but she knew an essence of him. It comforted me but made me miss him more. If he were to suddenly appear in front of me, I would shower him with tearful kisses. I would feel faint and cling to him with relief. Then he would go off to his concubine or his wife or his work or his books. He would not want to spend time with me, and I would not want to spend time with his desire to be elsewhere. That was the truth, but still I heaved myself up and did what I could to get him home.

My contact was waiting for me by the ferry. Taller than any woman I had ever known, as usual selling groundnuts and not looking at all like how a woman selling ground-nuts would look. You would think her unsuited to this job of espionage, but Nafissa was who she was. As clever as a serpent and a fervent believer in the Mahdi even though she had never met him. And now she was using me as an informer. I told her everything I had heard from the khawaja and his visitor, who turned out to be the British consul, living all alone in the palace. Yes, they are devastated after the victory in Sheikan—terrified. No, there is no plan to send in another army after Hicks. Instead, five hundred soldiers are to be sent to bolster the garrisons in the north. As for a new governor-general, they are saying that the next one must be someone who knows the Sudan well. Gordon's name was mentioned. How easy it had been to get information out of Robert! His Arabic was much stronger now and to him I was a tottering old woman carrying a guffa full of what he needed for his paintings. Like a child, he kept his eyes on the contents of the guffa and took delight in what I brought him. When I asked him a question about the news the British consul brought, he shared it without thinking. He knew about Yaseen, knew which side my family were on, and assumed our unflinching loyalty. But necessity makes its own rules. I munched groundnuts and answered Nafissa's questions as best as I could. When Robert was away with the expedition, I had given her drawings of the steamers, inventories of the boatyard. Before he set out, I had given her details of what he was taking with him and any information I was able to get about Hicks's army. Without taking a penny. Surely all this was enough. It was time for a recompense. High time to turn my requests into demands.

I spoke in a low voice, looking down as if I were made small with shame. Ashamed that my son was on the wrong side, could not see the light, did not believe in the Mahdi. "He deserves his imprisonment," I said. "Truly he does, and his life has been spared all this time because of the compassion of the noble Mahdi. I know this. All I want is that if Yaseen is foolish enough to escape, who knows, he might try, that the guards would turn a blind eye. Just that. No effort. No breaking any rules, nothing underhanded that would get them into trouble. Do you understand me? They just need to look away."

She looked at me as if expecting me to say more. When I was quiet, she said, "I understand you." I imagined her ruthless, capable of anything. She was in her late thirties, that age when women stop conceiving regularly but still might be surprised by an unexpected pregnancy. Her husband was shorter than her. It was something that amused people. He was actually a relation of mine, through my mother's side; that's how I knew her. "I heard that you would do anything for money," she said to me the first time we spoke.

I was taken aback. Was that what people said about me behind my back? It was not flattering. I certainly didn't make any money off of her. She was known to support the Mahdi and had been singing his praises and extolling his miracles for the past two years. Soon she was working for him too. When she found out about my visits to Robert, she took an interest in what information I could pick up. I only helped her because of Yaseen. It was not true that I would do anything for money. What was true was that I expected something tangible in return for my efforts.

Next step would be to send Halima, a message delivered by word of mouth from a trusted traveler—a letter would be too dangerous—urging her to help her brother escape, providing the necessary finances. I felt a huge longing for him. To see him safe, with us, here where he belonged. He had a baby son he had never seen. We had kept this secret from him, so as not to burden him in his imprisonment. But yes, he had a son.

I took the ferry to Tutti to see my grandson. He was seven months old. I held him in my arms. He could sit up on my lap now, fist clutched around a carrot. How dear he was, my own flesh and blood. Why was I deprived of seeing him every day, growing up under his father's roof where he belonged? Salha patted my hand and sighed. As soon as her morning sickness started, a week or so after Yaseen's departure, she announced that she wanted to return to her parents' house. "To be looked after," she said.

"Am I not looking after you well, girl? Are you complaining?"

"I am not complaining, Aunty, but I don't want to trouble you with my condition."

"How is it trouble? That child in your belly is my grandson."

She must have sent word to her folks behind my back because her father came to fetch her a few days later. I found him standing at the door, and I was too embarrassed to protest. And she had been here since then! Let me count. All through the pregnancy, the birth, and the forty days afterward. True, the last weeks of the pregnancy were her right, all women did that. They needed their mother's care, to be pampered and indulged through the difficult weeks, making demands and acting up. The kind of behavior not befitting for a woman staying with her in-laws. In my case, my family were in a different town, and I was denied this privilege. I cried hot tears, but it could not be helped. So, I understood that Salha needed to be with her family up until forty days after the birth. But then, after that—what was the excuse? "Come home with me, Salha." This was my refrain, week in week out.

She was not docile. And it was clear from before the wedding. That time when she refused to get her lower lip tattooed. Every bride did that, two weeks before the wedding. Salha refused without ever caring to give a reason. Her mother had no sway over her. Only when her father interfered did she accept. Her father had sent her to school when she was young as he sent his sons. Apparently, some families did that with daughters who showed exceptional promise. She was one of them and she learned to read the Qur'an. The result was that she started to see herself head and shoulders above us all. Yaseen liked that she was educated. They would talk for a long time I remember, quietly without raising their voices. Serious talk, without laughter or flirting. I remember listening to their reasoning back when he was home and she was with us. When everything was how it should be, proper. I would listen and to be honest I did not understand every single word they said. Abstract words, events that had nothing to do with them. But I would still follow their voices, pleased that my son was content with the wife I had chosen for him.

Today we went through the whole procedure again. "Come home with me, Salha."

"I will. Insha'Allah soon. Any news?" The weight she had gained during pregnancy was still on her, her breasts full with milk. She was comelier now than she had been as a bride.

"Halima is able to send him food."

She smiled a little, "He must be heartened, too, I am sure, my uncle certainly is, by the recent Azhar fatwa against the Mahdi. I don't know why they took so long in issuing it, but the wording is clear and the refutation strong."

"Does it matter, my daughter, if the man is fake or true? Surely peace and prosperity are all we want."

She made an impatient gesture with her head. "It does matter of course."

I did not wish to argue with her, so I reached for her arm. "Come home with me today. For Allah's sake."

"I am not prepared."

"I'll wait for you."

"What is the point when *he's* not there!" There was a desolate note in her voice.

"I need you near me. Seeing you, having his son close comforts me."

She looked down at the ground. Her father's farmland stretched out before us, watermelons growing all the way to the sandy banks of the river. She neither replied nor got up to make any preparations to leave with me. I held my grandson tighter.

Finally, she said, "I might go to Berber with my family. For my brother's wedding. He is marrying a girl from there."

Berber? Four days away. A wedding? When we weren't even sure if her husband was dead or alive! Was she not anxious? She gave me a long speech on how safe Berber was compared to Khartoum, well out of the Mahdi's reach. What does that have to do with it? We started to argue. "What is your uncle doing to secure my son's release? Nothing. Sheikh Amin Al-Darir, a big man. He has influence and a ready ear with the authorities. Isn't Yaseen working for him?"

"My uncle wasn't the one who sent him into danger," she retorted. "Why aren't his brothers doing something?"

"I am," I shouted. "I'm doing everything I can with no one helping me!" The child started to fret in my arms. I handed him over and left.

I imagined Yaseen arriving in Khartoum to find Zamzam instead of her. But how would he find Zamzam? Even if he searched for her and he probably would, it would not be easy for him to find her. I could tell him where she was, or I could keep it secret from him.

# 15

# Yaseen

**Khartoum, January 1884**

I escape from Al-Ubayyid while my enemies are softened
by their success. I slip away at night with the help of Ishaq
and Halima. My sister had not forsaken me, though her
new husband is part of this regime and she herself a fervent
believer. Halima bribes whoever needs bribing and persuades
whoever needs persuading. On a moonless night, Ishaq takes
me by the hand, eases me out of an unguarded frayed part of
the zeriba; we push aside thorns and run toward the forest.
There waiting is a man with a camel, perched upon which
is the special decked palanquin used to carry brides. "Come
with me to Khartoum," I urge Ishaq. He shakes his head.
He is earnest and keeps his thoughts to himself; he is not
talkative. His loyalty is to Halima now; she is the only mother
he knows. He is her adopted son, while to me he will always
be the baby brother in Zamzam's arms. I bid him farewell
and hide inside the bride's howdah, emasculated I cannot
help but think, until the safety of the north.

I am free. After a year in prison, I am home. My mother slaughters a goat in gratitude. My friends and neighbors gather to welcome me. Even the venerable Sheikh Amin Al-Darir pays me a visit and gives me leave from work to recover. I do not have cheerful news for my visitors. I am full of forebodings. Our enemy is strong and getting stronger. Our position is bleak. They, though, are optimistic. Gordon will arrive in a fortnight they tell me. Egypt had not forsaken us; help is on the way.

My wife and son are in Berber. I long to hold my child in my arms, to bestow on him a name, to unload the burden of my thoughts to his mother. Without them, I feel an acute sense of restlessness. There are my brothers, my nieces and nephews, there is my mother. I am surrounded by love and care and yet anxiety keeps me awake at night. I reach for my books or hold a pen, note with relief that my script is as fine as ever, breathe in the smell of ink, something that I had particularly yearned for in my incarceration, but I cannot focus for any length of time. Free at last, I walk the streets of Khartoum. I visit the tailor for a new robe. I walk for the sake of walking; I walk because I am unsettled, but I am also searching for Zamzam. No one watches my movements; there is no hostility, no constraints, but I cannot shake off a sense of oppression. It lies inside me, trailing me into mosques and friends' houses. I can go wherever I want, but it seems that what I want is her. Everyplace she might be found appalls me to the extent that I am relieved when I do not find her. It crosses my mind that I should look for her in brothels and then stop in my tracks, unable to breathe from anger.

"You are not well," my mother says. "Look how thin you've become! You need to rest."

I ask for her help in locating Zamzam. Everyone I was able to question in Al-Ubayyid said she would most likely have been brought to Khartoum. There are places here that are easier for a woman to penetrate. I sense a reluctance in her, a disapproval she cannot hide. I squeeze her hand. "Please, you have done so much for me, do this too."

She agrees to try and then says, "Why don't you go to Berber instead? You can bring back your wife and son." She is contradicting herself now. One minute telling me I need to recuperate, the next sending me off on a journey. I set out.

With Khartoum behind me, lulled by the movement of the camel, I start to feel a sense of clarity. My love for Zamzam is a burden. She herself a weight I picked up early in life, too young to apprehend the full responsibility. And yet as a believer, I should accept Allah's will. She was entrusted to me, and I tried my best. Is that not what life is? We are entrusted with health or security or wealth or position or family or skills or children or all these things and then expected to do our best.

She is not a burden but a gift. It is wrong to think otherwise. If Allah wills, I will find her, and she will become part of my family. I will do right by her, fulfill her needs, protect her from harm. I will substitute her days of hardship and wretchedness. I will cradle her and give her everything she wants. I will make her forget all the sadness of the past. When I find her, I will not ask her to tell me what happened. I will neither demand an account nor a narration nor a confession. We will pick up where we left off, seamless. As if we had never been separated, as if we had only turned away from each other for a short time.

It is like that with my wife. I speak to her as if we had never been separated, as if we had only turned away from each other for a short time. I hold my son in my arms, fill my eyes with the sight of him, bury my face in his neck, a new experience for me, this vulnerable flesh and blood, this faultless extension of me. I am amazed at his smile, his baby chatter, his royal command over his mother. That long-forgotten sound coming out of me—a laugh—I had not laughed in such a long time. Next to my wife and child I feel hollowed out by my time in prison, needy and sensitive. I am grateful for the change I see in Salha, how much softer she is. She had been an edgy bride, quick to complain of the discomfort marital life was causing her. It was off-putting at times. Now she is more open and accommodating, patient and flexible. Motherhood has done this to her.

"You must name him," she says. "I refused to let anyone else do it. And it is high time he has a name."

I am charmed by her manners; how vivacious she is and luscious! I am captivated by how she handles the child and nurses him. All this is novel to me. I can forget my cares, be hopeful again. Perhaps the memories of Al-Ubayyid will recede, perhaps I will be able to mention my time there without rancor.

"Rustom," I say.

She laughs. "Such a Turkish name!"

"Do you mind?"

"Not at all."

She says it again and again so that the child starts to get used to it. He sleeps in her arms, and she says, "I used to write you letters. At first, I did think I would get them to you. But even your mother had difficulty sending letters to Halima, so I kept them with me, and it became as if I were writing for myself."

"I would like to read them," I say.

This makes her happy. She lays Rustom down and fetches the letters. I pick one up and read.

*Today comes the news that Sheikh Ahmed has arrived in Khartoum. He had pretended to pledge allegiance to the Mahdi and then as soon as he found an opportunity, escaped. In the same way that in times of extreme famine, we are allowed the meat of pigs, so in extreme fear of death, it is permissible to pledge a falsehood. I wonder if you will do the same. I also wonder how "extreme" is defined. Is it up to the individual to judge? Or are there certain conditions that must be met for a situation to be rendered extreme and thereby altering what is usually prohibited and making it permissible for the time being.*

Such a fine mind. She understands what others do not, even men I consider learned and experienced. The basis of the law is to facilitate ease for people and not hardship. The strictest interpretation is not necessarily the best one. I open up about my friend Sheikh Isma'il and his visit to me in prison. I still hope that his position was taken under duress, but it is unlikely. Salha shares my distress at the error of his judgment.

"I do not think Isma'il is a true believer in the Mahdi," I say. "More a pragmatist who wants to be on the winning side."

"In your generosity, you are finding excuses for him," she says.

I smile and turn again to her written words. From her, I had expected sentiments but instead she is a thoughtful writer.

"You must not praise me too highly," she says. "I would rather you correct me so that I can learn more."

"Are you not kept busy with your duties as a mother?"

She looks flustered for the first time. "I am of course," she says and stands up to fetch a blanket to cover the child. "He is my everything, but I have always loved reading and writing."

As in Khartoum, there is a warm welcome from my in-laws, as well as additional family members I had not met before. Berber is expecting to host the newly appointed governor-general on his way to Khartoum. Preparations are being made. Gordon is traveling overland rather than by steamer; it is easier that way to visit the villages along the route. It is expected that his party might arrive tomorrow or the next day. I am asked by Salha's uncle, one of Berber's notables, to be part of the welcoming committee.

General Gordon, mounted on a camel, comes toward us. He has accrued considerable followers on the way—men on donkeys, on camels, on horses, and on foot. They approach us as one compact mass, brimming with optimism. I am reminded of the time seven years ago when I saw him in Al-Ubayyid. He was on a prancing camel then, and I was making my way into the city carrying Bol with Akuany by my side. So much has changed since then. The general is older I can see, but while age bestows on some men mellowness and gravity, it seems to have made him fidgety and slightly distracted. The town receives him with a military parade,

ululations, and a drum salute. He dismounts amid the crowd
and passes the guard of honor that leads up to the government
house. This popularity and warm welcome are due to the
promises he has been making. To cut taxes in half, to reprieve
those unable to pay, to waive off debts, to ban the use of the
whip, to grant amnesties for all offenses and the list goes on.
It is a great show of generosity and hope is infectious.

Indoors in the spacious reception room we—the chiefs,
merchants, ulema, and notables of Berber—gather to receive
him. With him is a young, slim man whom he introduces as
his agent, Lieutenant Colonel Stewart. Gordon says, in the
poorest of Arabic, that he is here without an army because
he brings peace and not war. The ulema who impose the
death penalty, who calculate (after years of study) the exact
compensation that must be paid upon the accidental death
of a Muslim—free, enslaved, or unborn—must listen as he
pronounces it a disgrace and a sin for a Muslim to kill another
Muslim. He says he is offering the Mahdi the sultanate of west
Sudan and sending as a gift a Turkish cloak and a tarbush. In
Al-Ubayyid men are killed for wearing the tarbush. Gordon
is misunderstanding our enemy.

He then lowers his voice and says that he has something special to show us, something important to share. A firman from
the khedive. Not the one that appoints him governor-general
of the Sudan but another secret one. Lieutenant Stewart is
taken aback. It is perhaps something they have not agreed
upon, something impulsive on Gordon's part. Gordon takes
the firman out, unscrolls it, and I cannot help but be enthralled
by the burnished paper, the gold tughra of the sultan, the red
and black elaborate script. The firman is a thing of beauty, of

art—separate from our gathering and our ambitions. I yearn
toward it for the security that it represents, ideals of order
and just authority. He reads, in his poor insistent Arabic, the
wordings. Those who are near the firman, follow with their
eyes; those of us who are far must pay attention. I am not listening to him, and I should be. What he is saying is important,
unexpected. He is announcing the independence of the Sudan
from Egypt and the Ottoman Empire. The wording of the
firman is that his mission in Sudan is the immediate evacuation
of Egyptian military and their families, and in those areas not
taken over by the Mahdi establish a Sudanese governing body
of tribal chiefs. But what he is saying is slightly different—the
establishment of a directorate in Berber made up of six of
the most notable men, independent of Cairo but subject to
Gordon as governor-general of the Sudan and commissioner
of the British government.

His announcement is met with silence. He goes on to say
that he does not want us to misunderstand him and to think
that his intention is to abandon us to stew in our own juice.
On the contrary, we should, he says, be spurred to organize
our own government. Getting rid of the Cairo government
and being independent under him—there could not be a
better future for the Sudan.

When the meeting ends and General Gordon and his party
leave, we speak among ourselves. Names are bandied about.
The obvious six men for the directorate of Berber. And what
about Dongola? Zubayr Pasha, Hussein Khalifa, even the
names of Salha's uncles are mentioned. But if the Egyptian
garrisons are to be evacuated, who will protect these towns
from the Mahdi? Independent but subject to Gordon as a

British commissioner—what kind of independence is that? Someone says, "I would rather serve the false Mahdi than a Christian who will force us all to become Christians," and he is cheered. We are being abandoned by Egypt, let down because she is under British occupation, not the same Egypt that invaded the Sudan with the help of these very same northern tribes. But why not seize the opportunity? Besides, what choices do we have when even as we sit the news comes in that Sinkat on the Red Sea has fallen. No one says it out loud, but the path of least bloodshed is obvious—to submit to the Mahdi. It tosses us like a vicious sleepless night.

I grieve for the decline of the Ottoman Khilafa. The crisis in Sudan is both result and symptom. The political glory of Islam is shrinking and weakening; the seat of the commander of the faithful is under threat. How many future wars can the empire withstand? Without its legal strength and independence, I fear for the Muslims of the future. They will be pawns and vulnerable; they will be divided.

Berber is colder than Khartoum and Salha frets over our child. She is eager to return to Khartoum. I tell her of my winters in Cairo, and she listens to my reminiscences. Stoves in homes and heating up water for baths—all are foreign to her. "I wish I had been with you," she says, and I echo her reply. She would have been the ideal companion during my studies, but everything has its time. Everything needs permission from the Almighty to exist.

We return to Khartoum by steamer. It is quicker and safer. I hold up my son and look down at the water. I recall that the river has always been Zamzam's first love. She would gravitate toward it. That is where I should have looked for her—down at the waterfront. I resolve to do that when I get back to Khartoum.

My mother is relieved to see us, delighted with her grandson. In the evening, I take her aside and ask if she had made inquiries about Zamzam.

"Yes," she says. "I found out all about her. She was with a British engineer who worked in the boatyard."

"Was? What about now?"

"He left like all the foreigners are leaving and he took her with him."

"Where to?"

"How should I know! His foreign country. See, you need not worry about her or have a troubled conscience. She is being cared for. You can forget her now."

I can't. Not her. Nor the times I traveled south, the affection I felt for her land and people. How I worshipped alone in places where shamans wielded power, where people kept company with the spirits of water and trees. Experiences I have never shared with anyone. Standing still, reciting sacred words and feeling the atmosphere around me shift, the subjugation of waywardness, the bowing down of nature, the sounds of listening. All these memories, she is tied up with them, borderless love, elemental. The house feels cramped, the baby's cries an irritant. I step outside, stand under the light of the waning moon. I digest the news. I sit under a tree and absorb it increment by increment. I sit until I hear my mother's voice asking if anyone had seen me. I get up and go indoors. Supper is laid out, and I am not a child to sulk and go to bed on an empty stomach. The next morning, I go back to work.

# 16

# Musa

## Al-Ubayyid, March 1884

I was there when Gordon insulted him. We all saw the cloak and the infidel's red tarbush. Sultan of west Sudan! "He offers me what I already have," my master said. "He is proud of his gift. But I am not boasting when I affirm that I am the Expected Mahdi. I am not a trickster, nor do I need a sultanate, nor money, nor prestige." We all swore revenge, we asked for permission to fight our way to Khartoum and bring back Gordon's head. But instead, the blessed Mahdi wrote him a long letter, inviting him to the one path, pleading with him to see the truth, warning and chiding, giving him every chance, time and space to change his position. I had seen this strategy work with tribal chiefs and Nuba kings, with all the enemies who were now fighting on our side. Perhaps it could work with Gordon too.

We were no longer in Al-Ubayyid. It had gotten too crowded, and its water supplies were limited. Instead, the Mahdi moved his government outside the town, southeast, past Sheikan where Hicks was defeated and near the deeper ponds and plentiful creeks of Al-Rahad. Here was enough water for us all, we in our thousands, tent after tent, straw huts, families, and livestock, spontaneous souqs that sprung up. Often the wind would blow in a fragment of that vast defeated army; or in the desert, not yet buried in sand, there would be personal items that belonged to the soldiers—photos of family members, pipes, scraps of letters. Anything that was useful, the main booty, had long been collected and distributed—a flintlock pistol became my most prized possession—but still things continued to appear. The desert brought forth buttons and handkerchiefs, a mug, a toothbrush. It had been such a vast, powerful army, and the Mahdi had reduced it to rubble.

I longed for him. I, Musa, here with him in the same town, a few steps away. I longed for the time when I used to fetch water in the pitcher, crouch down and pour it for him so that he could perform wudu. That was my happiest time, us together, close. Hearing him say my name, his gentle smile, and now there were thousands claiming him. I, long ago, accepted that I did not have much to offer him. But he told me that some delicate operations needed men like myself, men who were neither prominent nor in the public eye.

He gave me the responsibility of leading raids through the Nuba Mountains. These raids sometimes troubled me. I would charge my horse through a hut, swipe away with my sword chunks of straw, sneeze as dust fell on my face. I would gallop over meager possessions, bedding, cooking pots—simple, poor villagers, not government forces, not infidel foreigners but people like us. All because their leaders did not accept the Mahdi, would not swear allegiance to him. But this was not a time for wavering. I did as I was told.

All over the country our cause was glorious. News of victories reached us. After Al-Fasher in the far west, the east started to crumble. Most of it at least. We closed down the Suakin-Berber route. Tokar fell to us. We won the first battle of the Red Sea coast. We won the second battle of the Red Sea coast. Was it not time to move north, to take the big prize, Khartoum?

Permission was granted for some of us to proceed ahead of the main army. The honor fell on those who had been the first to support the Mahdi and I was one of them. We set out, the horsemen of the Mahdi. We left Al-Ubayyid behind us. With me were my wife and daughter. My father and stepmother. They had surprised me by wanting to come, refusing to stay in their house in Al-Ubayyid. The order for everyone to move, the time of the exodus had not yet come, and the Mahdi was still in Al-Rahad, but my parents wanted to accompany me. Each of them rode on a donkey and we had an extra one for supplies. We set out into the desert.

My little daughter was a joy in my life. Thin arms and long legs, no one could mistake her for any other child. I carried her even after she could walk. When we stopped to set up camp and I lifted her off the donkey, she was weightless in my arms. It was not possible to travel too close to the river. Government steamers patrolled the river and they shot at any moving figure they saw. This caused us difficulty with getting water and thirst became our greatest challenge.

I pitched a tent and left my family. I took one donkey and three waterskins to fill at the river. The slope was so steep that I lifted the hind legs of the donkey and we half skidded, half pushed ourselves toward the water. I lay facedown, clothes and all, guzzling until I was full. I let the coolness wash over me. Bliss. But looking up, I saw a government steamer approaching. I put the waterskins to soak, as they were too stiff to hold any water and I hid behind a bush. It was a narrow escape as bullets started flying, and one of the donkey's ears got blown off.

Days of intense heat and the struggle to get water. There were other families in the same situation as us; hardly any soldier traveled on his own. With them were wives and mothers, in-laws, children, and slaves. Sheep, goats, chickens. Extended families formed clusters, cooking and eating together. An informal market set up—women selling eggs, men selling water. Once, a worn-out donkey was slaughtered and its meat sold.

Walking with my daughter in the afternoon, I came across a shell. It was intact and buried in the sand. I unscrewed the top of the shell, emptied the container of powder, filled it with pebbles and gave it to her to play with. She smiled at the rattling sound, held it tight. We walked back to the tent together. The next morning, we set out early and inched our way farther north.

Sometimes we engaged the soldiers on the steamers. Rifle shots whizzing back and forth. The satisfying splash when one of them hit the water. Sometimes we spoke of taking on a whole steamer, making it ours. There was no command from high to do so—moving toward Khartoum was the priority—and so it remained wishful thinking. Instead, we taunted them from behind bushes. One youth stood tall on the shore brandishing his spear, jeering at them in plain sight.

The rest of us admonished him, "Stay low, lad. Fall back." He took no notice, laughing and boasted of our triumphs in Aba, in Gadir, in Al-Ubayyid, in Sheikan. Excitement lit up his features. He was the son of a general, a child when the Mahdi manifested, now barely an adult. Watching his reckless courage, the spirit that coursed through his body, we were all enraptured. His broad forehead shining, the tilt of his chin and thin neck, his sinewy arms and wrists. He made me feel old, though I was not old, but I could not let go like him. I had responsibilities and plans, orders to give and obey, a strategy to follow. He was unrestrained and an ecstasy took over him. "Infidels, whores," he goaded them even after the bullets started to whizz. "Losers. Cowards. You choose to stay safe in your boats! Come and fight! We will take you and Khartoum too." Some of us laughed or joined in assent until a bullet landed in his hip and he tumbled into the water. I risked my life rescuing him before he got swept away by the current. There were no physicians; the next day his wound putrefied, and he got worse by the hour. When the drum rolled, the army marched, and I never found out if the poor lad's family stayed with him or had to move on and leave him in God's care.

In the next encampment, we were sitting eating when my daughter got shot. She was on her mother's lap, a morsel between her fingers. A fragment of an artillery shell entered the tent and took off the top of her head. She didn't move or scream, just closed her small mouth. My wife did not move, and I wondered if she was shot too. Maybe I was shot. Everything seemed still and we expected more shots.

Finally, I stood up. I lifted my daughter, and she was as light as ever. Her blood flowed over my arm and her mother started weeping.

I walked out of the tent with her in my arms. People came running up to me wanting to know what happened. No other shots had been fired; no one else was injured or harmed. Just that one shot. We could not spare water to wash her. It would be a waste. I dug a hole in the sand and laid her there. I covered her. Her mother came behind me wailing; she threw herself on the grave and started to claw and shove the sand away with her hands. She unearthed the body and I had to bury it again. She then unearthed the body and I buried it for the third time.

The next morning, the drum rolled, and the army moved. I could not bear this spot and was eager to get away. My wife was the opposite. She wanted to remain by our daughter's grave. We quarreled and she got her own way.

# 17

# Zamzam

**Khartoum, May 1884**

As soon as she had arrived, the river—huge and strumming—claimed her. After years in the desert, she felt welcomed by the water, knowing it to be the timeless companion, the one that ran without effort, gave without needing, sang and sang the ancient tunes she had heard in her childhood, the songs she had yearned for and listened out for, that she had only half understood, but it did not matter, because listening was more important. She could strive to understand at her own leisure, tomorrow or the day after or the day after; the river would still be there for her, patient and strong, rich and always flowing in the same direction.

In the khawaja's paintings the river was stiff. It didn't move, it didn't sing. Instead of smelling like a river, the paints had an odious smell. And yet he thought well of his art, acted as if it were the most important thing in the world. Claimed that it was valuable, was curious about the color of her tongue, how it compared to other parts of her body. He disgusted her with his poking and examinations, his insistence on paralyzing her on canvas. In response, she would glare at his paintings, cursing them. Her curses, melodious and repetitive, unnerved him, and that filled her with satisfaction.

Every morning, she went to the river, washed and dawdled, bent her head and listened. She washed the khawaja's clothes and her own clothes. This reduced the amount of water she needed to carry. At the end of her river visit, she balanced a pot of water on her head and made her way back to the house that was near the boatyard. In the afternoon, she went back and half filled another pot even though there was a well in the back garden. She was fortunate in that she had time to herself. Most of the other girls she met were pressed and rushed, overwhelmed with busy households. She knew how they felt. Before Robert, when she had been with Hawa, who owned the fruit orchard, the work had been grueling. Back and forth from the river carrying pots of water. The pots so heavy that they compressed her neck, strained her back, pained her waist. The orchard was inland, at a considerable distance from the river. If she returned with a pot that was not full, she was punished. The punishment was to be deprived of a meal. She would eat rotten guava instead and end up with diarrhea. True, there were others with her, there was companionship, but they were all too exhausted to have any meaningful interaction. Worse than that was how they would be set against each other, forced to compete. Life was more comfortable with the khawaja; there was no doubt about that.

During the weeks he had been away with the Hicks expedition, she did as she liked, which was mostly sleeping. It was a change when he came back. Nursing him was interesting, taking instructions from the doctor who came to see him. Robert was calm and distant during his convalescence, wrapped in his own world. He would look through her as if he couldn't remember who she was; sometimes he even mumbled thanks. She would have preferred him to stay that way, but soon enough his stamina came back as did his obsession with painting. "Humor him," Fatimah said. "If posing for him is all he's asking, then you should be grateful."

Fatimah was easy to talk to. Even Robert chatted to her, and he was not a very talkative man. Fatimah understood all about the paintings. "He wants to show his people what they can never see," she told Zamzam. They didn't have rivers, they didn't have women? Zamzam was not convinced. And if their rivers were not like the Nile and even if their women were not like her, why did they want to see what was far away, what did not belong to them, what had nothing to do with them whatsoever? She certainly did not want to know about them.

Fatimah laughed. "Girl, everyone is taking something out of here. Gum, ivory, cattle. And we want things too. It's called trade. People exchange things. When it's fair trade, it's blessed, and when it's unfair it's an injustice. That is the way of the world. Everyone wants something and they barter to get it."

What did she want? She wanted Yaseen; that was what she wanted. And the river. And children. What was she meant to barter for these? What did she have?

Fatimah and her guffa, full of things for Robert's paintings. Henna, coffee, gum, horsehair—his consumption was huge. He was wasteful. He was acquisitive. Zamzam had never in her life seen a single person require so many items just to survive. He had so much furniture in his rooms. On the walls there was a baffling arrangement of spears, daggers, leopard and lion skins. A war horn made of hollowed elephants' tusks. Robert never used any of them. He possessed a wooden piece that had once been the leg of the Mahdi's bed in Jazira Aba—whatever for? His clothes were complicated and varied—shirts with collars and without, suspenders, tweed suits, footwear of different kinds—slippers, shoes, boots—all for one single person. He even surpassed Nazli Hanim with her finery, talcum powders, and hookah pipe. He had gadgets of all kinds—binoculars, pocket watch, revolver, compass, sword, shoehorn, medals. Zamzam spent considerable time examining these items, wiping the dust off them, enjoying their novelty and extravagance. It was only the paintings that filled her with rage. The ones in which he was clawing off layers of herself and pasting them on paper. The ones of trees, monkeys, and riverfront, all anemic, fake, smelly imitations, merited her derision.

She dreamt of Yaseen coming to the house, just walking in through the gate, like Fatimah did, like it was the most natural thing in the world. Like he was not imprisoned in Al-Ubayyid, like he was not dead, and he could be dead without her ever knowing, but he couldn't be dead because there he was right here. Walking through the gate and she runs toward him. She climbs him. She clings to him, wraps her arms and legs around him, feels his laugh vibrating against her stomach, can't hear it because she is the one babbling and screeching, squeezing him tight. And is this not the happiest of dreams, so sweet that she must have made it all up? If it were up to her, she would leave it at that, add nothing else, his arms supporting her weight; his laugh against her stomach and thighs is enough, but the dream goes wrong because he turns his head and she is still in his arms, legs wrapped tight, arms clasped well; he turns and sees the painting, sees her neck, her shoulders, sees her breasts and stomach like everyone else can see them, and if it were up to the khawaja's ambition the whole world will see them, and Yaseen peels her off him. He hangs his head and walks away.

When she woke up, she took a knife from the kitchen and slashed the painting.

Did he not turn into a lunatic, the khawaja! Stomping, shouting, even after he thrashed her. Face red and hair standing on end, holding the damaged canvas as if it were a child, shaking. She crept away and went to Touma's house. Touma wiped the blood off her face, washed the cuts, applied coffee to stop the bleeding. She did not ask questions. It was something that she did—put battered women back into place, hid them if they needed hiding, fed them when they needed feeding. Freed slaves who were penniless. Runaways who were lost. Criminals who were tired of crime. Those kicked out of their homes. The maimed who were friendless. The mad who knew too much for their own good. When Touma won them over, they became her girls—brewing merissa in her shop, entertaining clients in the dark back rooms, on the brass bed covered with sheepskin—earning a livelihood. Touma and her girls sang in weddings and at circumcision parties. Often for no occasion at all, they hosted gatherings.

It was on such an occasion that Zamzam had met her. Lured by the beat of the drum, she had left the house and followed the sound. Pitch-dark streets but she was not afraid, only curious. That was when Robert was away, and she had time on her hands. After sleeping off her exhaustion, the loneliness seemed more acute. She found Touma and her parties, dancing, and liquor.

Drums on hot nights, strum of a lyre, bodies lit by fire, the flames burning in the center of the dance. Chants of brittle joy, defiance, absurdity. She could dance like Hibra and Hadija taught her, long ago in Al-Ubayyid. She felt the beat of the drum inside her stomach, in her chest, where all the wildness was and the ululations were screams, not of joy, not of liberation, but of echoes of what should be. Sweat pouring, hoarse voice, turn to admire the one who jumped the highest, the one who bent her back the farthest. Better than dancing was the drink. But it cost money, and she found coins in the house. The khawaja was careless with what he left in pockets and drawers. She helped herself.

It filled her up, the millet taste, ancient food, something her father had drank and her mother and uncles. In thick forests and green grass, in the land of the wild buffalo. Intoxicating was it not, to go back and feel like a child again, huts safe, father smiling, friends her age who knew her name. Here on breezy nights, she could have that again, stare at the sky and not think of him. He would disapprove of all this. He was religious; that was who he was. But where was he now? It was difficult to cry during sunshine and work. But gulp, swallow, and the tears would flow easy.

The first time Zamzam met Touma, she said to her, "I know you from before. I met you years ago. We were traveling, my brother and the merchant from Khartoum. We stopped at your place. And you wanted to keep my brother, but the merchant said no. The following morning you gave me a shawl to wear."

Touma laughed and said, "I don't know what you're talking about, girl." She was stitching a love charm from the root of a wild fig tree. Men bought them to make themselves irresistible to women.

"It was you, I'm sure."

"Where was that?"

"Between Malakal and Al-Ubayyid. Don't you remember?"

"No, I don't remember. People pass me by."

"You don't remember him? Yaseen, the merchant. He was a merchant then."

"Names mean nothing to me. What's your name?"

"Zamzam."

She laughed. "You weren't Zamzam then, that's for sure."

No, she wasn't, and she was wearing her mother's jewelry. Smooth beads in red and black, tiny ones like seeds and ones as big as stones. Crisp shells, a beaded necklace in deep orange—all taken away from her, torn away, never to be returned. "Touma, it was you in that place. Before you came to Khartoum?"

"Me or someone like me. What does it matter?"

She was smiling but her evasiveness perplexed Zamzam. She was disappointed, wanting to connect with someone who had known her, had known him and Bol. She learned that in Touma's world one was not meant to ask questions; narrating the past did not erase it. Complications that were fatalistic or illegal, criminal or rotten luck, too much that needed forgetting and putting away. It was the worst of manners to ask, *Where did you get that scar from? What was your name before? Where is your first child?* Connect with others without asking them questions, without expecting them to explain themselves.

Tonight, as Touma packed coffee into the cut on her forehead, she didn't ask, *Who did this to you? Why didn't anyone stop him? What did you do to provoke him?* She made soothing noises and looked Zamzam straight in the eye to gauge if the pain was surface or deep inside. If she wanted to act strong and brush it off or needed to cry and be comforted.

It was the former. "I'm going to tear all his paintings. Burn them to smithereens."

"He'll call the police on you. Destroying his private belongings. The police have whips with metal pieces at the ends."

Zamzam fumed then settled. Went back—where else would she go—dusted and cooked and fetched water. Robert was working on another painting, and he ignored her. No words exchanged. He was fixated on a new project—the Khartoum souq. There were no women in that painting. Instead, it was centered around a man in a turban selling caged fowls of all kinds—hens, parrots, a peacock without enough space to spread its tail.

When he broke his silence he asked, "Where's Fatimah? She hasn't been coming."

Fatimah's visits had abruptly ceased, and he was starting to run out of supplies. He sent Zamzam to the souq and she got the wrong things because, as he said, she wasn't paying attention to what he specifically wanted. When he tried to buy his own supplies, he returned swindled and unsatisfied. Where was Fatimah?

He sent Zamzam to search for her. Fatimah had mentioned once that she lived in the Salama Pasha district, south of the souq. It was an adventure for Zamzam to head out in the morning to a place other than the river. She walked west past the palace and the government buildings and then turned inland toward the post office. She skirted past the souq and the houses built of brick, toward the modest ones made of rammed earth. She had to ask her way several times. From those who didn't know who Fatimah was to those who knew her but weren't sure where she lived. At the end she was given specific directions and found the house.

The door was open and there were people coming and going. She stepped inside and heard the keening, immediately saw the shrouded but recognizable figure. Fatimah, laid out ready to be buried. That was her face surrounded by a white veil. She must have been ill all those weeks; she must have been dying.

A woman sitting on the ground nursing a baby noticed Zamzam, looked up at her. She had wide, bright eyes, and even though she was in mourning there was a liveliness in her voice and gestures. "Did you know my husband's mother?" The baby stopped feeding and sat up in her lap. She adjusted her clothes.

"Yes," said Zamzam. "She used to sell supplies to the khawaja . . ." Her voice trailed because of the surprise in the woman's face. So, this was not common knowledge then; this was a secret of sorts. And now the woman was turning her head, hand on the baby who had pitched himself forward. She smiled up with concern at the man toward whom her baby was crawling, and it was him, him in the flesh. This was his house, this was his wife, this was his child—Zamzam had no idea there ever had been a child—and Fatimah was his mother.

She turned and ran out of the house. He was alive. He was alive and well. He was in one piece. He was free. He was not imprisoned. He was here in Khartoum. He was not in Al-Ubayyid. The Mahdi hadn't killed him, hadn't enslaved him, hadn't destroyed him. He was here, had been here for how long? In the same city, breathing the same air, drinking the same water. Had he not searched for her, had he not tried? Zamzam stopped running. But she had mentioned him to Fatimah, had she not? Said his name, said Halima's name. She had told her about Al-Ubayyid, about him being in prison, about how he was a merchant before he went to Al-Azhar. She had told her all these things. And Fatimah never said a word, never said he was her son. All those months and months . . . Unfamiliar alley, the river out of sight. She needed the river to be on her left, needed to head east back to the boatyard. Where was she now? She had lost her bearings.

She stopped. A child leading a donkey, a woman carrying a pile of driftwood, a door painted blue. She should ask for directions. There he was across the road. He had seen her, seen her running out, followed her, found her. "Where is the river?" she said.

He did not move closer but instead raised his hand. He looked different, gaunt and less solid, older with dark shadows under his eyes, his clothes too loose for him. It had been over a year. She must be different too. Well-fed, certainly more well-fed and rested since the Al-Ubayyid siege. But the fresh scar on her forehead, the long weal that ran from shoulder to elbow—new for him to see. The sun's rays beating down on them; it was already hours past dawn, and the freshest part of the day was over. He said, "You didn't leave? I was told you'd left. Who are you with?" He cleared his throat. "My mother said you were with . . . at the steamers . . . the boatyard. Are you still with the same people . . . ?"

She nodded. So, he had known all along. Known and done nothing. Known and neither claimed her nor checked up on her.

"Your brother is well," he said. "Ishaq used to come and visit me." He sounded hoarse, hesitant as if he was not sure why he had rushed out of the house. As if he was not sure what the next step should be. She had always known him confident, in control. Not like this.

The sun bore down as if it were intent on killing them. She didn't have anything to say. The smell of a lemon tree behind her but she could not step into its shade. He must go back to bury his mother. Afterward she would chide herself for not expressing her condolences, for not asking how he had escaped. She walked toward the river.

There was the riverfront. Head toward the boatyard. "I thought you'd left!" Where was she meant to go?

Her clothes clung to her body, not a single breeze. She lingered under the shade of a tree, but that did not help. Only a haboob could relieve this misery, sweep away the heat, bring a breath of fresh air. She sniffed the air for the smell of dust, but it was still far away. How low the river was! It would be months before the rains.

The news of Fatimah's death or, rather, the drying up of his art supplies made Robert bad-tempered. He wanted Zamzam to find a substitute, another source. He was irritable that she didn't care, didn't understand. She realized that he was like Nazli Hanim. He was British and she was Turkish, he was a man and she was a woman, but they were fashioned from the same clay. Moods and the inability to stay idle, a sense of entitlement for a better life. For them both, she was a toy—a decorative part of their lives. Robert would end up discarding her; already he was less fascinated. He had sketched and painted her enough. She was no longer a novelty or a curiosity. The sheen on her had faded, the exoticism sealed on canvas, ready to be consumed by someone else.

She was waiting. For a haboob. For a change. For a decision. She could run away. She could gather her things in a bundle and go to Yaseen. She knew now where he was. She could say to him, "You are my rightful master. I belong to you." She could do that, but she did not. Instead, she waited, and the haboob did come. How glad she was for its wildness! Burning orange and brown beauty that mocked the concoctions of the resident artist, a smoke from hell. It was right that earth to sky should be in turmoil, to rip up paper and possessions, to bend what was standing still. All worth it for the peace afterward, for the gentle coolness. Sand to sweep out of the room, sand piled up in corners, in grooves, even covering the grass and the leaves of trees. Sweeping, sweeping and grateful for the coolness. The sound of the breeze circling, carrying the scents of the river. It made the waiting easier.

Then one day his wife was at the door, carrying the baby. She refused to come in, and Zamzam, heart beating, stood with her in the street. Listened to what she had to say. That Zamzam was a member of their family, and she must be with them. That Yaseen had looked for her when he came back from Al-Ubayyid. That Fatimah had told him she was gone. All of this she must hear and not cry. She did not want to cry; she wanted instead to hold the baby and Salha handed him over. They sat down in the shade of the house.

"It was a long walk," Salha said. How comfortable she looked, leaning her head back against the wall of the house, at ease with herself! Skin oiled and shining, hair plaited tight. Even her feet, which she started to massage, were looked after, cool and dark with henna, silver anklet on moisturized skin. Her large eyes were on Zamzam's face. There was curiosity in them, a wish to understand.

"So, this is where Fatimah came behind our back. Yaseen didn't tell his brothers. They have been after her for years to stop working. She didn't need to; they were earning enough and giving her everything she needed. It must have been something she wanted to do, for herself." Salha's voice was slightly louder than that of the average woman. Her words clear and round. There were qualities in her that Zamzam had never seen before.

This was how a free woman looked and spoke, after growing up safe in a father's house and moving to that of a trustworthy husband. All through life protected and held firm. A virgin on her wedding night, chaste afterward, luxuriant in her modesty, never been whipped, never been violated. Bowing down only in prayer, eyes only downcast over books and ink. All these things must have given her that security, the permission to be energetic when she wanted to be active, languid when she wanted to rest. The placid ease of her body. Never been cowed, never been pushed or starved. True she must have struggled with her bossy mother-in-law, chafed at the restrictions of her life, yearned for the things only permitted to her brothers. But she had experienced neither violation nor violence. Her feelings acknowledged, her body precious. Fertile and healthy. Beautiful because that beauty had never been soiled, nor sold, nor twisted. It was a fact. As it was also a fact that Yaseen had left this woman, his well-connected wife, and went to Al-Ubayyid with the Mahdi's army camped seven miles away to seek her, Zamzam, the khadim in the governor's house. She could swoon.

"What's wrong, girl?" Salha grabbed her arm.

"Nothing, just the heat."

Salha took the baby from her. "You're not pregnant from the khawaja, are you?"

"Oh no. He never touched me."

Salha raised her eyebrows. "And I'm a newborn kitten with eyes closed!"

Zamzam laughed. The laugh cleared her chest.

Salha stood up and dusted her tobe. "I was going to come yesterday, but we heard the worst news from Berber. It had seemed so solid when we were there and now it's fallen to the Mahdi. Such a shock. I'm definitely not going to walk all the way back now. I'll get a donkey ride. Come and stay with us, as I said. I do need help with the baby."

# 18

# Robert

**Khartoum, June 1884**

He held the damaged painting. The only one he had done here in oil, smaller than the others, but it could have been one of his best. In fact, he was sure it would have been the best. Instead, it was a torn canvas, stabbed by a knife, ruined. He might as well throw it away. Why was he keeping it? To admire his work. That was one reason. The more distance he had from its execution, the more he assessed it with critical eyes, the more he found to admire. Why be modest when it would never be framed, never hang, never be gazed upon? He had captured the girl's blue-black skin with accuracy, the feminine muscles of her arms, the row of scarification on her stomach. She was seated in a three-quarter pose against a black background, looking over her shoulder, gripping and pulling the edge of a white muslin veil that covered her head but not her torso. The sheen of luminous skin, fierce eyes, her upper lip curved in a sneer not a smile. Robert sang its praises to himself—"a meticulous approach to detail," "as if carved in stone," "influenced by Jean-Léon Gérôme's nudes." He had tried to undo the damage, stitch the tear, smooth the canvas, and put it back together again. It was no use. During the joyful days of working on it and when it was first complete, he had looked after it with exceptional care, his only oil painting, susceptible to brittleness from the dry weather. He had constructed a little tent for it and hid it inside the cotton sheets, making sure to sprinkle the material regularly with water. The oil colors needed a moist atmosphere. He had also made sure that the damp sheets were protected from dust. No need to do any of that now. No use in getting angry either. Every day or every other day, he would take it out and look at it. He would look at the title he had given it—the script clear and whole, every letter safe. His signature, too, bold with the sense of accomplishment. Such damage to beauty shocked him and pushed him back within himself, stunted his creativity. Damage that was wilfully done, with intent and malice.

It made him stop painting. Days after she did what she did, he had not been able to hold a brush. It was as if he were ill again. Even when work was intense at the boatyard, he had managed to forgo his siesta and put in a few hours in the afternoon and later at night. When General Gordon first arrived and tasked him with building a new steamer identical to the *Abbas*. When the steamers needed radical adjustments to carry extra soldiers and ammunition. When they needed urgent repairs and the replacing of parts because of enemy fire. Even through all of that, his real inner work, his secret art had continued. But she had disrupted it. He had never hit a woman in his life. It sickened him. Heather would have been appalled. But there was no point in apologizing to Zamzam; his words meant nothing to her. She never listened to what he said; every mundane instruction was bungled or disobeyed. Language of course was an issue, but he expected common sense and decency to compensate. They didn't. She was nothing like the wonderful Fatimah, whom he now missed. So sharp that woman had been, and helpful, tottering with her basket, her thin gray braids and thick, dry lips.

He remembered Fatimah teaching him how to make brown paint by burning leather with tufts of wool until a paste was formed. Together, they had shaped the concoction into tablets. All he had to do after that was to mix the tablet with water to get ink or with oil for a heavier consistency. He had reveled in the particular browns the mixture produced, how in tune the colors were to his surroundings, how the shades were those of desert, sunsets, and skins. Fatimah had humored him, smiling at his enthusiasm, willing to go out of her way to help him. She had been his friend.

Weeks passed before he could pick up his brush again. He tackled the subject matter that had always felt challenging to him. The bustling souq. Away from the river, the boats, away from the girl. He should have done the souq long ago when he had first arrived and it was in prime health. Now, after the euphoria of Gordon's arrival and with disruptions all around the countryside, it was fast becoming a miserable place. Robert chose the focus of the new painting to be the man selling birds. He seemed not to have been affected by the deteriorating situation and was willing for Robert to sketch him. Back in his room, the sketches paled in comparison to the colors on the canvas, the radiant images in his head.

The girl interrupted him as he was focused on the eyespots of the tail. In the paintings he had encountered, mostly of

Indian peacocks, the plumage was metallic blue, green, and bronze. The peacocks in the Khartoum souq were chestnut brown with a violet tinge. She said, "I've earned my freedom."

He put the brush down and wiped his sweaty hand with a handkerchief. He was used to the heat now, the constant perspiration, and had taken to wearing almost nothing. Yesterday, it had rained, far too early for this time of year, and after a couple of hours the freshness dissipated. He listened to Zamzam without turning to look at her. She rarely spoke in such a direct way. Usually, her speech was a mumbled monotone, curses, he assumed, that were targeted at him. Today she wanted something.

"You told me that the painting I damaged costs more than me?"

It angered him that she would bring this up, that she would dare remind him of it. As if she had no regrets. Yes, he had told her that, to impress upon her the value of what she had destroyed. To make her understand her crime. To understand that the painting was important, a precious object that was going to be sold by his agent in London, something that would bring a high price, higher than the whole bloody lot of her, from head to toe, if she were to be displayed in the souq!

She said in a rush, "There were others that you sent away. Plenty. So, I've earned my freedom."

He did not know how to reply. He had always intended to free her. After that, she would remain his maid and he would pay her a monthly salary. That's what fair-minded people did. At this moment in time, though, he did not feel generous.

"No," he said.

"I will run away," she said.

"Where to?"

"My people. I have a family."

He grunted and dismissed her with a wave of his brush. Eejit. She could not even choose the right time to approach him, interrupting his work. Inventing a bogus family!

She became insolent after that. She would accidently break a plate, accidently burn the stew, forget to bring in his clothes from the clothesline when a haboob started. He had vowed not to hit her again, no matter how much he was provoked. Give her time; she would settle. He made sure all his paintings were locked away in a trunk. He had been doing that since she damaged the oil painting. Now he made sure that even the key to the lock was always with him.

The city had less food and security but there were more painting materials to be found. The mission school had closed, and the priests were happy to sell him supplies. The wife of one of the European consuls left him unused sketchbooks and paint before she was evacuated. Robert felt rich and ready, confident that he could produce more now that he had overcome the setback to his creativity caused by the damaged painting. At the boatyard, the tension was intense. When he returned home, though, he was able to put all this anxiety behind and settle. One painting after the other for Christina—peacocks, monkeys, a rhinoceros—it won't be long now before he would be with her. Once Gordon left, he would leave too. Another four months was the calculation. Then his dreams would come true—the move to Edinburgh, an atelier all to himself, a housekeeper to look after Christina.

One morning, after another burnt porridge, he gave in and freed the girl. He signed the necessary papers. She grabbed them and left without a thank you. What made her even more of a fool was that she was going back to the same Sudanese man who had first taken her out of the jungle. Robert was giving freedom with an offer of paid employment, and she was choosing a harem! To replace her, he bought and freed a young lad. He was a cheerful fellow, willing to learn, and though Robert was short on time to train him and things inevitably went wrong, it was a preferable situation. Besides, he was never going to paint Zamzam again. He realized that. After hitting her, after she had brought out the worst in him, she was finished for him as a subject. She had passed from his eyes, straight to his head, swirled around in his creativity, and come out again through the skill in his hand, to settle on the canvas. He was free of her.

An unexpected promotion at work. Malcolm Ramsay had decided to leave and suggested that Robert take his position. How could he not agree when it meant an increase in his savings! It meant, though, more responsibility, more time spent at the boatyard, more direct contact with General Gordon. On first meeting him, Robert had expected a Highlander, not a stuffy English officer. The man spoke like one, acted like one, and did not possess any sentiment toward Scotland. On his orders, all the steamers had been fitted along the sides with sheets of bolted-on boilerplate iron that were bulletproof. These sheets were the right height for the soldiers to easily fire over them then duck down again. Robert was invested in all these changes, in tune with Gordon's resolve to turn these steamers into war vessels.

Ramsay said to him, "Are you sure you don't want to leave with me?" It was tempting to exit. To say *I've had enough, this is not why I came here.* But Ramsay was going to another lucrative post in Suez. Robert could not go anywhere else. Christina waited for him in Scotland, she was talking now, there was his atelier, his career. He did not have time for another colony and another adventure. He needed to squeeze what he could out of this assignment. He would stay but certainly send his latest paintings with Ramsay to post to his agent. Choosing which ones to send soothed him. The torn oil painting of the girl was out of the question; no one must see it and ask questions he was not prepared to answer. Instead, he would send some of the earlier ones he had done of Zamzam. These decisions took his mind away from the tense city and the war drums beating at night.

He needed to start a new major project. The souq was near completion and would be ready in time to send away. He had put a lot of effort into the caged birds, and though the painting was not his best it was still striking. It was natural to be listless between projects, to experience a sense of emptiness, but that could also be anticipation, the poise just before springing forward. He must not let the siege interfere; it was not his responsibility. Let Gordon huff and puff and deal with the rebels. Robert didn't really care what happened or who won. Mahdists, Turks, Egyptians—all at each other's throats and once he was out of here, would he give Sudan a second thought?

He found his new subject. He was returning from Burri on the *Mansoura* after it had run into engine trouble. Burri was east of Khartoum, on the southern bank of the Blue Nile.

There the rebels had clustered and dug trenches, but they were pushed back in an organized attack. A victory but all the shots fired at the steamers had caused considerable damage and needed a full day's attention. It was close to sunset when he sailed back into Khartoum. The sun was straight ahead, large, and the sky above it layered in colors. A few heavy clouds now that the rainy season had started. The sky, which had been stark during the day, was softening into blue. Robert could see the palace on the left bank, the khedive's flag waving in the breeze. On the roof, Gordon, a small figure with his telescope. No doubt he was watching their approach now. On impulse Robert waved even though he didn't expect a response. A growing pleasant fullness spread through his body. Anticipation and arrival. This was what he was going to paint next, from this vantage point. The steamers, the river, the sunset, the palace, and a man on its roof, indistinguishable, standing behind a telescope.

# 19

# Charles

**Khartoum, March 1884–November 1884**

You like how they say your name, changing the *g* to the guttural *gh*, elongating the second syllable so that it sounds Scots. Ghur-*doun*. *Ghur-doun Basha*, they say. The title "Pasha" is Ottoman as are the decorations of the Order of the Osmanieh and the Order of the Medjidie. You do not mind honors, they sit well with your nature, they do justice to your achievements. Major General, Companion of the Order of the Bath, Companion of the Order of the Dragon, Chevalier of the Legion of Honour, the Imperial Yellow Jacket. It is monetary prizes that you shun. You detest the acquisition of wealth, the constant wrangling over salaries and benefits. It is pedantic and you do admire spirit. You admire your enemies, the fanatics led by the Mahdi, the dervishes who throw themselves into battle as if death will not touch them. You wish you were leading them. Instead, someone else is and you are in Khartoum with an army you are commissioned to evacuate. You are not here to fight.

This is what the firman from the khedive says. But you know that this is not why you have been sent here. You are here because no one else can be. This assignment is made for you. Is that not what you said to the *Pall Mall Gazette*? You said, "We cannot evacuate. We must either surrender absolutely to the Mahdi or defend Khartoum at all hazards . . . The moment it is known that we have given up the game, every man will go over to the Mahdi. All men worship the rising sun." That interview ran under the heading CHINESE GORDON FOR THE SUDAN; it was picked up by every other paper. You are the people's choice and so the very government with which you have publicly disagreed appoints you. You are in tune with the public. Beloved by the Queen. Evacuate, Khedive Tewfiq's firman says. But you know that with the Mahdi winning the country and Egypt abandoning them, even those Sudanese loyal to the Turkish Egyptian government will cave in. No, you can do better than that.

You can be a catalyst. Your very presence on this soil will stop the Mahdi in his tracks. Hold fast, bide your time. Who knows, a handful of poisoned dates and the self-proclaimed savior of the earth will keel over. All that fervor will frizzle out. And then slowly, area by area, you will bring Sudan back to the fold.

And when it returns to the fold, you will have advanced direct British influence. You are chipping away at Turkish Egyptian sovereignty, paving the way for a replacement. Never mind that it is the Khedive Tewfiq who is paying your salary. You, Ghur-doun, serve the interests of one empire, the British one.

Your arrival to Khartoum on February 18 is a legend. Pleasant weather, picturesque river, verdant green on either bank. In letters you play things down and say, "I was well received." In truth you are stirred by this welcome, ferried on the *Isma'ilia*, escorted by the *Abbas*. An artillery salute from Omdurman Fort and when the steamer veers left passing Tutti, the cheers rise, and you see the southern bank of the Nile lined up with Khartoum's garrison commanders, civil servants, crowds and crowds. It is as if the town's forty thousand inhabitants have all come out to greet you. A brass band starts to play. Chocolate street boys trill your name. Women break out in ululations. It is a ghastly sound, but love softens you today. You cannot help but love these simple people. There is no humbug in them, no pretense. They bring out the best in you. They trust you and you feel responsible. You will not let them down. You will not abandon them. You disembark with Stewart behind you; he is nervous at all this excitement. A most capable and amiable fellow. You could not have been blessed with a better aide-de-camp. You disembark into the warmth of a crowd that calls you Sultan and Father. They might as well call you Savior. At this day, this hour, Ghur-doun is their rising sun.

First is the military parade and the meeting with the city's notable, among them the blind senior cleric, Sheikh Amin Al-Darir, head of the Khartoum ulema. How could you possibly forget him? The man hardly looks a day older because he had always been ancient. Farajallah Bey Zein, the outstanding Black officer and former slave who in the 1860s fought for the French in Mexico and was awarded the Legion of Honour; you have big plans for him. More familiar faces, fresh introductions. "Welcome back," they say, and it does feel as if you have never left, as if you had only gone away months and not years.

You make your speech. You repeat what you had said in Berber—but not the contents of the second firman for perhaps that was not such a sound idea after all. You proclaim the independence of Sudan from Egypt. You reprieve debts, halve taxes, and offer concessions. The crowd yell their delight. Small boys leap and dance, chanting your name.

You are intolerant of corruption and crime, a just Christian. Born in Woolwich, conventional military training, a spectacular career service in China. Incidentally, in China you, too, fought against a religious fanatic. A man who claimed to be the Son of God—no, not Jesus Christ, but his younger brother. Hong Xiuquan first learned about Christianity from American missionaries. In hallucinations he saw himself as God's Chinese son, whose duty it was to destroy the corrupt Manchu dynasty and spread the teachings of Christianity. His following grew to the extent that he captured the city of Taiping. You took command of a militia, the Ever Victorious Army, and brought the rebellion to an end, thereby cementing British trade interests with China. Thirty years old and the press could not have enough of the triumphs of "Chinese Gordon."

The palace is familiar. Protruding balconies. Up there the spacious roof, vital because on it you will be able to stand with your long telescope. It allows you to see all the way to Omdurman and beyond. Fruit trees in the garden, immense and empty rooms. Spacious halls, impressive dining room, the telegraph room where the clerk can send telegrams not only to the local forts but also to Suakin and Cairo. You recognize your old servants, many of them slaves you had freed yourself. Smiles all around and more welcomes. This was your home when you were governor-general of Sudan in 1877. But instead of remembering that time, your mind goes back to your first visit. In 1873, when you were en route to take up your position as governor of Equatoria. Isma'il Pasha Ayoub was the governor-general then, and he held a dinner in your honor. You can never understand this need for dinners. Formality sickens you. Food and drink an unnecessary accompaniment to important conversation. On that day, the food was especially rich and assertively Turkish. The entertainment was a Nubian belly dancer. Scantily clad, brown layers of fat quivering, hips gyrating, full lips open in a cheeky smile, aimed at you the guest of honor; she stuck her tongue out, the drumbeat worked its way toward a crescendo and she with her movements followed. You threw your napkin on the plate and rushed out of the room. Of course, everyone noticed. Even then, as governor of Equatoria and not governor-general of the whole Sudan, you were still Ghur-doun. Not allowed to slip away unnoticed. Instead, your untimely departure from the dinner is what everyone talked about. That you had been displeased.

It is this memory that comes back now; you push it away. You are past fifty, you owe explanations to no one, you can do or not do as you please. Tonight's dinner in honor of your arrival is frugal enough for your taste. No waste, no fuss. Less fat in the food, less sugar in your tea. Upstairs, the corridor in front of your room is stacked with Hicks's packed belongings. It is a sorry sight. Not a day passes without a fresh reveal of the extent of the Sheikan disaster. Stewart, who occupies the adjacent room, launches into an uncharacteristic outburst.

Hicks would have succeeded had he not encumbered himself with a ludicrous amount of baggage! Tables and chairs! Carpets! Wines! Even tents are not necessary in this climate. His Indian army training was against him. English soldiers in India are coddled as if they are delicate women. It's a disgrace! You are in total agreement. The way Europeans live in India is obscene in its luxury. It had taken you two days in Bombay to figure this out. Two days as private secretary to the viceroy of India before you resigned. You leave Stewart fuming and stroll over to the balcony. There are fireworks over the river, naive and rudimentary but more enjoyable for being so. You pull a chair and sit late into the night. You are fond of Turkish cigarettes, their characteristic aroma and mild flavor. They have less nicotine. The air is divine, the stars twinkle, and there is so much that needs to be done.

In the following weeks, from the east and from the north, supporters of the Mahdi start to encroach on Khartoum. Their generals send you letters asking you to surrender, telling you that you are outnumbered. You order that they be pushed back. From the rooftop, you swivel your telescope east, follow the Blue Nile, and watch how the enemy had dug in fortifications at the shore, how they are shooting at the soldiers in the steamers. You send two more steamers as reinforcements. The result is a victory, and the citizens of Khartoum are reassured; they did not expect any less of you.

These are small battles but your superiors in Egypt are not happy. They don't want you saying that you will "smash the Mahdi"; they want you to evacuate. And you do evacuate, hundreds and hundreds. You expedite the transfer of one

Egyptian family after the other—the widows and orphans of
the soldiers who died with Hicks. The ill and disabled soldiers
unfit for service. You listen to the arguments of those who
don't want to leave. They say they believe in you, that you can
save Khartoum from the Mahdi. He is still in Al-Ubayyid,
after all. He will just stay there and leave Khartoum in peace.
Yes, you say, you have made him the sultan of Kordofan.

But no, he has refused your appointment. Two of his messengers arrive, distinctive in their patched jibbahs that are
alien to Khartoum. They wave white flags, and you allow
them to enter the palace. Swords by their sides, they refuse
to disarm. One of your sergeants moves in to disarm them
by force. You tell him not to and instead order two chairs
to be brought, invite them to sit down. You go through
the Sudanese rituals of hospitality. Your guests are fidgety,
hands not far from the hilts of their swords. No doubt they
remember the fate of the Mahdi's ambassadors who were
killed by the governor in Al-Ubayyid. They should know
better; you are Ghur-doun. Had they been more friendly,
you would have offered them your signature entertainment,
the one you delight with every Sudanese—the first sight of
their face in a mirror, the first climb up a flight of stairs. It
won't do; they are a glum pair. They hand over a letter from
the Mahdi. The letter, on translation, is a long lecture to you,
chiding you for your arrogance, inviting you to Islam. The
Mahdi does not recognize you as governor-general of Sudan.
He will not negotiate. He rejects your gifts of the red tarbush
and the splendid cloak; he is returning them. Instead, he sends
you the clothes of true humility and asceticism. Clothes like
the ones these two are wearing—muslin trousers, a jibbah

with patches of different colors and a straw skullcap. You are outraged by his words, his tone, his nonchalance, which is either supreme courage or a ploy—and both are provocative. You, who are on your knees every night praying to be the dust under your Lord's feet, are being lectured on humility. And by whom? You tear the jibbah with your hands. You pulverize the cap. Muslin, straw, they are not as flimsy as they look. You throw the pieces on the floor. You stomp over these fragments, and it is as if your boots are not making marks on the material but raising sparks, igniting heat. There is a din in your ears, pressing from inside, there is clanking, voices in half words, condemning, mocking, taking you to task. You stomp and you stomp. It is irrelevant that you are making a spectacle of yourself. You hear gusts, voices, and waves. You stomp and you stomp until you need fresh air.

Through your telescope, you see them. They are arriving every day, more and more of them. Spears and livestock, camping across the White Nile, their banners shifting in the breeze. Panning the telescope to the north you can see the others across the Blue Nile, the neighboring tribes who are threatening Khartoum. They are awaiting the arrival of the Mahdi. Men who have abandoned their land to fight the holy war. Or have been forced to do so because it is no longer enough for a village to pay allegiance to the Mahdi, they must fight for him too. Who is doing the cultivation now? No one, and starvation lies ahead. For everyone. Khartoum can only last a few more months.

From the palace steps, you watch Stewart embark on the *Abbas*. The river is favorably high, and the steamer is filled with ammunition, a mountain gun, and fifty soldiers. Stewart is taking the smallest of the steamers, shallow enough to navigate the tricky rocks of the waterfalls. With Stewart are the English and French consuls, the senior boatyard engineer, Malcolm Ramsay. They will fight their way downriver, through Berber and perhaps if the Sudanese in the vicinity rally, the city can be retaken. That would be such a feather in Stewart's cap! You have given him your journals to hand over, your codebook, inventories of the supplies of ammunition and food in Khartoum. The urgency of the situation, that is what he must convey to your superiors in Cairo and London.

They are divided. Some are on your side and others dragging their feet. Queen Victoria "trembles for your safety." She writes to Gladstone, the prime minister, "Gordon must not be abandoned," and Lord Hartington, secretary of state for War, agrees. But Lord Granville, the foreign secretary, is happy to abandon you. It is unthinkable but true that Gladstone himself has risen in parliament and expressed sympathy for the Mahdists! "These people are struggling to be free, and they are struggling rightly to be free." *Rightly*, he says. Rightly! After you warn of the danger for the whole region, for Suez, for the future.

It takes so long for news to reach you, for you to know what is happening in England. Eventually, you learn that all through the summer the debate about the Khartoum siege had gone on, with the press taking your side. Your anti-abolitionist friends had forgiven your misstep of reinstating slavery and rallied. Hartington threatened to resign. Finally, at the end of August, before Stewart sailed, Gladstone had given in, and three hundred thousand pounds were authorized for a relief expedition. It is on the way. You have forced their hand.

A month goes by. Delay after delay. Where are they? In the meantime, the Madhists are surging up through the desert; you see their arrival through your telescope. A whole army pressing in from the south across trenches and parapets. The Mahdi has set out from Al-Ubayyid, he is on the way. Khartoum is fidgety. It is worse at night once the war drums start. On and on, they are the sound of doom. Ghur-doun. Doun. Doom.

A group of women are agitating outside the palace. They blame you for the high prices. How are they to feed their children! They demand that you find a solution. Women yelling at you. Have you lost your prestige? When you inspect the lines, when you walk the city, people now skulk away.

Rescue coming from the north, the Mahdi advancing from the south. Who will arrive first? It is all about holding out now, waiting for the expedition led by your lifelong friend, General Wolseley. You've known him since the Crimea, and oh it will be grand to see him in Khartoum. Preparations must be made to receive General Wolseley and his officers. They will need accommodation. You rent out all the houses on the Blue Nile waterfront. This is precisely the language Khartoum understands. Solid evidence that the relief expedition is on the way. Everyone breaths more easily. Landlords are ecstatic. They throw out their tenants and hand over the leases to you.

One of the evicted tenants is the young Scottish engineer who oversees the boatyard. He is the last British national left in the city. You have him moved to the palace. At first the servants, assuming that all white men have been created equally superior, put him in the room adjacent to yours. You order him moved to the other side of the palace. He looks bewildered carrying all his belongings.

You do not need his company. At the beginning, Robert is far from talkative and keeps himself to himself. Breakfast, your favorite meal, passes in peace. Lunch, likewise. Perhaps you can forget that he is even here. However, after dinner and wine, he starts to talk. He is that type. Out on the terrace, there is whiskey, and the lamps throw shadows. You wonder how much longer you can tolerate his accent. Ten more minutes? Five? Not everyone must have a military bearing or the benefits of education. The colonies do this—the son of an Aberdeenshire fishwife, gutting cod for a living, now dines with you in a palace. Apparently the fellow fancies himself an artist. You tell him of the time you spent in the Crimea sketching maps and of the assignment snapping photographs in Armenia. Your accomplishments earned you an election as fellow of the Royal Geographical Society. Envy flickers in Robert's eyes; he aspires above his station. He is that type. After another glass of whiskey, he starts to share his opinions. What exactly is he saying? A detailed observation of how the enemy counts success by the number of heads they sever. A barbaric practice you have forbidden your soldiers. And rightly so. But an ancient practice Robert says. David and Goliath. This is said with the faintest of sneers. David and Goliath. Enough to irritate you. But you can hold out, can you not, for another few minutes?

Not when he announces that being captured doesn't worry him because he will surrender without a fight. He will pretend to profess belief in the Mahdi.

"Deny your Lord?" you ask.

"Yes," he laughs. "I will bloody well deny my Lord."

You are incensed. He continues with a blithe description of how he will wander Khartoum in sandals and a patched jibbah until help comes. Or until he finds a means of escape. You are livid and say that you would rather die.

He laughs and drains his glass, says he has a bairn waiting for him back home; he intends to stay alive. It is perhaps the word "bairn" that tips you over. You put your pistol to his head.

"Whoa," he says, raising his arms.

He must be more drunk that you realize. He thinks it is all a joke. His trust in you is as massive as your contempt for him. You shove his head with the muzzle. You shove his head with the muzzle, wanting to kill him. You have tipped over into another space. A space that is weird and exciting. It is as if you are outside yourself. Everything bright and dreamy, a charge emitting from you, molten, otherworldly, you are here and not here, you are more than human, above natural laws, made of another element. Gravity is different, so is distance and space, the pistol nothing to do with you, not in your control. But this mustn't go on, cannot go on. You move the pistol away and walk inside. Indoors, you catch your breath, lean against the wall.

You climb the stairs. Pistol in your hand. Fire in your head. Even the roof is not for you tonight. You enter your room and lock the door. You put out the lantern and pace in the starlight. It is a bare room, high ceiling, wide windows to bring in air. Thoughts propel through the crackling in your head. Ideas scramble to distract you from asking yourself what you were doing just now—a civilian—deranged, could you not control yourself, Ghur-doun, it's the drums calling, and they are starting now doun, doom, doun, Ghur-doun. No, drums don't say names. Someone is talking, a voice, and it is your voice. Your voice. You are taking Robert to task. He had better not be captured then by the Mahdi if he cannot hold fast to his faith. It is the fault of Gladstone, that Liberal, dragging his feet, dithering, rising in Parliament to proclaim that the Mahdi has a right to fight for freedom. *Rightly, rightly*, he says. Rightly struggling to be free. And yet he, Gladstone, sent an army to protect the Red Sea coast, did he not, without a qualm; Suez of course must not fall. And instead of building on that success, those Indian troops with Graham. Instead of putting up the pressure, he ordered them to fall back. Fall back and then saying the Mahdists are rightly struggling to be free. And the ones you butchered in Sennar, prime minister. Fine to rightly struggle in west Sudan, all very well and perhaps Khartoum, too, can be spared in Gladstone's equation but not the Red Sea coast, not Suez. Hypocrite politicians.

If you were the Mahdi, you would be now laughing at all of Europe. You wish you could be him. Why not? He is having a good laugh; he made a fool of one Turkish governor after the other. He is a strategist; he controls villages that have never laid eyes on him. Graham should have kept going. They didn't listen and now you are here penned in. Why is it taking them so long? People will go wild with hunger. They will eat cats and dogs. They will eat cockroaches, and no one must make a fool of you. You distribute durra and they pass it on to the enemy. Not the enemy, Ghur-doun Basha, they say, our own flesh and blood. But fools if your flesh and blood have gone over to the Mahdi, are they then not your enemy? No grain for them. You must start to punish and imprison. You pace the room. This is not a night for sleep. The will you have, the might you have, you will win at the end. One morning you will look north through your telescope and round the bend of the river, you will spot the British flag. Guns salute, band plays. Let them hear it all in the enemy's camp. Bomb and blast. Then they will skulk back to the desert. The Mahdi should stay put. Will he? Put yourself in his shoes. Sandals not shoes. Sandals not shoes, sandals not shoes. Not boots. Sandals. Put yourself in his sandals. Ghurdoun in sandals. Put yourself in his sandals. You put a pistol to a man's head, just now, but it was not just now, it is dawn.

You recover enough to face the blow that the *Abbas* had hit a rock. Stewart and his party disembarked. The steamer could not be fixed. Stewart started negotiating with the locals to buy camels to continue the journey overland. He and his party accepted the invitation of a local sheikh, trusted him enough to go unarmed. They were ambushed. It is confirmed that Stewart, the English consul, the French consul, the senior ship engineer—they were all killed.

From the corner of your eye, you notice Robert taking the news badly. He says he had given paintings to Malcolm Ramsay. They are now lost forever. He curses and you are provoked. But you do not respond. Stewart's death deserves nothing less than dignity. You must send Robert away from you somehow. He needs to leave. But you cannot engage with him now. Your journals, letters, plenty of them, that Stewart had been carrying are now in the enemy's hands. Detailed reports on the situation in Khartoum—how much ammunition left and how much grain. So much evidence. To land in the Mahdi's lap. Armaments, deployments, details of the ammunition in each steamer. The names of the city's ulema, government officials, and merchants. Even the code-book. Everything now in the Mahdi's favor.

You send the *Bordein* and the *Tel el Hoween* to fight their way to Shendi. There, they will wait for the Camel Corps to cross the desert. With the steamers is Robert and you have achieved two things—removing him from your sight and reassuring the citizens of Khartoum that help is imminent. But there is still no sign of the relief force. Every single day, you look north through your telescope, waiting for the sight of the red uniforms, the flutter of the Union Jack. End of November was your calculation. Food-wise and ammunition, Khartoum could only hold out until the end of November, otherwise "the game is up and Rule Britannia." Yet here you are weeks later, just about. Soldiers reduced to skin and bones, snoozing on their feet, people dying of malnutrition, so many corpses in the streets that you pay twenty piastres to anyone who will bury one. The city is shelled day and night. Shells fall in the Nile, scar buildings, kill children and horses. Shells shatter the windows of the palace that you insist on lighting up through the night. Lanterns and candles, lots of candles, to ward off the beat of the war drums. Ghur-doun. Doun. Doom. They are beating for you and no one else. Every night, murdering your sleep, raiding your nerves, turning your hair white.

It is white now—all of it. You notice it when you shave. You notice, too, that your hand does not tremble. You are not afraid. It is others who are afraid of you. The Mahdi now encamped across the river, hesitating to attack, even though he knows the appalling condition of the city. Your officers who in your presence cannot hold their hands steady to light a cigarette. Grown men reduced to stammering because they face Ghur-doun. Ghur-doun, who is not afraid of death. You could blow up the palace if the Mahdi takes the city. Two mines will be enough. But the plan stinks of suicide. It is the Lord's will to give and take life. You will not give up. But yes, blowing up the palace can be done. This way you can avoid capture, which would be loathsome, which would be worse than death, and you pray, every night, that you will not be captured, that you will not be brought low. Secretly and not so secretly you crave a martyr's death. This would involve capture, shackles, and being put to the sword, ordered to renounce your Lord or else. But you will not renounce, you will not weaken like others have weakened. You will hold firm and die like Peter and Paul.

A woman ambassador comes with a letter from the Mahdi. She is taller than any woman needs to be. She says that the Mahdi promises you safe passage. He does not want you harmed. He accepts now that you will not join him though he would have preferred you to do so. So instead, you may leave and go back to your people. You do not belong here; Sudan is for the Sudanese. The slut is wasting your time. You have no more words to say to the Mahdi. It is time for the language of lead.

# 20

# Yaseen

**Khartoum, September 1884**

I hurry down to the waterfront before the rain falls. It is deserted. Gone are the days when steamers floated past piled with ivory. Every palm tree and every fruit tree has been stripped bare by the hungry. Another blast of gunshots from Burri, certainly not thunder. There will be more funeral prayers for me to lead, maybe even today, if the bodies are gathered before sunset.

I am near the district office when a woman calls my name. I have never set eyes on her before. Tall, carrying a guffa. I turn and she mumbles condolences for my mother. One of her acquaintances perhaps. It has been three months now since my mother died, since I accepted condolences for her. An odd note is struck. The woman has more to say. "Your sister, Halima, has arrived." My heart starts to beat. She is, like my sister, one of them then. A spy in our midst, a supporter of the enemy. And yet she is not afraid to reveal herself.

"My name is Nafissa. Maybe your mother didn't tell you about me," she says.

This is worse. I have no need to know her name. I am not curious about her relationship with my mother. I ask, "Where is Halima?"

"In Omdurman."

So, the Mahdi's followers are coming north and just like that, without resistance, entering Omdurman. Strolling into the town, claiming space, settling down.

"She wants you to know this. And to tell your brothers where she is. She is waiting for you there."

I make a sound of annoyance. What does Halima want from us? To take a boat and visit her, sit exchanging pleasantries with her new husband, who is a staunch follower of the Mahdi. No, when the siege intensifies, she wants us to slip out and surrender. Nafissa takes out a letter. I don't want it. Consorting with the enemy.

"It's not from Halima," she says. "When you are ready to answer, ask for me. I sell groundnuts near the Tutti ferry. I will help you."

I take the letter from her. I find a secluded spot, away from prying eyes. The letter is from my friend Isma'il. I hear his voice in the familiar script. He is now leading one of the armies that are camped south of the city. He writes, after the customary salutations:

*Dear friend, your rightful place is here, by my side. Khartoum will fall. Gordon is deluded. The whole country is behind the Mahdi. All of us. Where are you? It is high time that you take your rightful place among the victorious. Are you comfortable being ruled by a Christian? Whose flag is it that flies over the palace? Don't pretend that you don't experience the humiliation.*

I unclench my jaw, clench it again . . .

*The Mahdi wants the best for you. Don't be stubborn. Don't turn your back to counsel. If you are afraid to lose your position, then know that you will be dislodged from it before long. If you are afraid to make your family destitute, this is exactly what will befall them when we win. These foreigners don't have our best interests at heart. The British, the Turks, the Egyptians—why are we in thrall to them. When you and I studied in Egypt did we not sense the way they sneered at us because they ruled over us? You understand. So why are you pretending not to feel the glorious pride that thousands of us are feeling? How can you be content to stay small under their thumb!*

His reproach is a scream in my ear. A drop of rain falls on the letter. I fold it away and put it in my pocket. But. But he is evading the core of the matter, or he no longer sees it as the core. Years ago, the two of us went to Aba, entered a cave, met the man who claimed to be the Expected Mahdi and the two of us concluded that he was not that man. He did not fulfill the conditions. What has changed, Isma'il? I know the answer. I won't pretend that I don't. What has changed is that this is now a massive rebellion against a major power. The Mahdi has coalesced the nation's sense of injustice.

Inside, Sheikh Amin Al-Darir is due in court. The windows are wide open and the smell of rain wafts through. Instead of talking about the case he will rule on, he says, "He got another prophecy wrong." The whole office—jurists, ulema, clerks, and tea boys—knows who he is talking about.

There is no one else. We bear the weight of this calamity. Something that has grown and spread wild. So that now we are in this grave predicament. So desperate that overriding General Gordon, we had written directly to the Khedive Tewfiq begging for help. Groveling. We have yet to receive a reply.

"What now?" I ask sitting next to him. Since marrying his niece, I am more familiar with him.

He is in a jocular mood. This tactic of jeering at the enemy is as old as time; it lifts spirits. They call us the scholars of evil, spiritually deficient, supping at the sultan's table. We call them dervishes and fanatics; we call him the Mutamahdi, the fake Mahdi, the imposter. Brave words and yet our nerves are on edge, our confidence in tatters. My friend's letter is awkward in my pocket. My friend, he should not even be my friend. And I should destroy his letter.

Sheikh Amin Al-Darir rests both hands on his walking cane and tilts his head up. "First the imposter claimed that Sennar had fallen after rebels infiltrated it from the west. But Sennar still stands strong; it was never penetrated. Then he turned his vain desires to Dongola and claimed that a great army of light was advancing to defeat British forces. No such thing. He prophesizes what he wishes, and whenever the Prophet visits him in a dream, he tells him exactly what he wants to hear!"

Sheikh Amin chuckles and others join in. Then he changes his tone and speaks with reverence. "Peace and blessings upon you Prophet of Allah, seal of the messengers." He breaks into the verses of the *Burda*, Al-Busiri's *Poem of the Cloak*:

*Muhammadun sayyidu'l kawnayni wa'th-thaqalyni*
*Wa'l-fariqayni min arabin wa min ajami*
*He is the beloved one, whose intercession is hoped for*
*Against all the terrifying things that take us by storm*
*He has called people to Allah, so those who cling to him*
*Are clinging to a rope which will never break*
*He is the one in whom meaning and form were perfected*
*And then the One who created all mankind chose him as His beloved*

One line after another continues and I join in the chorus, remember with an ache the time it was professionally recited at Al-Azhar and Isma'il was sitting next to me, shoulder against shoulder, knee against knee. Best of friends, brothers away from home, in awe of the atmosphere, the voice of the reciter, moved by the chorus we were repeating, the same one on my lips now: *My Lord, bless and grant peace always and forever upon your beloved, the best of all creation.* Until I know it in my bones, know more than I already know.

On my way home, I notice that it has not rained. Instead, the wind has carried most of the clouds elsewhere. I stop by the riverfront and reread the letter. Isma'il is doing what he had done in Al-Ubayyid when he visited me in prison. But I cannot go where he has gone, I cannot make the change. And what if the expedition never comes? If Khartoum falls? What becomes of me and my family? I cannot bear to think along this direction or make plans. I am hemmed in.

Someone touches my shoulder. I put the letter away and turn around to greet Farajallah Pasha Zein. He had recently been promoted by Gordon to the rank of major general and appointed as head of the garrison in Omdurman. He is tall and handsome in his uniform, and I experience a thrill of pride. Here he is a Sudanese, fighting for the cause of justice, fighting on the right side. There is a confidence in his manner that uplifts me. He is experienced and highly skilled. He had even fought in Mexico.

"Tell me, Sheikh," he says. "Now that providence has put you in my way, I have a query that only you can answer. My question is speculative. Do not hold it against me or believe it is a commentary on our military situation. I speak to you in confidence, and I also request that you answer me from a religious perspective." He takes a breath and continues, "In case of defeat, God forbid, when all is lost and the only choice is surrender, when the enemy says join our cause or you will perish, what is the right thing to do? Does one then profess faith in the false Mahdi?"

The layman always expects us to answer in binaries—halal or haram, permissible or impermissible. Whereas there are shades—what is makruh, disliked or nonpreferable, and even more subcategories. The general's question is pertinent. It had been asked before throughout history when Muslims faced trials and tribulations; it had been debated and answered. There is even the Oran fatwa issued in Al-Andalus, which catered to the needs of the Muslims persecuted by the Spanish Inquisition and forced to convert to Christianity. The situation here is different. Our enemy is a Muslim, and the defeated will not be asked to abandon the faith. It is the requirement to believe in the Mahdi that constitutes the oppression. So, what should one do? The answer is to choose life. Keep your faith within your heart even if your tongue is forced to say otherwise.

Flee if you can. If you cannot, live in the hope of better circumstances. Allah is All Knowing, All Forgiving.

I am restless after this conversation. I tear up Isma'il's letter and throw the pieces in the river. I head home. There were times not so long ago when I used to walk through the door carrying bananas or guavas or a bag of dates. Now I return every day empty-handed.

Zamzam is at the door. In the morning I had left early before the dawn prayer and had not seen her. It feels as if more than a day has passed. Her sweet smile and I feel relieved, grateful that after all that has happened and all that has gone wrong, she is here safe with me, in my house, where she belongs, where I had always wanted her to be, always intended her to be ever since the day she lost her father. I do not take her presence for granted. It is I who now welcomes her, I who now speaks as if she were the one who had stepped through the door and not me. She finds my words of welcome amusing. Perhaps they are. I feel blessed that she is here, settled and comfortable with my wife and family, that she feels she belongs, that she knows that this is her home, with me, in this space, my place, within the walls of my house, around the same cooking fire, under one roof.

# 21

# Zamzam

**Khartoum, June–November 1884**

Free, heart tight, expectant, in love, she was not sure what her position would be in the household, not sure about much except that she did not want to be anywhere else. Yet Yaseen was out of her reach, literally and figuratively, and others—women, men, and children—moved between them. He was not head of the household; the position belonged to his eldest brother who was stern and aloof. There was his eldest brother's wife, heavily pregnant, and their three daughters. There was the middle brother, his wife with their younger boys. Only Salha and baby Rustom were familiar to Zamzam. All the others needed figuring out. No one introduced themselves, and it was as if neither Salha nor Yaseen had taken the trouble to explain who Zamzam was! Some of the children thought she was a transient visitor, a poor relation lending a hand.

She was out of her depth. The eldest brother's wife was merciless in her demands; the middle one's wife was quick in noting her faults. It had been a long time since Zamzam lived within a family, not in the governor of Al-Ubayyid's kitchen, not with the bachelor khawaja engineer. This was an established family with customs specific to the tribe they originated from, their class and standard of living—all that she was not accustomed to. A house with an area for the men and an area for the women, guests coming and going, a stress on providing meals for the poor, the day punctuated by prayers. How was she meant to know that the colored bed-sheets were only for the women and everything plain white for the men? How was she meant to know that the sound of a man clearing his throat meant that he was about to enter the women's area? She could learn; she would not be beaten. She was so busy that the sound of gunfire coming from the outskirts of the city did not distract her. Yaseen's household was where she belonged, and she would assert herself in it.

Once she understood the power dynamics, she worked hard pleasing whoever needed pleasing, soothing whoever deemed her a threat, careful not to take sides, keen to be useful, relieved that she was already accepted and no one ever questioned her right to be among them. It was a marvel to watch how the family treated Yaseen. Because the family were proud of him, they made a point of putting him down, scoffing at his ways with gentle words or gestures. His broth-ers had to remind him that he was not better than them, his brothers' wives that he was the youngest. More challenging for the older wives was to keep Salha in her place. She blazed through them with her education and family connections; after giving birth her position was even more secure. Her circle of friends was wide, as was her popularity in the neigh-borhood and farther away. Zamzam, as her new maid, could be an additional asset or a weak spot. Any criticism of her was delivered with relish, a roundabout way to get back at Salha's superiority, to take her down a peg or two.

Zamzam enjoyed watching how Yaseen treated his nephews and nieces. All the hugs and banter, the ease with which they played with him and made demands. When the other brothers entered the women's area, the women covered their heads and lowered their gaze; they fell silent, and the children sat still. Not with Yaseen though, they joked with him freely, and he had no reservations in pulling up a stool to join them, his son on his lap, the other children fussing around him, 'Amo, 'Amo. These scenes reminded Zamzam of her own childhood. She, too, had loved him in that way before all the other ways. Now she yearned for his attention, but he did not belong to her; she wanted him, but she did not have the right. She was alone, as she had been alone before, words stuck in her head, needs unfulfilled, nothing like it had been in Al-Ubayyid. Nothing at all. But there was hardly time to feel sorry for herself. Day after day, she pushed through. It was enough; it had to be. There was no other choice to see him every day, to know that he was near. She learned to watch out for the times he left and the times he returned. She would make sure to hover by the door, so that he would bid her goodbye and so that she would welcome him home. Words exchanged, a smile.

Salha noticed this and took her aside. It was midmorning, and the baby was having a nap. They sat on stools in the room Salha shared with Yaseen, the one that had been specially built for them when they first got married. It overlooked the hoash and if they did not lower their voices any of the women sitting outside could hear them. Salha said, "You are free now, Zamzam. You do not belong to Yaseen anymore. Nor to any man. You understand that don't you?" Her voice was kind. Hers was a type of beauty that became more apparent every day, revealing itself little by little, until there were no doubts. Her voice dipped into a whisper. "You were so young when you met him, so attached to him, and it was his chivalry that made him respond."

Zamzam was not sure about the word "chivalry." The way Salha said it made it sound like it could be a reckless thing.

Salha was looking at her face, keen for her to understand. What was there to understand? That Yaseen had told his wife everything, did not hide the details; he was not ashamed. Salha continued, "Also, the circumstances. You were his but then you got taken away from him."

Zamzam's eyes smarted at the memory. How would Salha know what that was like? She turned her head and looked out of the door. One of the children was balancing on a stool with a missing leg.

Salha swallowed. "You are free now and he is not someone who would take what is not lawfully his. Do you understand? To have you again, to have you now, he must marry you. There is no other way, but . . . that is far-fetched."

Yes, it was far-fetched. She could not imagine it. A co-wife to Salha. It would not happen. Besides, none of his brothers had more than one wife. Salha squeezed her arm. "We will find you an excellent husband."

A sound escaped Zamzam's throat. She did not want to cry. But maybe she did. Maybe that thing inside her was the start of tears and not anger. What right did she have to be angry? Angry at whom?

"Once this wretched siege is over, we will find someone suited to you," Salha went on. There was relief in her voice as if this was what she had been building up to, this was what she had wanted to say all along. "Someone suitable in background. And you could still live with us here, the both of you. We would build you a room. Wouldn't that be nice? And I will be sure to get you your own pots and everything a bride needs. You would be near me, and our children would grow up together."

Zamzam nodded because she was expected to do that. The least she could do if gratitude was impossible. And Salha stood up, glad to end a conversation she had felt compelled to have. Moving on to what needed washing today and no, it was better to wait until Rustom woke up before pulling the sheet from underneath him. Such a pretty colorful sheet, it was part of her dowry. A new bride received lovely things.

Zamzam went to the cow for comfort. The house had a zariba and this was where the livestock were held—the cow, the two camels the merchant brothers traveled on (though they were no longer traveling because of the war), five goats, and a dozen chickens. She leaned her head against the cow's neck and breathed in. Childhood smells of hide and dung, faraway homeland. She belonged elsewhere, but this feeling of detachment was ugly. Cold and unnecessary. Salha was not pushing her away. So why did it feel like that?

When Yaseen came home that day, she was not waiting for him by the door. She heard his voice and felt his presence. She was conscious of him, but perhaps that could melt away in time. Unlike his brothers, he still shared Salha's room. His brothers had rooms in the men's diwan, which had its own hoash and a separate door to the street. At night, after putting the children to sleep, the wife of the middle brother would sneak off and visit her husband's room. She would then return and spend the rest of the night with her children. The eldest brother's wife was too heavily pregnant; she was expecting to deliver any day now. Six weeks after giving birth, she would steam her body, put on henna and perfume, and then resume her visits to her husband in the diwan. Yaseen would move to the diwan once his son was older. Now he spent most of his day there, had his meals with his brothers, received visitors. Late at night, he went to Salha's room. When it was hot, they dragged their angareebs outside. Zamzam slept near the storeroom, in the shaded area of the hoash, and because Salha kept her lantern on until Yaseen's return, she would, before falling asleep, catch a glimpse of him, head lowered, coming into the room.

There was rarely a day when the brothers did not receive visitors or bring guests back home with them. This started to dwindle over time, as the siege intensified. In one exceptional evening, heavy rainfall flooded the storeroom and brought the three brothers over to the women's area. After the matter was resolved and the family were gathered, Yaseen started talking about Zamzam's village. He spoke about its location, how far it was from Fashoda and how near it was to the White Nile. He mentioned the crops the villagers grew, described the first time he had gone there with his late father and the glistening gum hanging from the trees. He spoke about her father, mentioning him by name, how he built his hut, how many cows he owned, his skill the day he saved a calf's life in a complicated delivery. Zamzam, sitting in the shadows, hung on every word, lapped it up with broad smiles and expressions of assent that no one saw, delighting in the memories evoked, the sense of being grounded. The next day, she sensed a slight shift in atmosphere, a keener acknowledgment, a bit more respect. Yes, she was not a nonentity, a wild catch. She had a father and a mother and a village; she had an ancestry she could trace, a homeland she could return to.

It was the custom of the family to host orphans, to feed every beggar that came to the door, to distribute food at the mosque. As the siege intensified, the meals shrunk. Water was added to increase quantities, corners were cut, the women debated the merits of slaughtering another chicken that regularly laid eggs. They would prepare the best meals, save the chunkier bits of meat to send to the men in the diwan. In their turn, the men would urge them to feed the children first. Salha needed to eat well because she was nursing; the heavily pregnant wife needed to keep her strength up. The meals had to stretch. During the mornings, there were fewer women visitors too. The ones who came did not, as before, bring with them a pot of cooked breakfast or some ground coffee. Salha was reproved by the other wives for sugaring while their children had to do with less sugar. Zamzam was sent to the souq, where she battled crowds and endured harassment to return with less fish than was expected. She was scolded about this until their neighbor, too, reported that she had been able to get none. Even fruit was becoming scarce. Onions, limes. Meat became so expensive that they slaughtered another of their goats even though they only ever did that for special guests.

On Fridays, before the prayers, Yaseen spent time with Salha and the baby in their room. Zamzam would see him holding Rustom and hugging him. She would hear his laugh and Salha's voice. She was a talkative wife, and he would listen to her. Sometimes Zamzam caught snatches of their conversation—how it was unsafe for Salha to visit her mother in Tutti and could not her mother move in with them instead? Zamzam noticed all the preparations Salha made for him, how she made sure that her hair was oiled and her clothes clean, body scrubbed with dilka, perfumed from head to toe. During the week, when he was at work, she did not bother. She spent the mornings reading his books. Without cleaning her teeth or changing her clothes, she would sit on the bed and lean over the loose folio pages, pulling at her plaits. She would keep up a running commentary as she read. "Is that so!" she would say. Or "Dear, respected Sir, you have taken me by surprise!" Or she would murmur, "True, true, you are right, you are right, and I am the ignorant one."

On one occasion, only in a wrapper, she was rubbing sesame oil on one knee, leaning over an open book, the baby, newly woken, toddled and latched himself to her breast. He did not even need her to hold him! Zamzam was sitting on the floor sewing and listening to Salha's running commentary. "This is true. True. They did what? But I don't understand this word. Am I reading it right?" Salha suddenly screeched, "He bit me! Oh." She turned to the baby who, in surprise, let go of her nipple and was grinning, milk and saliva running down his chin. She started to tickle him. "How dare you bite me! I will bite you back, I will gnaw your cheeks and pinch you, see if I don't!" The baby chortled with laughter as Salha tickled and showered him with kisses. "How dare you bite me! I will wean you, see if I don't." Zamzam looked up and smiled. For the first time since she had come here, she remembered Robert. He had no access to this beauty. Everything he captured in his paintings was restricted by systematic evaluation. It was fair that he had never seen what she was witnessing now, that he never would. For a brief interlude, she understood something about the need to hide beauty, to shelter it and keep it away from prying eyes. The understanding did not come from instinct; it was not part of her heritage, but it wavered before her eyes, sweet and different. Salha was now stretched out on the bed; her oily knees threatened the book. Zamzam leapt up to rescue the pages.

"Teach me to how to read," Zamzam said to Salha. The lessons, haphazard and intermittent, brought a new pleasure to Zamzam's life. It would have been more efficient to join the children in their lessons, which Yaseen taught after work, but that would have been awkward. She did sit near them though and found herself understanding better what he was explaining, guessing the answers to the questions he addressed to the children. When she got an answer right, she was pleased with herself, even though she had not said it out loud.

One of the things Salha taught her was the meaning of the word "Zamzam." All this time, she had never heard of the well! Never known about its miraculous waters. Everyone who goes on pilgrimage to Mecca drinks from the well of Zamzam. People from all over the world drink and pray, pour its water over their heads, drench their clothes. "It is the best water in the world," said Salha. She told her the story of Hagar, thousands of years ago, left alone in the scorching desert with her baby. Thirsty and hot, without a drop of water in sight. The baby crying and fidgeting in the sand, while Hagar ran to and fro, up and down the hills, searching. And all the time, as the baby kicked the sand, a puddle of water started to swell beneath his feet. This was the healing water of Zamzam, after which she was named, the well that quenches millions. From that moment, Zamzam's perspective about her name changed. She who spoke the river's language, was named after sacred water. And was it not as if she knew Hagar and how she felt, enslaved as she had been enslaved, the thirsty child heavy in her arms, his cries scraping her peace of mind. Water springing out of the desert. The free, fast-flowing river was a thing of majesty but a contained well could be a miracle, too, powerful in its own way, yielding one surprise after the other.

When the wife of the eldest brother went into labor, the midwife was called. A rope was slung over the tamarind tree, the women in the neighborhood gathered, and Zamzam had her work cut out for her. She was so helpful to the midwife that the woman wanted her to start as her assistant. The idea appealed to Zamzam. She would get paid very little by the midwife, but often families, after a safe delivery, would give generous tips. Salha agreed to let her go. She herself was not paying Zamzam anything, the understanding being that Zamzam was a member of the family. She had bought her new clothes and promised to cover all expenses for a future marriage, but that was all. A chance for Zamzam to learn a skill and earn a living was to be welcomed. They were, though, a conservative household, she explained to Zamzam, and so she must be sure to come home at the end of the day and never ever stay away overnight.

Zamzam started a new stage in life. Fitting the household chores around her new role. Every delivery seemed to be different and there was a lot to learn. Moving around Khartoum, she also learned about the different areas. One day she even went with the midwife all the way to Burri village. It was now virtually under the Mahdists, and they were walking openly in the streets with their patched jibbahs and spears. The clothes made them distinctly different from the government soldiers and the civilians in Khartoum. The women, though, were indistinguishable and when assisting the labor, Zamzam forgot that she was in enemy territory. It was her first time to witness twins being delivered. One baby boy was smaller than the other—and the mother was completely surprised. Her young handsome husband was one of the Mahdi's emirs. Delighted, he gave the midwife a gold coin and Zamzam two Maria Theresa dollars.

In their household, they, too, had a naming ceremony for the new baby despite the deprivations of the siege. A boy after three girls was special and no expense was spared. To Zamzam's shock, the cow was slaughtered. Some of the meat was sold, some gifted, and the rest cooked for the ceremony's guests and distributed among the neighborhood beggars. More people were now destitute and hungry, and the house was almost mobbed. It was a harrying experience for Zamzam, who was involved in the distribution. Her mood only lifted when the women's party started and she saw her old friend Touma, with her drum, singing and entertaining what must have been every woman in the neighborhood. They hugged and exchanged news, but both were busy and Touma urged her to come and visit. "I will," she promised.

But she was not able to keep her promise. Salha said, "Touma is not the sort of friend you should have. We hire her as an entertainer. But she is not someone we mix with socially. And neither should you."

"Why not?" She should have gone without asking. She did not need Salha's permission.

Salha said, "Her reputation isn't good. And I won't speak any more on this matter." Such confidence in what was right and wrong. She did not know what Zamzam knew, that a man could hit you and your forehead bleeds, the blood turning your eyesight red, and you have nowhere to turn to, no one to run to, no one wants you, no one fixes your wounds or cares except Touma.

"She helps girls," Zamzam said.

"Does she now? I wouldn't call it help, Zamzam, when at the end they are led astray. She takes in freed girls who are homeless and needy and then corrupts them. They end up as prostitutes working for her! Is this not what happens?"

Zamzam remembered the room she had glimpsed at the back of Touma's house, the angareeb covered with buttered bull's hides. Still, Salha should not say bad things about her friend. She stomped off and for the rest of the day was slack in performing her duties. She did not find delight in baby Rustom's antics, and she paid scant attention to the loud conversations between Yaseen and his brothers. Their shop was near empty, all their supplies drying up. They might as well shut it and sit at home with the women!

The slaughtering of the cow and the naming ceremony had been the end of the good times. A defiance against the siege and its deprivations. After that, when even the dried meat was eaten and the earnings from the sold meat spent, things took a bleak turn. The brothers started saying that Gordon should surrender peacefully and save lives. The more stubborn he continued to be, the more the reprisals. They talked about moving to Omdurman, and Yaseen argued against them.

Fretful days and restless nights. The war drums, which had never troubled her before, reminded her of the dances held at Touma's place. She longed to drink merissa and dance like she used to. It had eased the pressures of her time with Robert. And he had not minded where she went, never asked questions, didn't care as long as she sat for his paintings. It was different here, all her actions accounted for, all her comings and goings. Day and night, she was under Salha's watchful eyes. This was family life; this was the price of belonging. But it was pressing on her chest; she was fidgety. What was the harm in dancing, in forgetting herself for a while, in letting go? Loosening the tightness, laughing. She would sneak off and face the consequences. Tomorrow she would go.

Salha must have intuited her intentions. Why else would she summon her to their room before Yaseen went out in the afternoon and say to him, "You speak to her!"

At first the couple sat side by side on the bed while Zam-zam stood with her back to the open door.

Apart from greetings, Zamzam had not spoken to him for weeks. How odd this situation was! She could tell that he did not want to have this conversation, that it was Salha who had pushed him into it. She could tell that he was not finding it easy. He said, "Is there anything wrong? Is there anything troubling you? You can tell me."

"Nothing," she said. It was awkward but she did not want to leave. These questions were better than nothing.

He went on, "There is a lot of crime now in the city. Because people are getting desperate. It's not safe for you to go out or stay out after sunset."

She nodded, enjoying the sound of his voice, wanting to hear more.

"Anything can happen, and I don't want you to be harassed or harmed in any way. We are in a time of war. There is no need to take risks. If you want to see anyone, let them come to you here. Send word for them and they can come."

Salha stiffened and stood up. She moved over to the chest of drawers and gave Zamzam and Yaseen her back.

He said, "If anyone was ever kind to you when you needed it, if anyone helped you when times were hard, then I personally owe them a debt. They are welcome in my home anytime. I mean it. Whoever they are. Your guest is my guest."

A calmness was beginning to cover her, the restlessness of the past days slackening. What was between them was dormant not dead, deep and unruffled, warm and at peace. She need never doubt.

He said, "Are you still happy working with the midwife?"

"Yes, I am happy."

"That's good."

A pause that could have gone on. It could have gone on, but Salha turned toward her and said in a quiet voice, "Bring me Rustom, will you? His cousins are teasing him."

Zamzam turned and walked out of the room. Her sense of rebellion started to dissipate; the feeling of suffocation lifting. He had reminded her that she had known him all her life, that he had known her before ever setting eyes on Salha. She was part of his youth and their love stretched from her village to his town. She must not feel lost or untethered. And there now was his son in her arms. He could say her name. Again, and again, for the first time, in his baby talk, he was saying her name.

It became easy to sleep at night; she was no longer keen to be anywhere else. Besides, with the difficulties of the siege, Touma might no longer be holding her parties or brewing her brew. Perhaps Zamzam was not missing out on anything after all.

One late morning sweeping the edge of the yard, a sheet of paper floated down from over the wall. Not a folded letter but what looked like a proclamation. She took it to Salha, who read it and became agitated, clasping her hand on her head and calling out loud. "The Mahdi is threatening us, the citizens of Khartoum. He is saying we shouldn't wait for the British to save us, they never will." Every woman stopped what she was doing and looked up at her. Some came close to look at the proclamation in her hand, but she was the most literate of them, the one who could read the fastest.

"The Mahdi wants us to go out to him instead. Oh, he has the audacity to send this! Oh, he is mentioning my uncle by name. By name. They are targeting us. Us in this house. And he has traitors here, right here in Khartoum, distributing this. Zamzam hurry, go out and find this man." She snatched the birch broomstick from her hand and propelled her out of the house. "Hurry, run. He can't have gotten far."

Left or right. Zamzam had no idea. And what sort of person was she looking for? She hurried in the direction of the river. An elderly man sitting next to a donkey turned his head and spat. A woman walking into her house. Children, who weeks ago would have been running and jumping, were huddled near each other playing marbles, lethargic and with sunken eyes. Was she meant to ask them? Perhaps the culprit had dropped off proclamations in other houses too. But Salha had assumed that he hadn't and that they were being deliberately targeted because of Yaseen's position.

Zamzam kept walking until she glimpsed the river. Ahead of her was the tall woman who sold groundnuts near the Tutti ferry. She was carrying a guffa and hurrying toward the river. Zamzam, too, might as well go to the river. She hadn't found the culprit, hadn't seen anyone who looked as if they had come from the Mahdi's camp.

Instead, the silky water. She had missed it. Carrying heavy pots of water from the river was no longer one of her chores; Salha deemed it too strenuous and unfitting. She did not want her washing clothes at the river, either, and preferred the task to be done at home. The result was that days passed without Zamzam visiting the river.

She greeted it like an old friend. Leaned over it with delight. Blue breeze, that familiar smell. She was like Salha poring over her books. The river was Zamzam's book, and she could read it. Today, it revealed stories of scorched water and bloodied shores. It trilled out warnings instead of familiar songs.

# 22

# Musa

**South of Omdurman, December 1884–January 1885**

We lapped up against the edges of Khartoum. We pressed at it from all sides—those of us who had traveled from Al-Ubayyid along the west side of the White Nile, those of us who had come up along its eastern side, the tribes on the south bank of the Blue Nile, those on the north. In places, we faced each other across the water, rivers in which no government steamer was now safe to travel. We heaved forward and squeezed the city. Thousands and thousands of us. Any vantage point—up on a camel, up a tree, up a hillock—and the sight was a glory. Banners swaying in their different colors, weapons bright in the sun, the thrill of the war drums, the cry of the great horn, and late at night the stomp of a war dance round a fire.

Energy bristled through the camp. I came across all kinds of people. Too often, there were those who had joined the cause for worldly reasons. For them, the looting of Khartoum was what drove them. The riches they would find, gold bracelets on the plump arms of Egyptian women, stores of grain hoarded by merchants, silver coins hidden in latrines.

This was all they spoke about. Were they afraid of death? No, but they were not eager for the hereafter either. A kind of recklessness pervaded us all. I found myself speaking in the same tones, saying the horsemen of the Mahdi will die for the Mahdi.

Khartoum roused my curiosity. Omdurman was in sight just ahead, but all I could see of Khartoum were the palm trees across the White Nile. When the time came to penetrate it, how would we know where to go? I spent time with people who had been to Khartoum. With a stick, they would draw lines on the sand to show me the layout of the roads and the position of the important buildings. Out of sight was that straight line of the Blue Nile, important because that was the area beloved to the infidels. They built their churches and their mansions overlooking the water, and Gordon's palace was there too. When I asked how one could recognize the palace, I got jeers for a reply. "It's like the one you saw in your dream of Paradise."

I decided to go for a reconnaissance trip. Ideally the water would be low when we attacked so that we could do so with our horses. Now it was still too high though visibly falling with each successive day. I needed to change my clothes to enter Khartoum undetected. To replace my patched jibbah with the kind of clothes I had not worn in years. I needed to leave my flintlock pistol behind. The rest was not difficult.

I was in Khartoum, walking its streets. No one stopped me, no one gave me a second glance. In this city, nothing marked me as suspicious. So, this was where the head of the snake lived. The blind (in every sense of the word) Sheikh Amin Al-Darir who, with the Mahdi among us, still had the impudence to carry the title of distinguished head of Sudan's ulema. His minion and kinsman, Yaseen, who escaped from prison in Al-Ubayyid. The one whose handwriting was on the evil proclamations that drifted our way. A church and not even one church—their flagrant crosses that we would break. They hoarded riches these priests. I tried not to be dazed, not to let my emotions sway me. I walked along the waterfront. I saw the steamers in the river, soldiers boarding carrying guns. I kept my head down.

Suddenly on my right, there was the palace. Its arched entrance, guards in spectacular uniform. I counted twenty-five of them. Majestic columns, an extravagance of gardens, greenery, and flowers. I wanted to destroy all this indecent luxury, to wipe it off the face of the earth. No doubt Gordon was inside. They told me he had sharp blue eyes.

I looked up and there was a khawaja officer on the roof looking through a telescope. Full elaborate uniform, the flag of the khedive flying above him. He moved back and I could now see his full face. He looked straight down at me. Why? But no, I was wrong, his attention was on the street boys who began to shout out his name. So that was him for sure. He rewarded the children with an indulgent smile and a wave. They needed more than this offhand kindness. When we liberated Khartoum, they would have a better life. We would take them into our homes, we would feed and educate them. We were one and the same with them, flesh and blood, not foreign rulers. Our Mahdi would live until the end of time.

I wondered how far Gordon could see with that telescope of his. One of the guards shouted at me. I was lingering and inviting suspicion. I had to move on. I cast a glance at the palace again. Such a building would have a ladder going up to the top level. Another or even more than one at different sides, leading to the roof. I had climbed ladders before, plenty of times, it was an easy thing to do.

The Mahdi had forbidden excessive displays of grief; women were not allowed to keen loudly, tear their clothes, or roll in the dust, and instead should be gratified that their loved ones were martyred. But this was exactly what they did when the news came of the defeat of our forces in the north. They had fought the British invaders in Abu Klea and the outcome was devastation for us. The invaders were here on our lands, heading toward us with rifles and machine guns to rescue Gordon and destroy us. The courage of our fighters had not been enough this time, even though the famous impenetrable British square was breached. In full gallop, with bullets whizzing around him, an elderly fighter reached the center, reined in his horse, dismounted, and planted his standard. He was martyred, of course, but we would avenge him, we must, we would not shirk or take fright.

In the following days, in one tense meeting after the other, we debated whether we should march north and meet the invading English army or focus on taking Khartoum. We decided to complete what we had already started.

After the dawn prayer, the Mahdi told us in the loudest voice, in the most earnest of tones, that if God grants us victory there were men in Khartoum who should not be killed—Gordon and Sheikh Amin Al-Darir. Gordon, because he wanted to exchange him for Urabi, whom the British had exiled, and Sheikh Amin Al-Darir, because he

wanted to win him to our cause. Then he said, "If a man bars
his house against you, do not kill him. If a man throws down
his weapons, do not kill him." I interrupted him, calling
out, "My master, in previous battles we had known them to
sometimes pick up their weapon from the ground after we
move on and then strike or shoot us from behind." He said,
"Whoever you encounter in the line of fire, kill him. Now
swear allegiance to me unto death." We swore to obey his
commands, we swore by God, and we swore by him that we
would not worship any but God, that we would not steal,
that we would not commit adultery, that we would not flee
from holy war, and that we would renounce this world and
choose the next.

In the first shrug of dawn, he raised his sword and pointed
it toward Khartoum. Flags unfurled, horns blew, and we
sprang forward. From across the White Nile and from south
of the city. We marched in from Burri and sailed in boats
from the north shore of the Blue Nile. On horses and on
foot. With spears and with guns. Banners in the cool dawn
breeze. We waded through the mud of the White Nile, leaping over the shoulders and backs of each other, nimble, able,
light on our feet. Trampling on those comrades who had
fallen, those stuck in the mud; it could not be helped. Once
the momentum was launched, nothing could stop us. Our
enemies surrendered at the sight of us emerging from the
dark. An unstoppable force, out for their blood. At Kalakla
gate, the Egyptian colonel stripped off his uniform and fled
into the desert. We could barely see but the way was clear.
So little resistance, even though Abu Klea must have boosted
their hopes. True, there were pockets of bravery here and

there, staunch resistance from soldiers who fought until their death. But it was nothing that we could not take in our stride.

I galloped through the streets of Khartoum, ahead of the others without stopping, determined to reach the palace before anyone else. When I tied up my horse, I saw that the sky had turned pale. But the palace courtyard was dark, and I stabbed two guards who fell without a fight. One did not hear me coming up behind him and the other was asleep at his post. Inside the palace there were lanterns everywhere, candles flickering, shadows falling. Only the stairs were in darkness; I crept up on all fours. I could hear someone moving upstairs. It was Gordon and he aimed his gun at me.

I ducked. My fingers clutched the step, my knees against my chest. The bullet pierced the wall behind me. I shuffled sideways and pressed my shoulder against the wall. I looked up and I could see him in detail because all the light was behind him. Would he come down the stairs or move back to the roof? He yelled out to the guards, and some called back to him. But our men had already reached them and behind me rose the sounds of fighting. He was all alone. No one was coming to his rescue. His eyes must have adjusted to the light. I could see him looking down at me. I needed to clamber up the stairs to reach him before the others did, to make sure I was the one who captured him and dragged him alive to the Mahdi.

I could hear the commotion coming closer, the palace guards putting up a fight. I could hear the cries of the servants and telegram clerks. I moved up into the light, nearer to him. No doubt he could see me now. If he shot, he would not miss. Instead, he sneered and made a gesture with his hand as if to say, "Stand up." Stairs were meant to be climbed standing up. They were not like ladders. They were not like rocks. His life was at risk, but he still had time for contempt. He would kill me while laughing at my backwardness. But I shot him first. Taken aback, he reached for his sword and lunged at me, lost his balance, and tumbled down the stairs.

I pressed my back to the wall and when his body was close, I kicked him. He continued to fall, cutting himself on his own sword, smearing the steps with blood, until he thudded at the landing. I could hear my comrades talking about him, speculating on his identity, confirming it, angry at whoever killed him. The Mahdi wanted to exchange him for Urabi. I did not want them to see me. It was getting light outside. The lanterns were dimming. I peered over the side and saw two men, one still clutching his standard, both kneeling next to the body. They rolled it over on its back. They searched the pockets, took out a watch and some coins. Then one of them brought out his sword and with one hack severed the head. He put it in his leather bag and rushed off. He would ride away and take it to the Mahdi.

In a daze, I made my way down the stairs, which were now swarming with fighters. Carrying axes and daggers, with sheer strength and bare hands, they were intent on razing the building to the ground. I pushed my way through clouds of dust and smoke. Outside everything was visible in the first morning light. Up above me, some men were climbing the roof and pulling themselves up the flagpole to bring down the flag of the Turks. One of them fell, right next to me. I heard the crack of his back and his scream of agony. It was drowned out by the shouts of victory that rose when the flag was dragged down and torched.

I joined the flow of fighters moving along the waterfront. Dead bodies filled the sides of the road. Smoke rose in the air. Bullets zinged and houses were raided, with emirs planting their flag and staking their claim. Daybreak and the first rays of the sun flared up the river. In sailing boats, our fighters were landing on Tutti Island. Boatloads of them overpowering the garrison there.

The cheering crowd surged, and I was with them. Here, along the river, were where the rich lived, the Christian missionaries and the Levantine merchants. They thought they owned this city! For the fighters around me, looting was the reason they were here. I could see it on their faces. Excitement when they seized stores of grain hoarded by greedy merchants, stashed gold and silver, women's ornaments. Slaves betraying their masters. Neighbors telling on each other. I did not stop for any of this. I kept on moving. News flitted through the crowd. Burri fort had been taken, all the bashi-bazouks holding out until they were killed down to the last man. Mogran fort had put up the white flag of surrender, but no one took notice. The fort was attacked, and every soldier was killed. The palace, the government buildings, and the Austrian consulate—all ours now. This rich city, this symbol of foreign rule and oppression. Khartoum had been captured in less than two hours. The time from dawn to sunrise. Victory over the infidels. Victory over the foreigners.

The crowd veered away from the river, they dispersed down alleys and around neighborhoods. Homes were broken into, and I could hear children crying and women screaming as they fought for their honor. We were already breaking the oath we had sworn to the Mahdi, unable to restrain ourselves. Like my failure to capture Gordon alive. I did not want to be in anyone's house. I wanted to fight outdoors, I wanted to raise my sword in the morning air. Suddenly the mosque was in front of me. It was surrounded by our fighters and those who had been praying fajr inside. "If God grants you victory, Sheikh Amin Al-Darir must not be killed," the man next to me murmured, and I saw the blind man wearing the Al-Azhar robe. No one would dare kill him now, not in plain sight. But the others with him had no protection, they had not been singled out by the Mahdi. We did not owe them any special treatment. One of them was Yaseen. I started to shout, "That's him. The culprit who wrote down those evil lies with his own hand, the proclamations against the Mahdi, the fatwa full of deceit. Infidel, traitor. Down with the evil scholars! Those who supped at the sultan's table." I pushed through and raised my sword. "Cursed be your day, Yaseen." He looked straight at me, and I saw the recognition in his eyes.

# 23

# Yaseen

**Khartoum, January 26, 1885**

Musa. I see him in the crowd. He is holding his sword up in the air. He is forcing his way toward me. I had not thought of him in months, pushed his memory away. But he is heading toward me now and I cannot run away, the crowd is too thick. I edge away from Sheikh Amin. I push my way through the crowd as much as I can and back to the mosque. But Musa is bearing down on me, moving faster than I can get away. The crowd heaves, this way and that. It is chaos. There are those of us who had just come out of the mosque and there are them. The crowd starts parting for him, as much as they can part. I can hear him now saying my name. It rings out in the morning air, and I repeat it. *Yaseen. By the Wise Qur'an. You are truly one of the Envoys. On a straight path* . . . I start reciting the surah in my mind, like we had just recited it in the mosque. It is the only weapon I have. He is bearing down on me. Will no one fight on my side? Will no one stand in his way or stop him from what he is about to do?

I am in the courtyard of the mosque, near the ablution area. This is as far as I can go. My way is blocked, men pushing me back toward him. His words are clear now, I can hear him. He is going to kill me because of what I had written. I brace myself for death and the memories of those past days at Sheikh Amin's house blaze and whirl—learned discussions and the new intimacy arising from the circumstances we were in, the surprise of Ishaq's visit and how upset I got when he said, "I came for my sister." All this, what I am, what mattered to me, is going to end. I surrender to the pain of the threshold. The threshold into eternal mercy, to lie down with my deeds, to sleep without moving, to wake for my judgment. Then I am snagged back by the wretchedness of my orphaned son, the grief of those who love me, and sadness shifts like a dark cloud. I entrust them to the Most High. I must not let them hold me back, they will be looked after. I am not irreplaceable. I am not essential. They will manage, they are strong. I can go. They will know that I could not stay. They will know that I wrote down the truth, every single word of it. I don't regret it. It was a privilege to speak justice and denounce falsehood. To say that, based on the evidence, the true Mahdi is yet to come.

"Infidel," Musa shouts, and most of the crowd now is on his side. They repeat the word. "No," I shout. "I am not an infidel." And the irony does not escape me, that here I am, in front of the mosque I just prayed fajr in, and I bear witness that there is no god except Allah, and I bear witness that Muhammad is His Messenger. I feel the force of his fury knock the wind out of me. He is clutching me now, swiping off my turban. He has a hold on me, pulling me by my robe. He grabs my arm, my right arm, the hand that held the pen, moved over paper, the hand that did the writing. He raises his sword and brings it down. Pain upon pain upon pain.

# 24

# Zamzam

**Khartoum, January 26, 1885**

She opened her eyes to the sound of gunshot, more persistent than of late. It was time to get up. The women's quarter was stirring to life. Zamzam, Salha, Yaseen, and Rustom had been in Sheikh Amin's house for a week. It had been Salha's idea to move in with her uncle. She started talking about it after the two elder brothers took their families and went to Omdurman. Every recent proclamation of the Mahdi had guaranteed safety to Sheikh Amin. If they became part of his household, they, too, she reckoned, would be safe. Today, Salha finished praying and then leapt up to clutch her baby. Suddenly Zamzam was subjected to countless orders. Bolt the door, run to the neighbors to see what's happening, where are the knives, we should arm ourselves. Instead, Zamzam dragged an angareeb near the wall and, balancing on it, she could see the fighters with their spears and banners, swarming the neighborhood, barging through doors.

Fear gripped her. This was all familiar. Just like Al-Ubayyid. She knew what would happen next. She knew what they would do to her. They were here now, already it was too late, they were at the door. Salha was standing barring their way. She was actually speaking to these men! Clutching the baby and having a conversation, reasoning with them. Saying, "Do you know whose house this is? You have no right coming in here, no right that is legal or religious." The fighters looked at her, incredulous. A woman with a baby on her hip, addressing them as if she had nothing to fear. But Zamzam, still standing on the angareeb, a live target, had everything to fear. Zamzam knew better. Salha's voice rose. "Don't you dare lay a finger on me! Get yourself out of our home! Out. I am not to be touched, not a hair. Don't you dare come near me!"

Zamzam fled. She jumped down and backed out of the women's quarters, through the men's, into the alley. Her heart was pounding, a long scream in her throat. She cowered and ran. She covered her ears with her hands. To stop herself from hearing herself, her own mutterings of terror, her own squeals. She ran through the streets, keeping close to the houses, slipping past the fighters, willing them to not see her. She ducked, hands reached out for her, a thumb poked her groin, she elbowed away anyone who pressed close. They did not persist. On a day like this, in this hour of triumph, they could do better; their sights were set higher. One of them grabbed her by the waist, lifted her up, she swiped at him and kicked; he laughed and dropped her. She screamed her way through their shouts of victory, through the thud of doors breaking down, shots and screams. Where was she going? She was going home. Home? To Yaseen's home.

Here it was and she dashed inside, bolted the door behind her, ran straight to the zariba. Not a single animal left, the last of the chickens had been taken with them to Sheikh Amin's house. The haystack was still here. She dived into it, as deep as she could go, into the smell of dust and straw, until she was completely covered. She crouched rigid, shook, stifled sobs, caught her breath. She could hear her pulse beating in her ears, the sounds of the streets distant. They will come in here because they had not already come, and they will find her in the haystack. Or they will not come at all. Or they will come and not find her in the haystack. She will be safe here, all by herself, crouched in the dark, dusty hay. She mustn't whimper, even if they raided the house, even if one of them stuck a spear through the haystack. But a spear thrust could kill her, and she would die here, right here. She should have gone to Omdurman with Ishaq. He knew this was coming. How delighted she had been to see him! Was that yesterday or the day before—she could not think straight. Carrying himself like a fine young man, strong and reliable. In his company, she had felt the warmth of kinship. It made her sad that he could not remember their village or its name; he did not know where it was. Even his original name, Bol, was something that she needed to remind him of. They should have always been together, never torn apart. He wanted her to come with him, to return to Halima's household, return to how she first was when Yaseen left her in Al-Ubayyid all those years ago. No, for sure she did not want that. Nor did she approve of his ambitions to fight in the Mahdi's cause and how he wasn't as young as everyone said! His mind had been addled she told him, and they had argued until he went back to Omdurman in a huff.

She was trembling less. She could not spread out, but she could make herself more comfortable, ease into this position, sink into the straw. She could ignore what was happening outside. It was impossible to know what was happening to Salha now, what was happening to Yaseen. What about Touma? Everyone in the city. Would it be like Al-Ubayyid? She was dozing, how could she be, the air was stale filtered through the dusty straw. She wanted to stand up, but it wouldn't be safe. Better to close her eyes, let her mind drift.

A bang so close, voices right next to her. She jerked into full consciousness, terror flooding her body again. No, they were not here but right behind the wall, in the neighbor's house. She knew these neighbors, their names. She had been in their house more than once, running errands. Now a commotion, she could barely make out the words. Screams. One of the men must have lied about hiding money; gold coins were found in the latrine as well as hoarded grain. The liar was shot there and then, his wife and daughter screaming, dragged away as captives. All this Zamzam could hear and piece together, sounds without sights, scenes she could imagine, did not want to imagine. That all this could happen on an ordinary morning and make it no longer ordinary. The cool January breeze, the sun rising over the trees, babies needing milk, a woman in labor. A day unlike any other day. And would this house be next, would they come here and search, drag her out of the straw and then. Then it would be like Al-Ubayyid for sure. She stuck her fist in her mouth to muffle a scream.

A banging on the door. A banging as if someone were asking to come in. Asking not barging, not invading, not taking over. She stiffened. A man's voice, "People of the house, Sheikh Yaseen has been injured." She stood up. She darted to the door, hesitated. Again, the knocking, more urgent. "People, open up, your son is here needing you."

When she opened the door, she saw him propped up by two fighters. He was barely able to stand, clothes bloodied, groaning. Only when he was inside, laid on an angareeb, did she understand what had happened to him, what he had lost. She must stop the bleeding as Touma had taught her, with boiled butter or coffee. The former was unavailable, the latter must do and there was not much of it either. She had to manage somehow, running back and forth.

The Mahdist fighter who had been knocking on the door planted his standard in front of the house. He spoke to Yaseen as if he knew him and asked her about Yaseen's brothers by name. She recognized him as the handsome emir who had given her the dollars in Burri when she assisted his wife in giving birth to twins. All this made her trust him. He did not, though, stop his men from searching the house. When they did not find any hidden valuables or hoarded goods, they left, apart from two who stood on guard outside to prevent anyone from coming in.

Zamzam and Isma'il nursed Yaseen through a difficult day and night. The worst part was cauterizing the stump after the coffee failed to stop the bleeding. Isma'il left the house and came back. He brought food and vinegar to soak the dressing. When Zamzam, at one point distraught and losing confidence, asked him to find a doctor, he said he did not think it was safe. She had to manage the best that she could.

The following morning Yaseen was weak but lucid, able to eat and speak. She changed his dressing. So far, the wound was clean. He asked her about Salha, and she told him the little that she knew. It was Isma'il who brought them more up-to-date and reliable information. Salha and all the women in Sheikh Amin's house had been taken to Omdurman. They were distributed among some families there. They were well looked after.

"Made captives?" asked Yaseen.

"No," said Isma'il. "The Mahdi ordered that any woman with a husband would be returned to him. The others will be placed with families."

Zamzam could see that this somewhat reassured Yaseen. He did not mention his arm and instead wanted news of the city. She left them together in the room and went and sat outside the diwan. Unlike yesterday, there were no sounds from the street. All was quiet and she could hear Isma'il's voice. Yesterday, the looting and killing had continued until the Mahdi put a stop to it in the late afternoon. All the citizens of Khartoum were now ordered to evacuate the city. Why? The Mahdi was moving his capital to Omdurman. He did not want the infidel's capital, the place that represented Turkish interests and foreign power.

She overheard Isma'il saying, "When you feel stronger, you, too, will have to go."

Yaseen did not reply. Instead, he said, "Thank you for all you have done for me."

"Why the formality! This is what friends are for."

"Even when these friends are on opposite sides." He sounded teary now, his voice muffled. She wanted to go back inside, to hold him and to mourn with him. Propriety held her back.

Isma'il, it seemed, was not willing to share his grief. He said, "I told you to join us. Time and again, I sent word to you, but you were stubborn. It is not too late. I can arrange for you to meet the Mahdi and I can intercede on your behalf, give you the chance to beg for his forgiveness and join his cause. In fact, he will be meeting your Sheikh Amin today."

"What I want you to do is help me escape."

Isma'il said, "There is a rumor that you are dead. This could be to your advantage and if you like, I can confirm it. But you are not yet fit for a long journey. Tomorrow, we must get you to Omdurman. I will find a trustworthy boatsman. Stay in hiding there and then in time we can plan your escape."

The following morning, after a more restful night, she helped him into the patched jibbah Isma'il had provided. Reaching the river, they saw what they had wanted to see these past months, what Gordon was straining for as he pointed his telescope north—soldiers from the relief expedition on the *Bordein* and the *Tel el Hoween*. English soldiers in their bright-red uniforms, Sudanese and Egyptian soldiers in their tarbush and brown uniforms. From the shores, the Mahdists opened fire. The steamers returned with heavy artillery but not much enthusiasm. It must have been obvious to them that the city had been captured by the Mahdi, all the smoke and damaged buildings, the crescent and star no longer flying over the palace.

Zamzam and Yaseen took cover under a tree. She thought she saw Robert on the *Bordein*, a man who stood out because he was not in uniform—just a glimpse and then he disappeared below deck. The steamers turned around Tutti Island and made their way back north, down the river. From the British perspective, the citizens of Khartoum were not worth saving; it had never been about them. If Gordon had surrendered, thousands of their lives would have been spared, but it had never been about them. She felt Yaseen leaning his weight on her. She must be strong and reliable for his sake. Cheers of victory rose all along the shore. The enemy retreating, the British skulking away with their tail between their legs, the foreign invaders pushed out. There must be more of these troops downriver; this was just a token force to check out the situation. All of them would now retreat knowing that the Mahdi was likely to pursue them.

Omdurman was a labyrinth of alleys, houses built from rammed earth. Zamzam and Yaseen got lost trying to locate the family's new home. Not wanting to draw attention to themselves and especially to Yaseen, they did not ask for directions. It was almost evening by the time they arrived, fatigued and hungry. Gratitude that Yaseen was alive (the family, too, had heard the rumors) and concern for his injury. The significant absence of Salha and Rustom. It was then that Zamzam allowed herself to let go, to sit on the floor and burst into tears. But even then, they must be careful. They must not make the neighbors suspicious, and although the Mahdi had ordered an end to the fighting, his men still roamed the streets and some of them were unruly. They could barge in at any minute. Word must not go around that Yaseen was alive.

A pit was dug in the ground to hide him. It was deep enough for him to stand up and just wide enough for him to lie down on his side, knees drawn up. Until the situation settled, he must spend the whole day down there, the rim covered in straw. Only at night could he come out for exercise and company. He was gaining his strength, doing more with his remaining hand, but still unusually quiet, as if distracted by complex thoughts.

Zamzam, who gave Yaseen his meals, helped him with his ablutions and continued to look after his injury, waited for him to confide in her. Inside the airless pit, so physically near to him, intimately involved, she did not find the closeness she desired. He acknowledged all her help, thanked her in a way that was natural and informal, but still there was a distance between them. His repetition of astaghfirullah confused her. This was not because she could not understand the words, but it did not make sense to her why he, the victim of injustice, was the one seeking forgiveness. When she asked him, he said, "I should be welcoming Allah's will with more grace."

She did not know how to reply. Salha would have known the right thing to say. But she was not here. Her absence, too, was part of Allah's will. Her absence and Zamzam's presence.

He did not need her to reply. He went on, "I must evaluate the options that I now have, what I can do for a living. And we can't stay here forever. I am thinking of where we could go."

The "we" gave her a rush of confidence. She said, "We can go back south to my father's village."

He was quiet. She wanted him to talk about their shared past, to tease or flirt with her. Instead, he just said, "Yes, we could do that."

A visit from Halima and Ishaq improved his mood. Halima was now in on the secret, too, and reassured them that people did indeed believe that Musa had killed Yaseen. Better still, Musa himself never denied that he had done so. Halima had aged since Zamzam saw her last. The resemblance between her and her mother, Fatimah, was pronounced. It comforted Yaseen to see his sister. It was evening and safe for him to leave the pit. The whole family could gather and although the house they were in was much smaller and more basic than their house in Khartoum, the occasion felt very much like old times. Ishaq's presence and his status as Halima's son enhanced Zamzam's position. He sat between her and Halima and she felt proud of all his achievements, which Halima was enumerating. She could also tell that Yaseen was enjoying the chance to quiz Ishaq on his learning. Has he really memorized all that Halima claimed he had? Let's put the lad to the test!

Another boy would have been nervous, but Ishaq was confident. Yaseen commented on this, too, and for a short while he sounded like his old self. It was Halima who changed the mood by mentioning Salha and Rustom. She would visit them, she said, and bring Rustom to see his father. "Must you have given him that wretched Turkish name!" she said to her brother. But these were the only words of reproach that she uttered. It was too late for any arguments or persuasion. Everyone had picked their side long ago. Now they would cling to the connections forged through Fatimah's womb. Family bonds stronger than political divisions.

He could not hold his son properly. Not properly in his arms. He was afraid to drop him, so wriggly a toddler Rustom had become. Halima brought him for a visit during the day. The time when Yaseen had to remain underground, away from the eyes of the neighbors, far from the open door lest anyone passing by in the street saw him. But Rustom did not mind the pit, he found it exciting and dug his fist in the cool earth. Zamzam wanted Yaseen's smile to change to a laugh. She wanted him to lift his head, to talk louder and be himself. Halima had given him a letter from Salha. He did not read it straight away and instead folded it away in his pocket.

"Salha asked for you," Halima said to Zamzam. "Come with me now when I take Rustom back to her."

They walked through Omdurman, Zamzam's first trip outside the house. They passed the open area of the market where vegetables and spices were on display and booths sold cooked food. She saw new arrivals building huts and families in the meantime making do with the shade afforded by bits of cloths stretched out on sticks.

They entered an alley, its entrance full of Mahdist fighters. Guards who were relaxed, some stretched out and others sitting, but their weapons were close at hand. The house Salha was in was wider than any Zamzam had ever seen. The women's quarter was full of women of all ethnicities and their children. A sense of disorder pervaded the place—unwashed cooking utensils, a baby with a rash screaming unattended, the carcass of a cat raised a stench. An Egyptian woman was scratching herself uncontrollably. A child bride was waiting for the henna on her feet to set, fingering the new jewelry on her arm. Some women were standing grinding millet;

several sat around cooking pots. Salha was in a room deep in the back. There was another woman there, asleep on an angareeb; she looked as if she was in her second trimester. In keeping with mourning customs, Salha had undone her braids. Her hair, frizzy and heavy, stuck out in a triangular shape around her face. Stripped of her jewelry, she looked unkempt and subdued, the skin thin and stretched on her face. Zamzam smiled at the reunion between mother and child. Only a few hours apart and yet they both reached out for each other to fulfill the most natural of needs. Salha's voice was still authoritative, though her eyes were watchful. When other women came into the room, she did not speak much. When Halima got up to say her goodbyes, Salha asked Zamzam to stay longer. It made her nervous thinking she must find her way home again by herself, but she, too, wanted to spend more time with Salha.

Anxious not to be overheard, Salha whispered, "Did Yaseen say anything when he read my letter?"

Zamzam shook her head. He might have read it by now but until she and Halima left, he had not opened it. "Be careful what you say. We can be overhead," Salha said.

"She is fast asleep," Zamzam said referring to the pregnant woman.

"There's two more of us outside helping," said Salha. "All widows together. This is the widows' room."

"Oh! Don't say that about yourself!"

"That's what they believe about me. They must. If the truth is out, I will be one."

A young girl walked into the room. She was about ten, dressed incongruously in a long silk dressing gown no doubt looted off the back of a European woman from Khartoum. She headed straight to Rustom, who smiled and reached out to her. "They are saying there is a Turkish infidel baby here," the girl said.

Salha snapped, "Does he look Turkish to you!"

The girl looked perplexed.

Salha glared at her. "Go and find someone your own age to play with. Go!"

The girl backed out of the room, stumbling over the long train of the flowery gown.

Salha started whispering again. "They are giving me time to mourn. It is not difficult to do that. I've lost my father and two of my brothers. My mother and sisters are still in Tutti. I don't know how they are faring. I found out today that my uncle died of a broken heart. They forced him to bow before the Mahdi, they pushed him on the ground so that everyone would see him groveling and know how magnanimous the Mahdi was! It finished him and then the Mahdi refused to lead his funeral prayer, declaring him a hypocrite."

Zamzam squeezed her arm. "We must get you out of here."

Salha shook her head. "There is no way. I've seen what happens to those who try and escape. There is no mercy. After the mourning period, I am to be married off to a high-ranking judge in the new administration. He is the head of this household and all of us women have been placed with him. This is the plan, for me, much better than for the others. And that is why I asked Yaseen to divorce me." Her voice broke and even though Zamzam gasped and shook her head, Salha went on. "Yes, he must do that for me otherwise I will be married to him and living with another man in sin!

Without a divorce this will be my awful position. There is no other solution to this predicament. Yaseen will not fail me. Believe me, I've thought about it day and night. Day and night, I have thought of nothing else. And he, too, must be coming to the same conclusion. I am sure."

Zamzam's mind was in a whirl. Is that what he was reading now? *Yaseen, divorce me.* Is that what he must have guessed to be in the letter?

"No," she said. "You must come with us. We are going to my father's village. We will be safe there. We can't leave you behind."

Salha said, "I don't have the courage for exile. I need to be among my people. The new rulers are allowing me to keep my social position, placing me with a compatible family. I must be grateful for this. It could be much worse. No, I can't make a run for it and live where no one knows me."

"I will help you. I will look after you."

Salha looked down and whispered, "Can't you see that this is an opportunity for you? Something that you've always wanted."

Can't you see? Can't you see?

Zamzam walked back through a town that was beginning to bloom as a new capital in an independent state. Immigrants pouring in, the families and tribes of those who had borne the rages of this war, who had paid the prices for victory. People who had always lived at the bottom were now rising to seize their rightful share of power, to have their stake in trade and administration. Nomadic tribes settling in Omdurman, rubbing shoulders with the riverine tribes who had always had the advantage over them. Now they were here to share their settled lifestyle, watered by the two rivers. Can't you see? *Divorce me, Yaseen.* Where was her opportunity? It shimmered ahead of her, like a mirage, but it might not be a mirage, it might be silver. Salha would not exaggerate, did not speak for the sake of speaking. Can't you see?

Zamzam saw Omdurman. It was heaving hot with hopes, heady with tomorrow. A town confident in its foundation, ready to be built. And here they were, in their thousands, armies of victory. She was not one of them, but she was like them. She was also one of the lowly rising, one of the poor benefiting, one of the featherweight children of this land, thrust up by this shake-up, loosened, and made free to stand up and grab what was there on offer, what she had always wanted.

She lost her bearings and found herself by the river. This was not the White Nile she had swum in as a child; this was not the Blue Nile that had comforted her in Khartoum. Instead, this was a union of the two, after the confluence in Mogran, one huge, vibrant flow, unrecognizable. Water that was more than water. And here she was wading in, like she had always waded in, to listen to the language of this river, what it wanted her to know. She could not face Yaseen right now, not yet. The world was rearranging itself around them, their lives rotating to fit this new structure. She would be the able one looking after him now; she would be the one taking him to her home and not the opposite. She was ready. The river's song had always been that she would follow him, but now a more compelling power was taking them back where they started. They would build on what already existed. Beginnings that did not have the chance to flourish, were suppressed by circumstances, strangled but not killed. Alive enough to be rekindled, nudged back to life. He might not be as bewildered as her. He might have already figured out what she was still absorbing.

She had never been shy. Why start now? There was still to come the adventure of their escape, details to work out. Such as circumventing the massive camp outside Omdurman. Such as traveling in the opposite direction as everyone else. They might not make it, after all. Many hurdles to overcome before she could be free and laughing in his arms.

They would have to take a donkey for the first part of the journey, so as not to arouse suspicion. Only after they traversed the camp would they find one of Isma'il's men waiting for them with a camel. Traveling by night, the camel's hoofs on the soft sand, that miraculous creation Yaseen had often talked to her about. How swollen with durra and water the camel's body would become, splendid and sturdy, so eager to run that it would need reining in. Padding over miles of sand, scrubland, galloping and galloping without needing a rest. And then over time, without food and water, its bulk would shrink, its neck become slender, its belly deflated, its movement sluggish. They would need to rest under familiar skies, look up and tell the time by the position of the stars, huddle from the cold under a sheepskin rug. They would be gentle with each other.

# 25
# Salha

My beloved son, I want you to know why I took this decision.
I didn't take it lightly. It burned me to let you go, to send you
away into an unknown world. But I would not have done
this had I not believed it was the best thing for you. To be
with your father. To grow up in his care. I know you can't
read this letter. I don't even know how to send it to you.
Insha'Allah, one day in the future, your uncles will resume
their trade and then I can give it to them, and it will reach
you. I feel I must explain everything. You see, I will not know
anytime soon if I did the right thing or not. Only when you
grow up and become a man able to raise his head high can
I be vindicated. I could not bear for you to be referred to as
an orphan. It hurt me immensely. I did not want you to be
scorned. You, an innocent baby, were subjected every day to
a torrent of abuse. An infidel, a Turk, son of an infidel, son
of the Mahdi's enemy—that is what they said about you. I
did not want you growing up hearing lies about your father,
believing these lies just to survive. I did not want for you the

secondary status of growing up in a stepfather's house, always lower in rank than his own children. That is why I sent you away with your father and Zamzam.

It was not an easy decision. First, the nebulous idea gaining a hook in my mind. This happened after the divorce. Even though the divorce was in secret, even though it was at my request and initiation, even though everyone around continued to believe I was widowed, its effect on me was profound. I will not talk about the pain of being separated from your father. Firstly, because I wish to keep it private, and secondly, it is your father or your stepmother who will read this letter to you—assuming I one day find a way of sending it and it reaches you—and I wish to spare them embarrassment. But as I said, first the idea of sending you with them was just an idea. Then, almost with disbelief, I weighed it, turned it round and round. It seemed extreme, unprovoked. Your father never once demanded that I do this. This was because, no doubt, he did not wish to cause me additional heartache; he was anxious about the safety of the journey and did not want to jeopardize you in any way. It is understandable. I asked myself if I had the courage to go ahead with it. I prayed for guidance. I prayed istikhara and waited for the signs.

The signs came. You refused my breast. Just like that, you lost interest, you weaned yourself. Ever since the day Khartoum was captured, my milk had been thin, my breasts floppy and reluctant to fill up. You would suck and suck and find little, get bored, and give up. This happened several times until I was only nursing you at night to calm you before you slept. I must add that we were never left hungry. From the moment we came to Omdurman, food was sufficient. Basic, but enough and you were eating solids well, encouraged by the other children around you. With time, my milk would have come back, I expected it to do so. But you weaned yourself. Just like that. Almost overnight, you did not need me anymore. This was the first sign.

Then I overheard the guards. They were probably joking, but how could I be sure? They might not have actually done it, but I was certainly not going to give them the chance. The "infidel Turkish baby," they said. "Let's toss him in the river!" Do you think I was quiet? Or that I was afraid of them? I gave them a piece of my mind and they did hang their heads in shame. Still, their words chilled me. This was the second sign.

Then finally, what made my mind up for me was the fever spreading among the children. At the time we did not know what it was. Fever and a rash, raised spots all over the body. It turned out to be smallpox. The pregnant widow, who had been my companion since we arrived, succumbed to it and died, but that was after I had kissed and squeezed you goodbye and gave you to your aunt Halima to take to your father.

After she took you, I could not breathe. Everyone assumed that the pox had got you; it was common at that time, children of all ages succumbing to it. After I gave you to Halima, I took to my bed. It was the separation from you, not the pox. And to think that I brought it on myself. It was as if I could hear you crying for me, whimpering even though Zamzam was trying to distract you. I tortured myself with thoughts of the new bride too enamored to care for my son. I pictured you neglected and uncared for. I told myself that I had made a mistake, taken the wrong decision. There were times when I thought I should run away and join you. Or come clean and confess everything. I weakened. In the middle of the night, unable to sleep, I weakened. When I watched other children playing. What was odd was that I could hear your voice clearly. I could feel you in my arms. But I reminded myself that I was making a sacrifice for you. For your well-being. I took comfort in the story of Moses's mother, how she put her baby son in a basket. His life was at risk from Pharaoh's soldiers. How the basket floated down the river until it reached the palace and baby Moses found a new mother. I repeated these verses from the Qur'an to myself, time and again. They helped to stabilize me through all the doubts and tossing and turning.

I want you to know all this. I pray for you every day. I long for the time when we will be united again.

Your uncles are resuming their trading journeys to the south, and they will take this and look out for your father. What joy it will be to hear any news about you. Any news. I need reassurance that I made the right decision in sending you away from me. You have left a wide vacancy in my life, time sits heavy on me, the days pass slowly. Ramadan brought me some relief. Fasting took the edge off my longing for you. I felt courageous and at peace. But I was not able to carry this feeling for long afterward.

During Ramadan there was the shock of the Mahdi's death. He had been ill with a severe fever that came on suddenly, meningitis most likely. He deteriorated so rapidly that when he passed, it was a shock. For a few days his followers were wild with grief and the rest of us holding our breath, hoping the whole order would collapse. Surely, I thought, now people would see clearly that their Mahdi was not the Mahdi. What happened to all the prophecies of him praying in Damascus and Mecca? Did he rule for seven years as the hadith says? And why hasn't the world ended or any of the other signs of the Last Days manifested themselves? I thought of your father often, I thought of my uncle and all those who dared speak the truth. They are vindicated now. They have won the religious argument. But religion was only the outer shell, powerful slogans to attract the poor and the illiterate. Shining rhetoric to whip up support. The Mahdi was never the Mahdi, and this was a revolution happening under our noses and not only a religious deviancy.

Before his death, the Mahdi had appointed his successor. Abdullahi al-Ta'ishi is now the khalifa. He ordered his tribe who are normally nomadic and cattle-owning to move from their ancestral homes and come to Omdurman. This is not new. They have been immigrating steadily since the capture of Khartoum. But now it is government policy. To facilitate the building of new homes for them, Khartoum is being dismantled. Its buildings knocked down and the wood and bricks carried by boats across the river. Against all advice, I went to see it. It was my first outing after the end of the mourning seclusion. I wanted to see our old home. Instead, I found a place full of ruins, all the elegance destroyed. At times I lost my bearings finding singular walls left standing, bushes and debris where people used to live. I wanted to lament like the Arabian poets did over the ruins of their departed beloveds' homes. I wanted to weep as they did over the ashes of those who had gone, but my eyes were dry. I was full of anger; I was choked by the injustice of it all. I am clearly no poet. All that came out of my mouth was curses. It brought me no comfort, that visit. Just the humiliation of scrambling over rocks and dried mud. My hopes of salvaging some of my uncle's books or your father's books came to nothing. I thought they would have been overlooked by the looters, but Allah only knows whether they burnt them or whether they are being sold in secret.

The Mahdi's death made no difference. The khalifa is intent on following his strategy. He even claims his own visions. Modest ones, with the Mahdi telling him what to do, rather than the Prophet Muhammad, peace be upon him. I am not the only one cynical; there are others who think as I think, who wait as I wait. We keep ourselves to ourselves. Slowly I am making new friends, linking up with old acquaintances, finding out what happened to so-and-so and so-and-so. Some of the stories are hideous, but others fill me will courage. I tell myself it is pitch-dark now, the early part of the night or the middle part, but dawn will surely come. My dawn is seeing your dear face again.


## February 1886

Oh, the joy and gratitude in getting your news. You are well. You are well, your uncles tell me. To think that they were able to hold you, hear your prattle, see your smile. To them it would have been a small pleasure but to me it would have meant the world. My dearest beloved, how delighted I am to hear that you have recently been blessed with a brother. A playmate for you so that you will never be lonely. You must be the best example to him too. You are the older brother, and you must always be protective and caring. Slowly, slowly you will both grow and then you will attend your father's new school and he will certainly expect you to excel. I need not worry about your education; you will be getting the best. Better than anything you would get here and that is a great comfort to me.

Your uncles must have passed on my news too—my marriage and how I have been able to bring my mother over from Tutti to live with me. Her presence brings me comfort and I am blessed with the chance to look after her in her old age. Here is another sign for me that I took the right decision in remaining in Omdurman. I am constantly asking Allah Almighty for reassurance; I am in desperate need to believe that I did the right thing.

Life is stable here. The khalifa has established a special souq for women. This is excellent. A whole area of the regular market set aside for older women to sell and buy. It is a safe and vibrant place where one could buy anything from cloves to yeast to sesame oil. Your grandmother, Fatimah, would have loved it. She was a true merchant at heart!

The khalifa has also spared no expense in building the Mahdi's tomb. From the outside it looks like a rectangular building with a huge cone of the qubba on top. On each corner of the building there is a small minaret. Inside the building is where the Mahdi is buried. The windows are especially pleasing, all oval and identical. I enjoy visiting and seeing it being constructed. It is more elaborate than a traditional qubba and on the very top there is a spear instead of the traditional crescent. This is because of the erroneous belief that the crescent is Turkish! Apart from that, I cannot help but feel a certain pride in it. Unlike the buildings in Khartoum that were of foreign design, this was something designed by us Sudanese. Truly made by the people out of genuine love. Nothing imposed. We are an independent country. That is the result of all the bloodshed. I might have mixed feelings about the methods used to achieve this, but one can never defend foreign occupation. Independence is natural and just.


## November 1888

My dearest son, I send you my love and blessings. I revel in the news that your uncles brought me. I hang on to every word they say. What would I give to accompany them and see you, spend time with you! Your younger sisters, Almassara and Rowda, so close in age, take up all of my time and most of my energy. I do want you to love them and to know that one day you will be an older brother to them. Every mother wants her children united, to bask in the sight of them together, to muse on the likeness between them, to listen to their voices as they talk to each other. I do long for that day. I know that Allah has blessed you with another younger brother. Masha'Allah. I picture the three of you and I know that you all must be a source of happiness for your father too.

Your uncles tell me that you have indeed started learning at your father's kuttab. They tell me about it. How it is the only one in the area and even though the people are not Muslim, they are eager to send their children for an education. This is a good thing, and your father is a patient teacher, I am sure. There is no use in me saying that he is overqualified and that his Al-Azhar education could be put to better use! This is his fate, and we must accept it. I believe that Allah Almighty has chosen your father to spread Islam in the south because he had traded with its men and loved its women.

Who goes from here to the Al-Azhar now! No one. Even Hajj is prohibited. Such a disgrace. A flagrant disobedience to Allah's rules. The khalifa wants total commitment to his holy war. War, war, he and his men can't have enough of it. They are so used to it now; I believe they are fit for nothing else. This country used to be a route for the pilgrims coming from Mauritania, Mali, and Senegal. They traded their way until they reached the boats at Suakin. Where are they now! We are cut off from the rest of the world and scandal upon scandal, the khalifa even wanted to gather the Muslims here for the pilgrimage. Yes, he proposed that they visit the Mahdi's qubba instead of the Prophet's grave in Medina. He wanted to build his own Ka'aba! Thankfully, he was persuaded away from this atrocity by my husband and others in the legislative assembly. There are still those who are enlightened among us and who know deep down that we are in the grip of a travesty but are unable to speak out.

## July 1890

Dear Zamzam, here is the whole story about Ishaq so that you know. It was Halima who told me that he was joining the army heading to invade Egypt. I met her in the women's souq, and she made this announcement very proudly. Of course, I knew that neither you nor Yaseen would approve of this, so I went to speak to Ishaq myself. I tried to dissuade him, but he insisted. I had done Halima an injustice thinking she was the one pushing him to go. Instead, he was the one full of enthusiasm. He said he had missed out on all the other battles because he was too young and now for the first time, he can achieve what he had always longed for. The army set out in the thousands, but things never went well. They were led to believe that the northern villages would come out to join them. Nothing of the sort happened. Ishaq was one of the lucky few who managed to escape. Alhamdulilah for his safe return. He is skin and bones, his eyes huge in his face. With Halima's care and nourishment, he will be fine. Alhamdulilah he was not injured. Truly, Zamzam, not a scratch. Rest and nutrition are all he needs.

As for me, I have not been well. I had a difficult labor and after two weeks lost the child. We buried her in the hoash, and I insisted on having my angareeb dragged next to her. All day I would lie on my side and reach out to stroke the sand over her grave. My little angel in her patch of Paradise. I spent almost the whole of the rainy season in bed but alhamdulilah I am now regaining my strength. Alhamdulilah that my mother is with me. She is a great comfort to me and looked after Almassara and Rowda while I was bedridden. My health is restored now, alhamdulilah. I even forced myself to go to a wedding last week. It was a big one and especially merry. Lots of dancing and I remembered you, Zamzam, and your love for dancing. Your friend Touma was there with her drum. She asked after you, but I could not tell her your news. It is still not safe. There are still people holding on to old grudges. I told her that you ran away on the day Khartoum was liberated and I have never seen you since. Touma looked well. I wish I could say she looked like her old self. Suffice to say she looked well. None of us look like our old selves. War is not kind to a woman's beauty.

After my illness, I resolved to put more effort into my women's classes. Remember when I taught you? Oh the memories of our house in Khartoum. They are vivid in my mind, always. But yes, during my illness I had time to contemplate the shortness of life and how little I had done with mine. I am not naturally a teacher, not like Yaseen; he has the patience for it. I am prone to impatience and abhor stupidity. But I do try, and I have found that I get a better response from older girls. I spend considerable time teaching them their religious duties and how to read the Qur'an. How fortunate I was that my father, may Allah have mercy on his soul, sent me to the kuttab with my brothers. I took it for granted, but it was a rare occurrence. Ignorance is darkness and everyone deserves to be rescued from it. How sad and shocking that women could believe that praying is only for men! Is this not a catastrophe! They see their menfolk heading to the mosque but they have never seen their mothers pray and so they conclude that a woman need not pray at all. Hajj, which women were always keen on (alas no longer a possibility under these rulers) did encourage them to start praying and older women who returned from Hajj continued to pray. But here another erroneous idea took hold, that praying is only for elderly women who have completed their Hajj. I am forever contradicting and haranguing. Now my reputation is that I have a sharp tongue and that I am difficult. Neither endearing qualities but someone must speak the truth.

I have never really told you about my new family. My husband as I explained before is a senior judge. He has always lived in Omdurman and though he is part of this new order now, he was never one of its fervent adherents, nor did he ever fight with the Mahdi. He has grown-up children from his first wife who passed away two years ago. He remarried but did not have children until I gave him Almassara and Rowda. In the women's quarters are my co-wife and her mother, my stepsons' wives and their children, as well as their maternal grandmother, who is very old and troublesome. I understand she is mourning her daughter and resentful of me for taking her place although that is not true because my co-wife is the one who took her place except that she is the silent, passive type very much in the background. The old shrew therefore focuses her ire on me; I am the one who is in her face day and night. She resents that I am now in charge of the women's quarters. But you remember how poor the conditions were and now they are much improved after my efforts. Her resentment is understandable, but really, I feel she is out to destroy me. When I was ill, it even crossed my mind that she had poisoned me! I am extra careful with my nail clippings and any hair that falls from my head. If anyone were ever to intentionally harm me with a spell, it would be her. I am utterly grateful that Rustom is out of her reach. She is nasty to the girls, no doubt about that, but she is mindful of who their father is and would not go so far as to harm them. That would indeed be biting the hand that feeds her! May Allah Almighty protect us all.

## November 1894

I had a sly chuckle today, and you must tell your father. A new Mahdi has appeared in the west. Yes indeed, an imposter and the present regime does see him as such. No one knows his parents; he is young, and they say he just popped out one day from a sycamore tree. Apparently, the tree follows him around and that is why he is called Abu Jameiz. He claims divine access and has gathered a large following around him. They even beat the first army that the khalifa sent out against them. This fresh ardor for a new Mahdi is because people have been let down. Neglecting agriculture in favor of war—how are people expected to live! Fatwas have been issued against this new fake Mahdi denying his claim, and today a stronger, better-equipped army is setting out to destroy him. Certainly, the chickens have come home to roost.

Masha'Allah you are eleven now. I don't know if the years have passed slowly or quickly. As I told you before, Almassara and Rowda have nieces and nephews who are their age or even older. One of them, Ali, my husband's grandson, is the same age as you. I often watch him and think of you. I notice the first time he was sent out on an errand, the first day he went to kuttab, the day of his circumcision ceremony. I like talking to him and imagining that you would talk like that too. Of course, being your mother, I believe you to be superior to him in every way—manners and learning. Every mother must think of her son as the best. This is our prerogative.

## January 1897

It broke my heart that you did not accompany your uncles and return to me. But they are right, and your father is right too; it is still too early. It is still not safe. When you are self-sufficient you can come and set yourself up in Omdurman, live with your aunt Halima or your uncles. We would then see each other regularly. Every day if you wish. You can come to me, and I will go to you.

We recently had a lovely celebration. The wedding of Ishaq to Halima's youngest daughter—your cousin marrying your stepmother's brother. You must be mindful of all these connections, know who is who and how they are related to you and each other. Halima spared no expense, and everyone ate their fill and we enjoyed ourselves for days. Ishaq danced with great enthusiasm carrying his sword, and his bride was all decked out. Still, Omdurman is somewhat gloomy these days I will confess. Everyone worried and mistrustful. The English, under Kitchener, have taken over Dongola, and the speculation is that they are intent on advancing south. They want to take vengeance for what we did to Gordon and Hicks.

# 26

# Christina

She carried the bundle into the library, where the maid had laid the fire. Beneath the layers of cloth, her fingers pressed against hard rectangular edges. This could be what she was looking for—some of her father's overlooked paintings. His death, in his prime and at the height of his creative power, had triggered a spike of interest in his work. A gallery in Glasgow was preparing an exhibition and the owner had asked Christina if there were any more items she could add. In the atelier, apart from the painting of Bennachie Robert had been working on when taken ill, there were five completed commissions ready to be collected and three other works in progress. In the drawing room there was the painting of her mother, which he never intended to sell, and another that never sold—a remake of the peacock in the market in Khartoum, a recreation of the original he had lost in the *Abbas*. All these she had gathered and now came across this in her father's bedroom, hidden deep at the bottom of his cupboard.

She placed the bundle on the desk. It had always been her favorite room. It was warm, and the windows bathed it in autumn's light. Orange leaves on the tree outside brushed the windowpane, complimenting the curtains. She began to peel off the layers of cloth, one by one. The deeper, the dirtier. Fine sand the like of which she had never encountered trickled down to the floor, a thick film smeared her black silk mourning dress. She sneezed. This was what she had hoped for, a portfolio. Large with a stiff cover, it must have been black at the time and now was a dull charcoal, brittle under her fingers. It almost creaked when she lifted it up and there, she could tell straight away, was one of her father's best works. It was like receiving a message from him, kind words, his loving smile. It was like she was a child again and from across the sea, from a land far, far away, from the depth of the desert, he had sent her sketches of monkeys and parakeets. Now before her was a wide river, the view as if from a barge, one of the steamers he had worked on, perhaps, heading toward the setting sun, an Oriental palace rising in the left-hand corner, exotic flag flying on top, and underneath it on the roof, the small figure of a man, indistinguishable, holding a telescope. You would not see who he was, that man; you would not tell him apart from others. But she knew he was Gordon because she had seen the other painting. The other painting that put her father's name on people's lips, that brought tears to Queen Victoria's eyes, that captured the public's imagination, their grief over their hero, forsaken in Khartoum, gazing out north every single day awaiting the relief expedition that came too late. Christina did not need to look at *Gordon's Last Days*, now hanging in Leeds City Museum, to compare it with this one.

The painting was etched in her mind and in the minds of others. It had helped in drumming up support for this year's military expedition, in stoking public feelings for the need to put things right in the Sudan. One of the last letters she had read out to her father, after he had taken to his bed and was too ill to handle his correspondence, was from a soldier heading out to Sudan. It was the painting, the soldier wrote, seen as a young lad, which instilled in him the desire to join the army and set out to avenge Gordon. Of course, the *Times* obituary had mentioned the painting; every tribute did along with the observation of the timing of her father's death, on the eve of the conquest, days apart from the victorious Battle of Omdurman.

But what was this then in her hand? A preliminary attempt, a trial? But it was too well executed for that, and her father would have known. It must have been painted first though. But it was different. A view from far away so that the perspective was broader. How confusing it was! On the one hand, she could see all its merits, her father's fine work, very much his style. On the other hand, it was a distortion of *Gordon's Last Days*, in which the river was a stream, the palace small and rudimentary, the British flag fluttering above it and no other, and most important of all Gordon was an imposing figure, the center of it all. How strange to see this version! It was as if it were a parallel reality in which the river ruled supreme and Gordon was any other administrator serving under the Ottoman flag, foolishly awaiting what would never come. No wonder her father kept this painting hidden!

This was the original painting; this was Gordon's last days as witnessed by her father. And then what? Gordon died and her father returned to Scotland and made a second painting. One in which the river was small, and Gordon was a hero. Robert had then put this one away, not sure what to do with it. He could not bring himself to destroy it, nor could he allow it to complicate the version of Gordon the public wanted to see. Now she, as his executor, must make the decision. To show it to the world or not? It was entirely up to her.

Outside, a cloud covered the sun, and it was the flames of the fire that shone on the colors of the painting. Perhaps her father's retrospective exhibition could include the watercolors and sketches he had sent her as a child. The monkey clambering a tree, the two hippos, the rhino who looked straight at her. Her childhood was resplendent with these images that arrived from far away. Her father painting specially for her, thinking of her, struggling to stay alive so as to return to her. She was nine when he came back. She had been with her grandparents all that time and then suddenly here he was, a stranger, gaunt and tanned. How terrified she had been to see him, bursting immediately into tears! It took time to get used to him, the new gust of life he brought back, the change in her circumstances. Gifts, attention, visits to the zoo and the Scottish National Portrait Gallery. But best of all was to soak up all his stories! All the adventures and wonders. She remembered his descriptions of all the marvelous things he had possessed but could not bring with him—the war drum, the leg from the Mahdi's bed, the elephant tusk. The months he spent on the *Bordein* downriver awaiting the relief expedition, as were Gordon's instructions, shaking off attacks from the rebels, dangerously going onshore for the men to collect firewood and for him to try and sketch. Four long months of uncertainty and waiting, much longer than anyone expected, at times firing in support of villages that were loyal to the government, then spending hours repairing bullet holes and damage from rocks. When the relief expedition finally arrived, her father accompanied them to Khartoum. They found it all smoky and ruined. "Any news of Gordon?" the general called out to some villagers on the shore, and the answer was a barrage of fire. Enemy shots that fell in the water and zinged past her father, and then having to turn back when they realized that Khartoum had fallen, that they were too late to save Gordon. Even the sketch in *Punch* had used the same words—Britannia in anguish, her arm covering her eyes, lamenting "Too Late."

Within a short time, her father became one of Scotland's leading art figures. It was all there, the recognition he deserved. He could pick and choose between commissions and the opening nights of his shows were sold out. It helped that he had spoken with authority about Gordon, that his painting *Gordon's Last Days* was instrumental in focusing public grief, in shaping public opinion in support of the conquest. Fourteen years it took for the army of revenge to be put together, fourteen years in which her father bought this house and a new atelier, was admitted into the Royal Society of Arts, held exhibitions of his work that were met with rave reviews. The town council of Edinburgh conferred on him the freedom of the city and he was appointed to sit on the committee of the Royal Fine Arts Commission. His name was linked to some of the finest artists of his time, his paintings in such high demand that they could only be afforded by a minority.

She shifted the painting away. The one beneath it rose to assault her. The shock of a nude Black woman, pitch-black, like no other Christina had ever seen. Breasts thrust forward as if they were real, torso as if carved in stone. Such savage eyes, the long veil on her head grasped so tight that her knuckles were clutched and rigid. She was holding up and pulling back the material in a gesture reminiscent of a fighter pulling back a cloak to take out a loaded pistol. Obscene. Far too explicit. The eyes luminous and lifelike, the lips as if they were about to part in speech. Nipples . . . This presumably was the same woman in the watercolors, with a pot of water on her head, indistinct, blurred. Never a nude—unless there were others lost in the *Abbas*. This, here, was unlike any other nude Christina had seen. Not like the sensual Orientalist paintings where the women were demure and reclining on pillows. Always reclining, languorous, hookah pipe within reach. This woman bore the ugliest of scars all along her shoulder; her muscular arms were unfeminine. She looked out—at whom? Robert—with utter disdain, unspeakable insolence. Christina shuddered. She would not have that woman soiling her father's name, his memory. How could he! The painting was damaged. It was right that it was damaged; it deserved violence. It should not exist, it was gratuitous, why did he keep it? She threw it in the fire. The flames leapt up to devour it, flaring, spitting, they scrunched the canvas with relish, releasing an acrid smell. Then at a slower pace, the title was burnt, one letter at a time, one word at a time. She only now noticed it—*The Negress of the Nile*.

# 27
# Salha

**Omdurman, September 1898**

My condolences, dearest Zamzam. May Allah grant your beloved brother Paradise and accept his martyrdom. I feel your pain, your loss. May Allah give you patience. What can I say to you? It has been terrible. He did not want to go out to meet the enemy. And he was not the only one. The khalifa's men went banging on doors compelling the men to go out, threatening that if they sneaked back to Omdurman during the night they will come in broad daylight and slit their throats in front of their homes. Halima didn't want him to go either. She is distraught and pays no heed to anyone. If Ishaq had started life in her stomach, she would not have mourned him more. Till now she has not run out of tears, her daughter widowed while pregnant . . .

And then fresh anguish when we were told that the British shot all the wounded. What can one say?

They had a new cannon, too, aimed at the Mahdi's tomb. I went to see it and found the qubba itself cracked like an egg and half of it blown off. The whole building destroyed.

And that was not enough for them. The Mahdi's body was dug out and dismembered. To copy Gordon's death, his skull was detached and preserved while his bones were thrown in the Nile.

Then on Sunday, the British flag was raised in Khartoum alongside the Egyptian one. For the very first time, the khedive's flag is overpowered now by the other one. Britain is now sovereign over all Ottoman lands that had been under Mahdist rule. This is what we Sudanese have unwittingly brought upon ourselves? We got rid of the Turks, branding them infidels; now we are ruled by the British who are not Muslims. They will drive a wedge between us and Egypt. They will set their missionaries loose in the south.

I am told to be hopeful. Things will improve Insha'Allah. There will be safety and Khartoum will be rebuilt. I long for the day I can write to Rustom and tell him to come home. I have waited for this for so long, for years. Insha'Allah I can hold him again and have him by my side. But today, Zamzam, I share your grief. May Allah recompense you in your children and keep us all safe. Ishaq was felled in his youth. His wedding feels as if it were yesterday. His bride dancing, her hair freshly braided and skin glistening. All the ululations and drums. Oh, I wish you had seen him and shared his joy. He was certainly the grand bridegroom—stamping in the circle of dancers, with the kohl rimming his eyes and fresh henna on his feet, raising his sword in the air, and jumping.

# Acknowledgments

In 2018, I was awarded a fellowship at the Rockefeller Foundation Bellagio Center in Italy, based on a proposal to write a novel set in the early 1900s when Khartoum was rebuilt following the British invasion of Sudan. However, following conversations in Bellagio, I changed my focus, went further back in time, and started to work on what was to become *River Spirit*. I am grateful to the Rockefeller Center for providing me with my first-ever residency experience and the opportunity to discuss my work with other fellows. Many heartfelt thanks to David Lewis for being the one to suggest that I not only write about General Gordon but also fictionalize his unknown assassin. I am also indebted to Urvashi Butalia for urging me, rightly, to unearth the hidden histories of Sudanese women. My experience in Bellagio and discussions with David and Urvashi was captured by the BBC World Service program *In the Studio* and a podcast is available on https://www.bbc.co.uk/programmes/p094cmml.

In researching the novel, I wish to express my profound gratitude to Dr. Omar Fadlallah for sending me the text of various sources, for sharing his own Mahdist novel, *Aisha's Vision*, and again for helping me research information about women during this period. I am also grateful to Reem Alhilou for tirelessly supporting my research especially with regard to the historical figure of the revolutionary Rabiha, featured in the prologue of the novel. Gratitude is also due to Professor Badreldin Hashimi and to the writer Fatima As-Sanoussi for help with social details that were small but immensely significant.

I "found" Zamzam in the Sudan Archive of Durham University, in a bill of sale and in a petition concerning a runaway slave girl who stole an item of clothing from her mistress. Many thanks to Francis Gotto, archivist in the University Library and Collections. And to Fergus Nicoll for pointing me toward useful resources, answering my numerous questions, and reading an early draft of the novel.

I am grateful to Sokari Douglas Camp for her warm interest in the predicament of a nineteenth-century artist without materials and for granting me many insights. Many thanks are also due to experts Lisa Williams, Gráinne Rice, and Freya Spoor for helping with my research into nineteenth-century Scottish artists' representation of Black women sitters and the titles of their work.

Nadir Mahjoub, Vimbai Shire, Stephanie Cabot—I couldn't have got this far without you!

It has been an honor, a joy, and a wonderful learning experience to work with my brilliant editor, Elisabeth Schmitz. I am immensely grateful to her and to the team at Grove Atlantic—Deb Seager, Amy Hundley, Lilly Sandberg, and Kait Astrella.

It was a delight to read the many books, papers, etc. written on this period of Sudan's history from various points of view. Here are the highlights, the ones that I depended upon and/or provided me with breakthroughs:

*The Mahdi of Sudan and the Death of General Gordon*, by Fergus Nicoll

*Fully Equal to the Occasion: Frank Power and the Siege of Khartoum*, edited by Fergus Nicoll

*Fatwa and Propaganda: Contemporary Muslim Responses to the Sudanese Mahdiyya*, by Fergus Nicoll

"Domestic Slavery in the Nineteenth- and Early Twentieth-Century Northern Sudan," by Heather Sharkey

*The Journals of Major-Gen. C. G. Gordon, C. B., at Kartoum*, by Charles Gordon, Alfred Hake

من ابا الي تسلهاي - حروب حياة الإمام المهدى – عبد المحمود ابو شامة

تاريخ حياتى الجزء الأول – بابكر بدرى

تاريخ السودان – نعوم شقير

مذكرات يوسف ميخائيل

تاريخ السودان الحديث ١٨٢٠-١٩٥٥ – د.محمد سعيد القدال